AGAINST THE LAVISH BACKDROP OF A MYTHIC EMPIRE, A WORLD OF EXOTIC PLEASURES AND SAVAGE TERRORS . . .

KUBILAI KHAN—His mighty empire stretched from the Persian desert to the China Sea. His taste for glory won him power; his hunger for power made him infamous.

EDMUND DE BEAUCHAMPS—In spite of honors and riches, he longed for his homeland. Then events swept him into battle, and even in victory there would be no turning back.

MEI-LING—The pampered daughter of a Chinese governor, she was ill-prepared to bear her destiny as Edmund's bride—or to bear the son of the Golden Barbarian.

MARSHAL SÖGATÜ—Shrewd, heartless; once the brightest star in the khan's military firmament, now he'd stop at nothing to see that star rise again.

GENTLE BREEZE—She was unaware of her own courageous spirit until she embarked on a reckless crusade following a bold knight in glittering armor.

Books by Franklin M. Proud

RALLY-HO
TIGER IN THE MOUNTAINS
   (with Alfred F. Eberhardt)
BRAVO ONE
THE GOLDEN TRIANGLE
THE TARTAR
THE WALKING WIND
WHERE THE WIND IS WILD
WARLORD OF CATHAY
PRINCE OF CHAMPA

PRINCE
OF CHAMPA

Franklin M. Proud

A DELL BOOK

Published by
Dell Publishing Co., Inc.
1 Dag Hammarskjold Plaza
New York, New York 10017

Dell ®™ 681510, Dell Publishing Co., Inc.

ISBN: 0-440-16933-X

Printed in the United States of America

First printing—January 1985

Author's Foreword

For the most part, place names used throughout the following narrative have been updated to conform with present-day usage. Exceptions, however, have been made in some cases.

In China, the notable exceptions are the ancient capital of the Han dynasty, Ch'ang-an (Sian), the erstwhile capital of the Southern Sung dynasty, Lin-an (Hangchow), and the imperial capital of the Yuan dynasty, Cambulac (Peking). It should be noted that, at the time of our story, Peking was known as Chung-tu to the Chinese and called Khanbalic by their Mongol overlords. Patently, "Cambulac" is a distortion of the Mongol name.

Since it no longer exists, the Kingdom of Champa should be treated as a special case. The kingdom flourished from the 2nd century A.D. until it was overrun by the Annamites (North Vietnamese) in the mid-fifteenth century. Thereafter, a truncated remnant of the kingdom lingered on in the south for a further two centuries before it, too, was swallowed up by the rapacious Annamites.

Today, little or nothing remains of the Cham cities of Mu Cheng, Indrapura, Faifo, Vijaya, and Panduranga. They are believed to have been located, respectively, at or near the present-day Vietnamese cities of Dong Hoi, Hue, Hoi An, Binh Dinh, and Phan Rang.

The mountain sanctuary of Ban Son cannot be located with any reasonable degree of accuracy. However, from the descriptive detail given by Edmund de Beauchamps, it is safe to assume that Ban Son was situated somewhere in the jungle-mantled mountains to the west, or southwest, of the city known to the colonial French as Tourane and called Da Nang by today's Vietnamese.

FMP

Fuengirola, Spain
December 1983

Caravan route from Acre to
Cambaluc (Peking) via
Balkh - 6,000 miles.

Chapter One

On the last day of September in the Year of our Lord 1276, the Army of the Blue Dragon broke camp and marched south from Changsha to join the combined force commanded by Marshal Sögatü. The campaign being mounted was designed to crush for all time the remnant forces of the Southern Sung dynasty still resisting Mongol authority in South China.

Forsooth, it had been so long since I'd been exposed to European culture that I had all but abandoned thinking in terms of the Christian calendar. For the better part of three years, when I'd been a prisoner of the Saracens in Aleppo, my daily life had been governed by Moslem concepts. For the last eighteen months in Cathay I'd found myself relating to Chinese chronology. Had it not been for the companionship of a Nestorian friar, Brother Demetrios, I'd have lost track of Christmas, Easter, and, mayhap, my own birthday. Almost seven years had elapsed since last I'd seen England's shores.

It was not, therefore, until later that evening, when it was brought to my attention by Brother Demetrios' reminding me that my twenty-fifth birthday was but two weeks away, that I associated our day of departure with the date of September thirtieth. I had thought of it only as the fifteenth day of the Month of the Monkey in the lunar Year of the Rat. In dynastic terms I also knew it to be the seventeenth year of the reign of Emperor Shi-tzu, though I doubted there were many people outside the imperial court who used dynastic years as frames of reference. Shi-tzu was the Chinese name the *khagan* had adopted when he'd founded the Yuan dynasty in Cathay. To all but a select few the supreme ruler of Cathay and the far-flung Mongol Empire was better known as Kubilai Khan. What, after all, is in a name? Here, only Maffeo and Niccolò Polo, Niccolò's son, Marco, and Brother Demetrios called me by my rightful name, Edmund de R_____ blond hair and beard, and fair ____ as a form of address, and nickname, *Chin man-tze* ____ thereafter it had been formalized into the name by which I became known to the Chinese. To all within the ranks of the Army of the Blue Dragon, I was General Chin Man-tze.

I was in Cathay not through choice but solely owing to circumstances beyond my control. That I now commanded the Army of the Blue Dragon I owed to the khan's whim—though Brother Demetrios was convinced a larger purpose lay behind the seeming caprice. Certainly, as was becoming increasingly evident, Kubilai meant to detain me in his realm for an extended period. The khan's plans, however, did not mesh with mine.

I hadn't expected to get much sleep the night before the scheduled departure of the army. It would be many months before Gentle Breeze and I would again be in each other's company. We had retired early and had coupled with a passion born of mutual need well into the small hours of morning before we'd fallen into a slumber of sated exhaustion. Yet, withal, I awoke as dawn blushed the eastern sky.

Gentle Breeze assisted me in dressing. I donned a silken shirt and loose trousers tucked into calf-length felt boots. Over my shirt I wore a leather jerkin faced with gold-plated rectangular bronze plates. Next, with Gentle Breeze helping to secure them, I laced the overlapping plates of my hip and shoulder armor. Those as well were plated with gold. Over my shoulders I draped an ermine-trimmed cloak of azure silk on the back of which was embroidered a fierce-looking cobalt-blue dragon. My gilded helm was topped with a feathered plume that matched the blue of my cloak. Only in the arms I wore did I depart from Chinese trappings. Belted at my waist was the English broadsword with which my father had girded me at the proud moment of my investiture to knighthood by England's Henry III.

That day in early June, seven and a half years ago, when I'd been knighted and had taken the cross, came to mind as I buckled my sword belt. How proud I'd been, how confident of winning glory on the field of combat and bringing added honors to the de Beauchamps name and coat of arms as English crusading knights won the day against the infidel. Vaulting ambition doomed to frustrating failure, I thought wryly. I'd neither tilted lance nor drawn sword against the Moslem foe. Even had I not been taken captive in Syria by pure mischance, the ill-starred Eighth Crusade would have afforded little opportunity for me to test my mettle. It had not been until this very year, far removed from the Holy Land and farther still from England, that I'd faced the test of full-scale battle at Hengyang, where the Sung warlord had made a stand against the Army of the Blue Dragon.

Gentle Breeze stepped back two paces. This was the first time she'd seen me arrayed in the full trappings of my rank. Her head tilted to one side, she regarded me appraisingly.

"Magnificent, my lord," she said approvingly.

I was pleased, yet observed self-deprecatingly, "Plumage makes not the bird."

She flashed me a smile. "But it makes him stand out from the flock."

"And a tempting target for falcons," I added dryly.

She sobered. "May the Lord Buddha protect you, my lord."

I drew her close and gazed fondly down at her upturned face. "Fear not, little one."

The courtyard was still in shadow, but long-slanting rays of the rising sun glanced off the green-glazed tiles of the roof of the Hall of Ancestors. In the flagged courtyard Scimitar, my sable stallion, was saddled and caparisoned, attended by the stablemaster. Wong Sin was supervising servants loading teak chests containing my personal belongings, plate armor, and assorted weaponry into a horse-drawn cart. I watched the scene of frenetic activity for a few moments before making my presence known.

My appearance on the scene acted like a wave of a magician's wand. All motion in the courtyard ceased and silence descended. That is not entirely accurate. Scimitar seemed unaffected by my entrance. Nor did the human actors remain long frozen. Almost immediately activity was resumed and the shrill babble of voices, the ever-present background music of China, swelled anew.

Just why my entrance had caused such an unexpected response didn't strike me until I had swung myself into Scimitar's saddle. Of course! This was the first time *any* of my household staff had seen me garbed in the full finery of my exalted rank. Ah, vanity. I must confess to posturing. Before touching spurs to Scimitar, I struck what I thought to be a suitably heroic pose.

Scimitar's hooves clattered on the flagstones as I rounded the spirit screen and exited through the moon gate. On the roadway outside the walled enclosure of my residence compound, Major Chang, my aide, waited with my cavalry escort. When I'd completed my inspection of the mounted guard, I set off at a brisk trot in the direction of the army's encampment. Major Chang took up a position close on Scimitar's right flank. When I'd given the cavalry escort time to form into columns to my rear, I spurred Scimitar to a canter.

The encampment site was on a plain to the south of the walled city of Changsha. From my residence in the city to the encampment was a short distance of some two li. It took but a short time for us to cover that distance, though we didn't do so directly. We circled to the east and reined in atop a hillock overlooking the campsite.

I should say former campsite. When I'd left the encampment the previous evening, it had been a sprawling collection of tents and pavilions. Long lines of horses had been tethered to ropes strung between the tents. Smoke from cooking fires had drifted skyward. Then, it had been a veritable hive of activity. All that was now changed. The camp had undergone a miraculous transformation during the night and hours of predawn. All the tents and pavilions had been struck. Cooking fires had been long extinguished. The plain now was a vast expanse of scarred earth and trampled grass distantly edged by ploughed and stubbled paddy fields. Drawn up in serried ranks on the roadway bisecting the erstwhile encampment was the Army of the Blue Dragon.

It was a sight that never ceased to astonish me. The cavalry, banners, pennants, and horsetail insignia stirring in the morning breeze, was positioned in the van. The cavalry numbered close to five thousand. Next came the foot soldiers, comprised of musicians, pikemen, cooks, archers, ostlers, artisans, crossbowmen, officers' body servants, catapult operators, baggage handlers, and the like. Taken as a body the foot soldiers numbered in excess of twelve thousand. To the total strength of eighteen thousand could be added an indeterminate number of camp followers.

Had I had no frame of reference other than the Army of the Blue Dragon I would have had no cause to be astonished, but I was wont to draw comparisons. In England eight hundred knights had rallied to the holy cause. Together with their retainers and men-at-arms the crusading force led by Prince Edward had totaled less than four thousand. The Mongols raised cavalry *touman*s of more than twice that strength. The cavalry of the Army of the Blue Dragon alone numbered more than Prince Edward's entire army. Yet, by Asian standards, the Army of the Blue Dragon was a small force. The army that the Sung warlord had fielded against us at Hengyang had numbered more than six times the present strength of my army.

There were, of course, great differences in the employment of European and Asian armies. The heavily armored European knight rode into battle astride a barded war-horse bred for size and stamina. The European knight was armed with battle lance, broadsword, battle-ax, and mace, but never, even if a skilled archer, did he enter the fray armed with a bow. The Mongol warrior was, essentially, a mounted bowman whose horse was bred for speed and agility.

When my cavalry escort had formed on either side of my position on the crest of the hill, I gave over my profitless speculation on the relative size and respective employment of

armies. The army assembled below me awaited my signal to
pass in review as it moved out.

I nodded to Major Chang, whereupon he swung my dragon
banner in a wide arc, then steadied it again in the upright
position. Below us the reaction was immediate. Shrill orders
rang out. The martial music of string and wind instruments,
cymbals, and drums was borne to us by the morning breeze.
Then, at a measured pace dictated by the sonorous cadence of
the drums, the army advanced in unison. As each unit passed
my hilltop position, pennants and banners dipped. It was an
impressive spectacle.

We stayed atop the hillock until the siege engines rumbled
by, followed closely by the strung-out baggage train. Only
then did I wheel Scimitar and, followed by Chang and my
mounted escort, set off at a gallop to take up my position in
the vanguard of the advancing army.

I maneuvered to bring myself ahead of General Wu, my
second-in-command, and slowed Scimitar to a walk to match
his gait to the drumbeat. I gazed southward toward where
rising mist betokened the westward curve of the Siang River
and to the haze-blurred hills beyond. I wondered idly what
lay in wait for the Army of the Blue Dragon in the southern
provinces beyond those hills. What was more to the point,
what had Fate in store for me?

Chapter Two

Our immediate destination was Kweilin, where Marshal Sögatü had established field headquarters. The distance from Changsha to Kweilin was ninety leagues. I estimated it would take us about three weeks to cover that distance. Although there was little chance that we would encounter any Sung harassment until we were well south of Hengyang, I deployed cavalry units ahead and on both flanks of my advancing force as a precautionary measure. That taken care of, I settled comfortably in the saddle. Lulled by the warmth of the autumn day, I allowed my thoughts free rein.

The ancient Greeks believed man's destiny was governed by the Fates—Clotho, Lachesis, and Atropos—three goddesses whose duty it was to spin, measure, and cut the thread of life. The Turks and Arabs attributed all the vicissitudes visited on mankind to kismet. Gentle Breeze, of Buddhist persuasion, believed that one's karma determined one's lot, for good or ill, in this life and the next. I, on the other hand, had been raised in the Catholic faith to believe that, while subject to God's will and answerable to Him for our transgressions, it was in our power to shape our destiny within reasonable limits. Considering all that had befallen me, it would have been easier had I subscribed to the Greek, Arab, or Buddhist concepts of predestination. The suspicion that I'd brought such harrowing experiences down on my head through my own doing was hardly reassuring.

My thoughts roamed back some sixteen months to my first meeting with Kubilai Khan. When news of my presence in his domain had reached the khan's ears, I suppose it was only natural for him to have been intrigued.

Not that I was the first foreign devil to stray into the Middle Kingdom. If Brother Demetrios was to be believed, Arab seafarers had traded in seaports of South China for untold centuries. Certainly, silks, spices, and gemstones from Cathay had found ready markets in ancient Rome, though I doubted that the Romans had known where fabled Cathay was located. There had to have been merchants—Syrian, Armenian, Persian, and Greek, to name a few—who had braved the appalling perils of the mountains and the horrors of the Taklamakan, Lop, and Gobi deserts in order to profit from the lucrative trading opportunities afforded by Cathay. Niccolò, Maffeo, and Marco Polo might have been the first Venetians to find their way into the Middle Kingdom, but they'd followed well-defined caravan routes already centuries old. I venture to say, however, that I was the first English knight the khan had encountered.

So, with Brother Demetrios acting as my interpreter, I'd been summoned to a private audience with the khan. I had been an oddity. Never before had Kubilai seen a fair-haired, blue-eyed Englishman of my tall stature. My hauberk and coif of chain mail had aroused his curiosity—as had the de Beauchamps coat of arms embroidered boldly on my surcoat. The upshot of that audience had been that, at the khan's suggestion, Brother Demetrios and I were to accompany the khan when the court moved from Cambulac to the summer capital at Shangtu. The reason advanced was that this would provide me with an opportunity to become familiar with Mongol weaponry and tactics. Manifestly, I'd found favor in the khan's eyes.

There was tangible evidence of Kubilai's goodwill. During my audience I'd mentioned that I had no war-horse and that my plate armor, having lain packed in an oaken chest for some four years, had rusted so badly I feared it was useless. The khan stated offhandedly that he would give orders that I could choose any horse in the Imperial Stables and that a metalsmith would copy my armor. The khan was as good as his word. I chose a magnificent black stallion from the Imperial Stables, naming him Scimitar. A metalsmith copied my plate armor faithfully and, additionally, fabricated a chamfron and bards for Scimitar. In addition I had a woodworker make me an iron-tipped battle lance from seasoned teak.

Yet, despite the khan's openhanded generosity, I had no wish to accompany the court on its move to Shangtu. All I wanted was to dispose of the trade goods we'd brought with us in order to finance a westbound caravan. My one desire was to quit Cathay and begin the long journey home to England. It was more than simple homesickness. I had grievances in England that cried out for resolution.

Brother Demetrios set me straight. I wasn't to look upon the khan's suggestion as an invitation that could be rejected politely. A suggestion from the khan was tantamount to a royal command. Nor should I be taken in by the generosity displayed by the khan. What had been given could just as readily be taken back. At the moment I appeared to have impressed the khan favorably, but should I displease him, a slow and painful death well could be my recompense.

We went to Shangtu.

I found myself attached to a cavalry troop commanded by a Mongol, Captain Toghu. I was subjected to ridicule and humiliation and treated as the veriest of raw recruits. Yet I learned to master the Mongol composite bow, a weapon that eclipsed the English longbow in both range and accuracy, and gained an appreciation of Mongol cavalry tactics.

I managed to contain my resentment of the treatment accorded me. I did, that is, until a Turkoman officer provoked me beyond the limits of acceptability. The ensuing incident was brought to the khan's attention. Kubilai's reaction was to order that the dispute be settled according to trial by combat. In Mongol terms that meant a fight to the death.

Happily, I emerged from that contest victorious. Almost immediately I was summoned to the khan's presence. Kubilai publicly conferred on me the honor of commanding a cavalry *touman* then being raised to be sent south to Changsha to join the Army of the Blue Dragon under the command of General Hsü Ch'ien. I was stunned by this unexpected development.

A few days later I again was summoned to a private

audience with the khan. Since, thanks to the tutoring of
Brother Demetrios in Merv and during the many months of
our long journey along the eastbound caravan route, I was
reasonably fluent in the Mandarin dialect of the Chinese
tongue, I wasn't accompanied by the Nestorian friar on this
occasion. During this audience Kubilai explained what he
wanted of me. Mine was a nominal command. Actual com-
mand- was vested in Mangatei, a Mongol cavalry officer
distantly related to the khan, whose official capacity was
tactical commander of the *touman*. I was informed by Kubilai
that he wanted me to report objectively on the military situation
extant in South China. To provide me with credentials to
facilitate this function, I would be promoted to general of the
third rank on my arrival in Changsha. At the conclusion of
that private audience Kubilai commented, facetiously I thought,
on my amatory adventures in Cambulac. He suggested that
female companionship more appropriate to my station could
be made available.

Shortly before that audience with the khan, I'd visited
Cambulac in company with Brother Demetrios and Marco
Polo. My purpose had been to take delivery of my armor,
which had been duplicated in bronze instead of steel. During
the course of that visit Marco had explored out-of-the-way
shops in search of items with possible commercial application.
He'd returned one evening describing devices that used black
powder to propel projectiles and launch explosive-headed
rockets. These he'd uncovered in the storeroom of an ancient
foundry. I'd been intrigued and had questioned Brother
Demetrios concerning these engines of destruction. He stated
that he'd heard of such devices being employed more than a
century ago in naval warfare between the Sung and Chin
forces but, to his knowledge, they hadn't been put to use
since that long-ago conflict. I arranged for a demonstration
and was so impressed that I placed an order for two each of
the mortars and rocket launchers. My intention was to field-
test them in land combat. When I informed Mangatei of this
acquisition, it served to exacerbate the differences growing
between us.

It had been on that visit to Cambulac that I'd sought out the
company of singsong girls in the teahouses and bathhouses of

the capital. Marco had objected to such conduct as unseemly. It must have been through Marco that news of my libidinous escapades had reached Kubilai's ears.

Four days before the *touman* was to break camp and move south toward Changsha, I had an unexpected visitor. I returned to my field tent to find a young woman awaiting my return. She was a seventeen-year-old concubine sent to me from the khan's harem.

She was not a gift without precedent. The khan had been known to bestow concubines on visiting dignitaries, but that he should honor me in like manner was an unheard-of gesture. I quite naturally was delighted. It served to raise me in the esteem of the troopers of the *touman*.

I imagine her selection had been due to the fact that in appearance she was more European than Asiatic. Only her high cheekbones bespoke an Oriental heritage. Her father had been a Turcople, a Syrian of mixed Greek and Turkish blood. Her mother was a Tartar. The daughter had been born in the Turkestan village of Bakhty and raised in the oasis of Turfan. Her name at that time had been Karla. When she'd entered the khan's harem as a concubine, she had been given a Chinese name, Wei Feng—"Gentle Breeze." Whoever it was who had chosen her as a suitable gift for me had not erred. I found her exquisite in face and form. What was even more remarkable was that she came to me a virgin.

Almost a year ago to the day, the *touman* had moved south from Shangtu. I'd divided it into two sections. One section, commanded by Mangatei, was to proceed overland. The second section, under my command, would embark on a flotilla of river craft at Tientsin and follow a waterborne route via the Grand Canal to Nanking and thence upstream on the Yangtze Kiang. With me aboard the flagship of our flotilla were Gentle Breeze, Brother Demetrios, Marco Polo, and my body servant Wong Sin together with his number-one wife, Ah Hsing. Marco had been ordered south by the khan to report on regional economic conditions.

The lengthy voyage absorbed the better part of three months. During that time I came to know and appreciate my bewitching concubine. She became both an inventive and sexually responsive bed-companion, and a sympathetic confidante. She was wise beyond her years, high-spirited, and possessed of a delightfully earthy sense of humor. All those who came to know her were enchanted. Brother Demetrios became her advocate and staunchest ally. I suppose that was only to be expected, since he, as well, hailed from Turfan.

We disembarked at Changsha on Christmas Day of the Year of our Lord 1275—the twelfth day of the Month of the Boar in the Year of the Boar.

A military aide conducted me to General Hsü Ch'ien. The Chinese general was a formidable battle-scarred warrior in his middle years. Somewhere along the way he'd lost his right eye and received a disfiguring facial wound. With every evidence of hostility he learned of my promotion to general of the third rank. I doubt that he knew aught of the reason for my promotion, but I strongly suspect he guessed its purpose. To my surprise I learned that Mangatei had received a similar promotion and been appointed as the army's cavalry commander.

Something else came as a surprise to me. General Hsü Ch'ien evinced keen interest in the engines of destruction I'd brought with me and claimed that they *had* been used in land actions by his grandfather, Hsü Yung, who had commanded a Khmer army in actions directed against the Kingdom of Champa. According to Hsü Ch'ien the black-powder devices had proved to be highly effective. He had no idea why their use in warfare had been discontinued. He authorized me to test them in battle.

I'm sure it was my acquisition of the mortars and rocket launchers that prompted the general to appoint me to the command of the right wing of our battle formation.

Shortly before the army's departure for Hengyang, Marco, accompanied by Brother Demetrios—who would act in the capacity of Marco's interpreter—left for Szechwan. I didn't expect to see either one of them again in Changsha.

We were confronted by the Sung army, a numerically superior force, in mid-February. It was a bloody battle from which, despite heavy losses, the Army of the Blue Dragon emerged the victor thanks to Hsü Ch'ien's generalship. I like to think that the use of my mortars and rocket launchers contributed to our victory.

I was wounded in the fray, but not seriously. In all modesty I believe I acquitted myself in a manner that would have won my father's approval. He would *not* have approved of the action taken after the Sung force had been routed.

Acting not on orders from Hsü Ch'ien, but on a mandate from the khan, Mangatei directed his cavalry in the razing of the walled city of Hengyang. Its hapless inhabitants were slaughtered to a man.

After our return to Changsha, when my wounds had mended sufficiently, I rode north to report in person to Kubilai. I intended to request that he put a time limit on the duration of my services. It didn't work out the way I'd intended.

My share of the profits from the disposal of the trade goods we'd brought with us to Cathay were to be held in trust for me by the Polos. When I reached Cambulac, Niccolò Polo blandly informed me that my share had been reinvested in goods now westbound in a caravan entrusted to Lorenzo Roccenti. With an empty purse I'd no choice but to postpone any plans I'd had to buy into a westbound caravan.

A few days later I met privately with the khan at his palace in the Forbidden City. What Kubilai disclosed to me after I'd rendered my report left me dumbstruck.

General Hsü Ch'ien had told me that he'd recommended me for promotion, but he'd said nothing about a request to be relieved of his command. Kubilai informed me matter-of-factly that my promotion to general of the second rank was approved, that Hsü Ch'ien had been transferred to a command in the Kingdom of Korea, and that I'd been given command of the Army of the Blue Dragon. He also told me that Mangatei had been transferred to Tali, in the former western kingdom of Nan Chao, and that the cavalry of the Army of the Blue Dragon had been ordered to join him there. A replacement cavalry *touman* was being raised at Cambulac but I couldn't expect its arrival at Changsha until sometime in the Month of the Ram.

At the conclusion of the audience Kubilai advanced a suggestion. He advised me to find a young woman of good family and, subject to his approval of the bride-to-be, take her unto me as a principal wife.

I stayed in Cambulac just long enough to order additional mortars, rocket launchers, black powder, explosive-headed rockets, and iron projectiles, then started on the return journey to Changsha. During the trip I had ample time to reflect on the radical changes that had taken place.

I suspected that the khan, who had paid informers in every corner of the land, had had no need of the information I'd carried north to Cambulac. I had a suspicion that the anger Kubilai had exhibited when I'd criticized Mangatei's massacre at Hengyang had been feigned—but that was something I didn't want to put to a test.

I should have seen it sooner. During my initial audience, when Kubilai had voiced objection to the ravens in my family coat of arms, he'd been testing me. That objection, which I'd ignored, had been to determine whether I would put honor above risk. Since then he'd tested me repeatedly.

Toghu, of course, had reported on my progress under training. I was almost certain the Turkoman's provocation had been at Kubilai's instigation. The trial by combat, which just as easily as not could have seen me killed, had been an evaluation of my courage and ruthlessness.

Had Toghu continued to report my actions and reactions to the khan from Changsha? Probably. And Chang! I knew he'd reported on everything said beneath my roof to Hsü Ch'ien. Could he, as well, have been reporting to Kubilai through an intermediary?

At the Hengyang battle I'd been in the forefront of the action. Had that been Hsü Ch'ien's doing, or had the general been acting on instructions from Kubilai?

It was entirely possible that the Polos had reinvested the funds due me on orders from the khan. Everything indicated that Kubilai intended to keep me in the Middle Kingdom. Why? Why me?

Kubilai's "suggestion" that I find a suitable wife hadn't been inspired by solicitude. It had all the weight and force of an imperial edict designed to tie me ever closer to Cathay.

I likened it to a chess game played with living pieces. Having survived a number of threatening moves, I was becoming increasingly important to the khan's game. It was too early to divine his strategy, but if Brother Demetrios was correct, I was destined to survive a few more moves—possibly all the way to the khan's end-game.

I thought I saw a way to be both a piece in the game and a player. No longer did I hold a nominal command. True, I would come under the orders of Marshal Sögatü, but there appeared to be a way to circumvent both Kubilai's and Sögatü's supervisory direction.

I would have to bide my time, but the final move would be mine, not the khan's. That Brother Demetrios had returned to Changsha, unaccompanied by Marco, shortly before the army's departure, had been a godsend. The Nestorian friar was the key I needed to open the door to freedom.

Chapter Three

The first thing I did when we made camp that evening was shed my finery. Clad in a cotton robe and felt slippers, I received General Wu, Toghu, and the wing commanders, Liu and Yin Po, informally in my pavilion. They had nothing untoward to report. Toghu requested permission to increase the strength of the outriding flankers. This I agreed to even though it would be some days before we reached hilly terrain where trouble, if it arose at all, could be anticipated. When all our business had been attended to I had my servants bring wine. We drank to the success of the campaign. At the conclusion of the toast I observed that we'd made a grand and impressive exit from Changsha for the benefit of relatives and friends but that now, when our audience was reduced to farmers, oxen, and water buffaloes, it behoved us to revert to working garb. The officers left my pavilion with smiles lighting their faces.

I turned to Major Chang, who awaited my instructions. "Have you seen aught of the Nestorian?" I asked.

Chang grinned. "I understand he roistered well into the night. Fearing he might miss our departure, he crawled into a baggage *mappa*. I'm told he slept through the better part of the morning."

I chuckled. "If he's spent the day eating dust, I doubt he'll be in a happy frame of mind. Send someone to fetch him . . . if he can find him."

I was all but finished eating when Brother Demetrios put in an appearance. He looked decidedly the worse for wear. Brushing ineffectually at his stained and dusty cassock, the friar sank down on cushions beside the low table.

"You wanted to see me?" he queried.

"To invite you to share my evening meal," I replied, placing my chopsticks beside my rice bowl, "and, in return, seek spiritual guidance. After all, you *are* my secular and spiritual adviser. I thought we'd left without you. I'm happy to see that's not the case. I trust you enjoyed the first day of our march."

The friar's chubby cheeks reddened slightly. "Sarcasm ill becomes you, Edmund, my lad."

I grinned. "Don't you think you'd be more comfortable astride a horse? An ox-drawn baggage cart hardly seems like an appropriate mode of transport for a man of the cloth."

Brother Demetrios bridled. "Our Savior was not above riding a lowly ass."

I was enjoying the friar's discomfiture. "Are you inviting comparison?"

"I—ah—" He broke off and grinned weakly.

Relenting, I pointed to a number of dishes. "Duck and ginger. Shredded pork. Crisp noodles. Can I interest you in food?"

His face mirrored distaste. "The mere thought of food repels me . . . but a cup of wine wouldn't go amiss."

Pouring wine into a porcelain cup I said, "Actually, I do have a question for you. It's been some days since I've had a chance to talk to you. As you know, the prospect of marriage is an unwelcome complication. Is there any way, without putting herself at risk, that Gentle Breeze can prolong the negotiations?"

The friar downed its contents and extended the wine cup for refilling. "What negotiations? As your concubine she shouldn't be involved in the process in any way."

"I'm fully aware of that, but I've no relatives or friends to speak for me. As matters stand, I've no one but Gentle Breeze to act as a marriage broker. She raised no objection. In fact I think she welcomed the task."

Brother Demetrios wiped his mouth with the back of his hand. His eyes widened. "Did she, now! Has she opened these—ah—negotiations?"

"She's approached the House of Wang. She has in mind Yü-huan, or her young sister, sixteen-year-old Mei-ling. Of the two she favors the latter."

"The governor's nieces. Either of them should meet with Kubilai's approval."

"God's teeth, I've no doubt on that score. That's not the problem. What's at issue is how best to delay the proceedings."

The friar ran his hand across his bald head, then tugged at his earlobe in a characteristic gesture of contemplation. "I don't see how you can prolong them without angering Kubilai. On the other hand I fail to see any reason for delaying tactics under the circumstances as they now exist. It will take Gentle Breeze some weeks to finalize arrangements with the House of Wang before names are submitted to Cambulac for Kubilai's approval. The Year of the Ox will be well advanced before word of his decision reaches Changsha. But that need not concern you. The wedding ceremony must await the conclusion of this campaign."

"What if the Army of the Blue Dragon is withdrawn from the campaign before we reach Canton?"

Brother Demetrios regarded me through slitted lids for several moments before answering. When he did so, he switched abruptly from Chinese to Greek. "Are you still determined to seek sea passage to the Persian Gulf? You haven't changed your mind about returning to your homeland?"

"My mind is unchanged," I answered in Greek.

"Gentle Breeze?"

"I cannot leave her here. E'en though I believe she will find life in England difficult, I must take her with me."

"Have you told her what you plan?"

"How can I when the plan is still conjecture? All I've told her is that I want her to join me when we near Canton."

Brother Demetrios sighed. "I swear I don't understand you, Edmund. You command an army. Your prospects are bright. Wealth is within your grasp. Here, your future is assured, yet you yearn to return to England where you know not what awaits you."

"Here, I'm a 'foreign devil' whose bright prospects depend entirely on Kubilai's whim. In England I am among my own people. Besides, a wrong has been done me that must be put to rights."

The friar snorted. "Your lands and title were stolen from you. A great wrong, I'll grant you that. But you have no guarantee they'll be returned to you. What you had in England was bequeathed you. What you have here you've earned. Which has the greater value?"

I gazed on the portly Nestorian friar affectionately. For three years he'd been my constant companion, with the exception of the months he'd spent in the west as Marco's interpreter. I valued the friar's counsel highly. In this instance there was substance to his argument, but he, of all people, should have understood what drew me toward my homeland.

Brother Demetrios referred to himself as a desert-born Greek. His father had been a Byzantine Greek, his mother a Uighur Tartar. He had a broad face and almond-shaped eyes, and no one would have suspected him of having even a drop of Greek blood in his veins. By his own admission he'd been no closer to Byzantium than Bokhara, yet he truly thought of himself as Greek and always spoke wistfully of one day going home to Constantinople.

"What you say is true," I countered agreeably, "but that doesn't alter the fact that England is my homeland. I don't belong here, little father. Surely you can appreciate that."

Brother Demetrios shifted his position uncomfortably. "Ye-es, Edmund, lad. 'Tis a compelling argument."

During the next few days my vagrant thoughts kept winging back in time. The friar had given voice to the truth. I had no guarantee that Ravenscrest Castle, the estates of my barony, or my earldom would be restored to me.

It wasn't a question of my identity. I'd but to put in an appearance at Windsor. I'd served with Prince Edward during the crusade. He knew me well. But now that he was England's Edward I, political considerations could weigh against me. I

did not believe for a moment that my claim would go
unopposed, and the longer it took me to present my petition
the more opposition I could anticipate.

I'd been on a fact-finding mission for Prince Edward when
my squire and I had been shipwrecked off the Syrian coast in
the autumn of 1271. It was at about the same time that my
father, Geoffrey de Beauchamps, Earl of Hartleigh, had been
killed in a hunting accident, though I didn't learn of this until
informed by letter early in 1273.

It is a wonder that any of us survived the shipwreck, and
even more wondrous that my squire, Hugh *fitz* William, and a
sailor had managed to salvage my oaken trunk from the
wreckage. In all likelihood, in fact, I owed my life to the
knightly trappings stowed in the trunk. Had it not been for
that proof of my station, I'm sure Hugh and I would have
been summarily executed by our Saracen captors. We were
questioned at length in Antioch, then imprisoned in Aleppo.
A demand for ransom had been dispatched to England.

When it became known that a storm had overtaken our
Genoese sailing vessel, it had been assumed that we had
perished at sea. Under those conditions, when word of what
was presumed to have befallen me reached Ravenscrest, I
suppose it was only natural that my lands, all except those
estates bequeathed to my young sister Catherine, had been
passed on to my half-brother, Thomas de Beauchamps, together with the earldom rightfully belonging to me.

Half-brother? I hadn't even known of the child's existence
until the letter from Brother Bartholomew apprised me of that
fact, together with the sad news of my father's demise.
Although he hadn't said so outright, the Dominican monk had
hinted strongly that Thomas was not the seed of my father's
loins. Everything indicated that the lad was the product of my
fleeting illicit relationship with my stepmother, Ethelwyn of
Hebb. There was little doubt in my mind that Thomas de
Beauchamps was my bastard son.

In any event the demand for ransom forwarded by the
sultan of Damascus, together with a note penned by me, had
not reached Ravenscrest until the spring of 1272. My stepmother had declared my note a forgery and, in consequence,

had rejected the ransom demand. Moreover, according to the monk's letter, my stepmother was betrothed to Simon de Broulay, Earl of Croftshire. Without doubt, by the time Brother Bartholomew's letter reached me, Ethelwyn of Hebb had become the Countess of Croftshire. In de Broulay she'd acquired a powerful protector.

When I learned that no ransom would be forthcoming, I'd seen but one course open to Hugh and me—escape. Disguised as mendicant pilgrims, we'd struck out afoot for one of the two enclaves in the Outremer still in Christian hands, Tripoli. Our freedom had been short-lived. On the fourth day we'd been apprehended by a mounted troop of Turkish cavalry.

It had been a traumatic experience I would have liked to erase from memory. We'd been brutally and repeatedly sodomized by the Turkish troopers. Hugh had been decapitated before my eyes. I'd been knocked senseless and had regained consciousness to find myself incarcerated in a stinking oubliette that I later discovered was located in the Syrian town of Hama. Convinced that I'd been condemned to a lingering death, I'd given up all hope. Then, more dead than alive, I'd been returned to Aleppo and restored to health.

My natural assumption had been that someone in England had raised and paid my ransom. I retained that beguiling misconception during the weeks of my recuperation. It wasn't until April, when I'd fully regained my strength, that the true reason emerged. The emir of Aleppo had realized a profit from another source. I'd been sold into bondage.

The man who purchased me from my Turkish captors was a Venetian Nobleman from the Ionian island of Kefallinia, Count Leonardo Orsini. With no commercial experience Orsini had been persuaded by Niccolò and Maffeo Polo to finance an expedition, a trading caravan bound for a far and mysterious realm, Cathay. Apart from a Bedouin guide and Arab camel drivers, Orsini's party was comprised of a young traveling companion named Carlo, six Lombard retainers, sixteen Greek men-at-arms forming a mounted escort, and a Venetian merchant from Acre named Lorenzo Roccenti.

Had Orsini had even the vaguest conception of what con-

fronted him, wild horses couldn't have dragged him on the
expedition. Yet perhaps I wrong him. Orsini was driven by a
compulsion to prove himself in an arena completely foreign to
his nature. He had dire need of my services as a military
commander. Neither his retainers nor his Greek men-at-arms
had had the benefit of any military training whatsoever.

The journey took two years and three months from Aleppo
to the imperial capital of Cathay, Cambulac. Count Orsini
was among those who did not complete the appalling trek into
the unknown.

The first leg of the journey, from Aleppo to Merv, took
from April to September. We crossed the Syrian desert, the
Zagros Mountains, and the Persian desert. Three of the mounted
escort and five of our horses perished in the desert sands.

At Merv we paid off the Bedouin guide and camel drivers.
Shortly thereafter we contracted with Brother Demetrios, the
Nestorian cleric who had been recommended by the Polos as
a qualified guide for our onward journey.

We wintered in Merv. In March we began our journey,
though we didn't enter the mountains proper until May, at
which point we traded our string of Bactrian camels for pack
mules and our horses for shaggy surefooted mountain ponies.

Regionally, the mountain ranges were known collectively
as the Roof of the World. They defy adequate description.
Soaring peaks perpetually mantled in snow and ice, passes
where the thin air left us gasping, plateaus bereft of growth of
any kind, gorges down which roiling streams rampaged, yawning chasms thousands of feet in depth, all of which conspired
to present us with well-nigh impassable barriers. The crossing
exacted a heavy toll in men and beasts.

Six mules, four ponies, four of our men-at-arms, one
muleteer, and one of Orsini's retainers lost their lives by
falling to their deaths or being swept downstream by raging
torrents. Then, when we were descending toward more hospi-
table terrain, we were ambushed by Tibetan bandits. Four
more of our party lost their lives, among them Count Orsini.

If it served no other useful purpose, Orsini's death released
me from bondage. In fact I was chosen by the survivors as
their leader for the remainder of the journey.

Early in September we emerged from the mountains at the oasis of Yarkand, our party reduced now to half its original number. To my dismay I learned that Yarkand was but the halfway point of the transit from the Outremer to Cambulac.

We skirted deserts boasting giant restless dunes, stopping briefly along the way at Kashgar and Turfan. We suffered no further casualties, e'en though the Taklamakan, Lop, and Gobi deserts made Persia's Dasht-e-Kavir look like child's play. Then, in January, the rock-strewn expanse of the bitterly cold Gobi desert gave way to the gently undulating frost-brittled grasslands of the Mongolian steppes.

In mid-February we beheld an awesome spectacle, a massive crenelated battlement studded at intervals with watchtowers stretching as far as the eye could see. I was told by Brother Demetrios that this fortification stretched from its western extremity at Shanhai Pass in an unbroken line to the Eastern Sea, an incredible distance of *seven hundred leagues*.

As the twin-humped camels of our caravan ambled sedately through the gaping gate in these long-abandoned defenses, we entered Cathay. Brother Demetrios referred to the realm as "China." The Chinese were wont to call it the "Middle Kingdom."

Such was the immensity of the realm that it took us another four months to reach its imperial capital, Cambulac. And that lengthy peril-beset journey had been but a prelude to adventures awaiting me in fabled Cathay.

God's bonnet, I thought glumly, on my return to England who would believe me? Who would credit that I'd traveled steadily eastward for two years without once setting foot outside realms over which Kubilai Khan held sway? If I told of a realm bounded on its northern frontier by a single battlement seven hundred leagues in length, or that boasted a manmade waterway extending southward for three hundred leagues, I'd be labeled a raving lunatic. Who would give credence to cities with populations in the millions?

What would it profit me to recount how I'd commanded an army of battle-tested veterans well before I'd reached my twenty-fifth birthday?

If I didn't want to be held up to ridicule, or have my sanity questioned, much would have to remain unsaid. I'd have to speak with Gentle Breeze about that. She'd have to guard her tongue as well, lest she be taken for an imbecile.

Chapter Four

On the eleventh day of the march our scouts reported contact with elements of the Army of the Jade Panther. Our sister army had Yungchow under siege. Marshal Sögatü had moved north from Kweilin and established temporary field headquarters near Yungchow.

When we made camp that evening I sent for Toghu. When he arrived I came directly to the point. "The khan has authorized your promotion to general of the third rank, to become effective in the Month of the Cock."

I watched Toghu closely. Though he tried to keep expression from his features, a momentary widening of his eyes betrayed surprise. I took this to mean that he'd not heard, directly or indirectly, of the pending promotion and probably had no idea that it had been in response to my recommendation. It could also mean that he no longer reported to Cambulac on my activities.

"Since the Month of the Cock is only a few days off," I continued evenly, "I've taken the liberty of advising you early so that you can attend Marshal Sögatü's briefing on the morrow."

"Thank you, sir. I wasn't expecting promotion to banner rank."

I smiled. "It normally goes with a cavalry command. Now, General Toghu, if you'll join me in a bowl of kumiss we'll drink to your promotion . . . and future promotions."

*   *   *

One of Sögatü's aides met us on our approach to Yungchow bearing word that we should make only temporary camp and that the marshal expected me and my senior officers to attend him in his command pavilion within an hour after our arrival.

Generals Wu, Toghu, and I arrived at the appointed hour. I'd expected the marshal to be an imposing figure. In appearance this was not the case.

Even by Mongol standards Sögatü was short of stature. He was lean almost to the point of emaciation. Above hollow cheeks his cheekbones flared like hawk's wings. His slitted eyes were all but hidden beneath bushy eyebrows. A moustache bracketed his thin-lipped mouth, but no beard adorned his pointed chin and his head was completely bald. Despite his unprepossessing appearance, however, a palpable aura of arrogant authority enveloped him like a suit of armor.

Sögatü greeted us brusquely, then launched immediately into a briefing. From time to time he directed our attention to a large-scale map.

The Sung forces were contained within a giant arc anchored in the east on the seaport of Swatow and in the west on the coastal town of Kochow. The northernmost limit was a mountain village called Kweitung. The major cities located on the perimeter were Kanchow, Yungchow, Kweilin, and Linchow. The eastern sector, from Swatow to Kweitung, had been assigned to the Army of the Golden Boar. From Kweitung to Kweilin was the responsibility of the Army of the Jade Panther. My army was to take over the western sector from a point midway between Kweilin and Linchow to the coastal extremity south of Kochow.

Sung forces occupied most of the cities and towns within the containing perimeter, their major stronghold being the heavily fortified river port, Canton.

Our arrival boosted the Yuan forces to a total strength of about ninety-five thousand. Sögatü's sources of military intelligence estimated that the Sung forces enjoyed a numerical superiority of approximately four to one but were ill-equipped, had few cavalry units, and were composed largely of untried conscripts whose morale appeared to be at a low ebb.

The marshal stated matter-of-factly that the task confronting his forces was straightforward. It was to wrest the towns and cities on the rim of the arc from Sung hands, then shrink the perimeter inward until the surviving Sung forces were squeezed into Canton. When Canton fell, as fall it must, the conquest would be completed by driving any resisting remnants into the sea.

Sögatü was coldly realistic. He didn't picture the mandate as an easy undertaking. Few, if any, defended positions would surrender without presenting stiff resistance. In his estimation we faced no major battles in the field. Besiegement appeared the more likely course of confrontation. He stressed that the campaign was not seasonal in character. Pressure would be exerted relentlessly and continuously until the last vestige of Sung resistance had been obliterated.

At the conclusion of the briefing Sögatü, his mouth compressed into a thin line, regarded me disapprovingly for a moment before dismissing us curtly. The animosity was almost tangible. I made a mental note to exercise caution in any dealings I had with the Mongol marshal.

Early the following morning we broke camp and continued toward Kweilin, still some ten days' march to the southwest of Yungchow. For the most part we followed the course of the Siang River where it cut its way through rounded hills and low mountains.

Our advance met with little opposition. The flanking cavalry units skirmished with harassing elements but the main body of the army saw no action and our progress wasn't slowed. We reached Kweilin at the end of the first week of the Month of the Cock.

By the time we arrived on the scene, Kweilin had been under siege by units of the Army of the Jade Panther for well nigh two months and showed no signs of being even close to capitulation. I discussed the situation with the commanding general of the Army of the Jade Panther. He was resigned to a lengthy siege and was of the opinion that I'd face similar conditions both at Linchow and Kochow. Were it not for the siege engines in my baggage train, I would have concurred with him.

Having agreed upon a reliable communication link between
our armies by means of manned outposts at strategic intervals
and mounted couriers, we parted company and continued our
march to the south. Linchow, the larger of the two population
centers on the outer rim of the sector assigned to the Army of
the Blue Dragon, lay but a week's march to the southwest. I
planned to stop there just long enough to place the city under
partial siege by ringing it with a detachment of cavalry. My
major thrust would be directed first against Kochow, some
seventy leagues to the southeast.

My reasoning was strategically sound. I wanted to put my
mortars and rocket launchers to the test as siege engines
against the smaller community before engaging the larger
target of Linchow.

We arrived at Kochow in early November, as the Month of
the Cock was drawing to a close. Through an emissary I
offered the city generous surrender terms. I wasn't at all
surprised when the terms were rejected.

The east-facing defenses looked to be the weakest. I positioned my battery of mortars and rocket launchers accordingly,
but to achieve maximum effect, I withheld the bombardment
until the hours between midnight and dawn.

To the militiamen manning the eastern battlements it must
have seemed as though the gates of hell had been flung wide.
The mortars belched flame. Wave after wave of rockets streaked
toward the ramparts, etching fiery wakes against the night
sky. The predawn stillness was shattered by a roar like a
thousand demons howling in agony. The defenses rocked and
trembled as projectile after projectile slammed into the earthworks and stone ramparts. As the rockets exploded at the end
of their trajectories they limned the battlements in a hellish
lurid glare.

It was spectacular, but the question was: What damage was
being inflicted? I ordered the bombardment to continue while
I went about preparing myself to determine the answer to that
question.

One of the duties of my servants had been to remove my
armor, piece by piece, from its storage chest on a weekly
basis to keep it burnished and lightly oiled. I'm sure that none

of them guessed the purpose for which the curved and molded bronze plates and sections were intended. Until now no one but the armorer who had duplicated my rusted steel armor in Cambulac had seen me girded in plate armor.

Under my direction my servants assisted me as I donned full armor. Outside my tent Scimitar was being barded, trapper-draped, and saddled.

I clanked stiffly from my tent, uncomfortably aware of the unaccustomed weight of the armor. I was assisted into the saddle and handed up my arms-emblazoned shield and a battle lance from which two pennants of de Beauchamps colors fluttered. Then, with Scimitar at a sedate walk, I made my way to the command pavilion, where my staff officers awaited me.

My appearance was greeted by an awed hush. In fact both Liu and General Wu shielded their eyes against the glare of sunlight reflected off my burnished armor.

I would be less than honest if I didn't admit to the sin of pride. Certainly vanity played a part. Yet the armor was prompted by more practical considerations.

Sending Chang ahead to call a halt to the bombardment, my staff officers and I approached the forward siege line at a leisurely pace. When we were nearly upon them, the mortars and rocket launchers fell silent—a sudden stillness that was a welcome relief for the eardrums. Motioning my officers to stay where they were, I lowered my visor and rode at a slow canter through the thinning smoke toward the city walls.

The Chinese are uncommonly superstitious. I was counting heavily on that fact. Just as I'd started the bombardment at a time when the human spirits are said to be at their lowest, so had I timed my entrance on the scene to take advantage of midmorn sunlight. Suddenly, after six hours of thundering noise, silence! Then a lone rider materializes out of the drifting smoke. The rider's horse is armored and richly caparisoned. The rider is faceless and gleams like gold in the sunlight as he approaches unconcernedly to well within bowshot. It should be an unnerving spectacle.

Of course, I had expected to be greeted by a hail of arrows. That was the prime reason for donning armor. But the specta-

cle I presented seemed to have paralyzed most of the archers.
A few arrows glanced harmlessly off my armor, then none
followed even though I now was clearly within range of both
bow and crossbow.

When I could descry the condition of the wall, I reined in
and subjected the stonework to critical scrutiny. The fortifications had sustained damage, but not as much as I'd hoped to
see after six hours of steady bombardment. Wheeling Scimitar,
I rode slowly back toward my silent mortars and my waiting
staff officers.

What happened next took me completely by surprise. As I
neared our lines, I raised my visor. It was as though that were
a signal. A spontaneous cheer went up from the crews of the
siege engines. It was picked up and echoed by the troops
within range of my vision.

If I'd achieved nothing else that day, my show of bravado
had added a broader meaning to my acquired name, the
Golden Barbarian.

As a proving ground for the siege tactics I'd devised,
Kochow served admirably. I soon perceived one reason that
might have led to the mortars and rocket launchers' having
fallen into disuse. After prolonged use they posed a threat to
their operating troops. Two mortars were blasted into flying
fragments that killed and maimed their attending crews. On
more than one occasion rockets loaded into heated launchers
exploded prematurely. Another drawback was that my supply
of iron projectiles and rockets was limited and had to be
conserved for the action I contemplated against Linchow.
And, lastly, while they were effective and fearsome weapons,
as siege engines they had limitations.

Pounding the lower earthworks served no purpose. Projectiles directed against the thick base and lower portions of the
stonework might crumble the battlements eventually, but it
looked to be an agonizingly slow process. Accordingly, I had
the mortars moved closer to their target and elevated so that
fire could be concentrated on the upper battlements. This
necessitated the construction of heavy wooden shields to protect the mortar crews from arrows and crossbow quarrels.

The rockets were my biggest disappointment. Against an

advancing battle formation they'd been lethally effective, but as a means of battering defensive stonework they proved virtually worthless. For one thing the timing of their detonation could not be controlled with accuracy. For another, their flight paths were far too erratic. I had the launchers moved forward and set to higher elevations. Now the rockets were directed to clear the battlements and rain terror and destruction within the besieged city.

To conserve projectiles I ordered that a number of catapults be constructed as a backup for the mortars. In my estimation the traditional Chinese design for such siege engines left much to be desired. I suggested some changes along the lines of the mangonels and petraries I'd seen used by French artillerymen at the siege of Tunis. Within four days the catapults were built and were hurling massive boulders against the fortifications.

From dawn to dusk the battlements were pounded relentlessly for the next nine days. Shortly after dawn of the tenth day the walls were breached sufficiently to allow my foot soldiers to stream into the city. We suffered casualties, but resistance was much lighter than I'd anticipated. In a matter of hours the northern gates of the city were opened from within, permitting Toghu's cavalry to sweep into Kochow at full gallop. By midday the beleaguered city capitulated unconditionally.

The Sung *chün fa* of Kochow was a tyrannical warlord who was both military commander and supreme civil authority. He was captured attempting to flee the city.

I had the warlord, his senior officers, and the mandarin civic officials brought to the square fronting the governor's palace. The warlord was brought before me. Coldly, I ordered his decapitation. Sentence was executed on the spot.

The military officers and civic officials stood with impassive faces stoically accepting the fate they must have thought in store for all of them. Their resignation changed to wide-eyed disbelief when I addressed them in Mandarin stating my terms of surrender.

First, all arms within the city were to be surrendered immediately. Second, the contents of the treasury and the city's food stocks were to be turned over respectively to my paymaster and quartermaster. Third, my troops were to be accorded the freedom of the city. Fourth, the assembled military and civic officials were publicly to swear allegiance to Kubilai Khan and the Yuan dynasty, in return for which their lives would be spared and their property exempted from seizure.

Lest this leniency be mistaken for weakness, I bluntly outlined the rest of my conditions. The city and prefecture would be governed by a military commander appointed by me. He would be responsible for the distribution of food, the allocation of labor, and the collection of taxes. He would govern by edict. He would be assisted in his task by a council of advisers, also to be appointed by me. To enforce his decrees he would have at his disposal a Yuan military garrison. Any infractions of the regulations promulgated by my military governor would be punished by public execution of the culprit and his entire family and the confiscation of all his property. Any civilian or former Sung soldier found to have brought false witness against any of my troops would be summarily tried and executed.

An hour later I gathered my unit commanders and issued strict orders that the townspeople of Kochow were not to be molested except in cases of infractions of the military governor's decrees. Any cases of murder, rape, or looting involving Yuan troops were to be investigated by the unit commanders, and if found culpable, the guilty soldier was to be publicly executed.

The generosity of my terms was not inspired by softheartedness. I intended them to serve a dual purpose. The Army of the Blue Dragon was understrength and faced with a shortage of available manpower. I wanted to create a climate that would be favorable to replacement by local recruitment. A secondary objective was to reestablish Kubilai's erstwhile reputation for magnanimity.

It took but four days to install Yin Po as military governor, appoint an advisory council, detail and quarter the garrison troops, and restore order in Kochow. Two days later General

Toghu reported that Sung units attempting to withdraw to the west had been intercepted and killed to a man and that mopping up operations had been successfully concluded in the immediate area.

The subjugation of the city and prefecture of Kochow had been concluded in less than three weeks.

Chapter Five

The autumn months of the Cock and Dog are delightful in
South China. The humidity drops, the days are warm and
sunny, and the nights are pleasantly cool. In the waning days
of December, as the Month of the Boar comes on the scene, a
cold dry wind blows from the north.

The Army of the Blue Dragon was marching north toward
Linchow when the seasonal change overtook us. Christmas, a
day of no significance except to me and Brother Demetrios,
came and went. We were still two days' march from Linchow
on the eve that ushered in the year of our Lord 1277.

Wearing a quilted robe, I was absorbed in the task of
trimming my beard when Brother Demetrios pushed aside the
rug-screened flap and entered my tent. Over his frayed cassock he wore a quilted jacket. He'd abandoned sandals in
favor of felt boots. He stamped his feet, blew on his fingers,
then walked over to the brazier and extended his hands
toward the glowing coals.

"There's a bite to the wind," he observed.

I pushed the bronze mirror to one side, laid my razor on the
table, and reached for the wine jug.

"Here," I said, extending a cup. "This will warm you on
the inside."

The friar accepted the cup of wine and sipped from it
appreciatively. "In another couple of hours we'll toast in the
New Year."

I lifted my cup. "It's been an eventful twelvemonth."

"That is has, Edmund, lad, that it has. Had those thieving Polos not choused us out of the caravan profits, I'd be on my way west by now. When last we toasted in a year, I'd have called anyone mad who suggested that a year from then I'd be attached to a Mongol army on the march."

I grinned. "If Orsini hadn't been killed, we'd have had no profits to share."

"True, but in that case I'd have hired myself out as a guide and still have been on my way west . . . at least as far as Turfan. Instead, I allowed you to persuade me to join this insane adventure."

"How are they taking to your presence?"

"Remarkably well. Many armies have shamans, or Buddhist *fan seng,* or both, traveling in their trains, but I know of no army in China that has a Christian cleric as spiritual adviser to its commanding general. The men look upon me as added proof of your eccentricity."

"And the officers?"

"The junior officers subscribe to the thinking of the troops. With the senior officers it's a different story."

"How so?"

"They recognize the duality of my role. They consider you uncommonly astute to use me as a religious-cum-financial adviser. Most of them applaud your sagacity."

"Most? Who are the exceptions?"

"Actually, only one. General Wu. Before I came along he was taking advantage of your ignorance to line his purse at your expense. Now that I've cracked his rice bowl, he looks on me with a jaundiced eye. I have it on good authority that he thinks me to be filling *my* purse at your expense."

"Which, of course," I commented dryly, "you wouldn't think of doing."

Brother Demetrios lifted his eyes toward the smoke-filled peak of my tent. "Heaven forbid . . . except within reasonable bounds. But if I *did* want to cheat you, it would be the simplest thing in the world. I had no idea how much *kan hsieh* was involved in military procurement. Why have I devoted my talents to caravans all these years when armies—

thirsting for spiritual guidance and ripe for plucking—roam the land?''

Brother Demetrios drained his winecup, then wiped his lips and chortled. ''You don't know it, Edmund, lad, but you're well on your way to becoming a legend.''

''An oddity. That I'll grant you. How could it be otherwise, given my marked differences in features, size, and coloring? But that hardly constitutes a legend.''

''Height, features, coloring—and the fact that you're the youngest general commanding a field army—certainly are part of the growing myth, but a small part. The image has been abuilding piece by piece for more than two years.

''Think on it, Edmund. First there was your astonishing mastery of the Mandarin dialect and Chinese pictograms. I'm the only one who knows that it took you the better part of two years to acquire those skills. Rumor has it that you mastered the language almost overnight. Then there was the trial by combat from which you emerged the victor. Following that you were placed in command of a cavalry *touman* and—wonder of wonders—were given a concubine from the khan's harem. And no one has lost sight of the fact that you introduced the awesome black-powder engines of destruction.

''When you reached Changsha, you were promoted to banner rank, a further mark of the khan's esteem. At Hengyang you rode into battle wearing strange garb, wielding unconventional weapons, and mounted on an armored steed. To hear some tell it, you practically won the day single-handed. It is said you lived a charmed life. It is stoutly maintained that the sable birds depicted on your escutcheon have magical powers which confound your enemies and protect you from harm.''

''Utter nonsense!''

''Not entirely, Edmund, lad. Legends grow from factual backgrounds, even if the facts tend to get distorted in the telling and retelling. As a point in case, you would be hard put to believe, let alone recognize, the stories already being circulated about your performance at Kochow.''

I was sure he was referring to the appearance I'd put in before the siege line, but I wanted it confirmed. ''What performance?''

Brother Demetrios chuckled as he extended his winecup.

"Innocence ill becomes you. You know perfectly well what performance. E'en though I was with you when you ordered the armor copied, I'd not seen you arrayed in all its gleaming splendor until Kochow. I gather no one had. It was awe-inspiring. I'll grant you that it afforded you immunity from arrows but all the rest—your shield, pennant-festooned lance, and Scimitar's silken trapper—was purely theatrical. It had all the elements of Greek drama."

I grinned as I refilled his cup. "I don't deny it . . . but it wasn't done to impress my officers or men. It was done to play on the superstitions of the Sung militiamen. As the siege engines fell silent, and before the smoke cleared, I rode toward the battlements like an avenging angel coming to proclaim the city's doom."

"More like a demon from the netherworld than an angel. I would say that you achieved the desired effect. I strongly suspect that the reduced resistance we encountered was due to the fear you instilled in the hearts of the city's defenders. I can assure you that your fame is no longer confined to the Army of the Blue Dragon."

"I hope it hasn't caused you embarrassment."

Brother Demetrios laughed. "On the contrary. Since it's well known that I'm your friend and confidant, I take advantage of the situation. It allows me to bask in your reflected glory." He raised his winecup to eye level, and added, "Here's to a happy and prosperous New Year. May it add luster to the legend."

We joined up with the cavalry units surrounding the city. The following day the siege of Linchow began in earnest. I anticipated a lengthy siege, since the Sung defenders had had more than enough time to make overtures to the containing cavalry units with respect to surrender. Surely, by now, the Sung warlord had learned of the fall of Kochow. On the other hand, since Linchow was much closer to Kweilin than to Kochow, the attitude of its Sung defenders probably was being influenced by what was transpiring at Kweilin. There, the besiegement by units of the Army of the Jade Panther was well into its fourth month and its defenders showed no signs of wavering.

We positioned the mortars, rocket launchers, and catapults to direct the major thrust of our assault against the south-facing battlement. The bombardment had been under way for the better part of four days before I called a temporary halt.

I debated leaving aside my shield and battle lance. As Brother Demetrios had said, they would play no part in my inspection. But, no, they were part and parcel of an English knight's accoutrement. I'd as lief have sallied forth without my sword as leave my shield behind. After all, I'd established the precedent at Kochow and there was nothing to be gained by abandoning it on this occasion.

I rode forth at Linchow as I had at Kochow, in full equipage as befitted a Norman chevalier.

The first thing that struck me as odd was that not so much as a single arrow was let fly at me despite the fact that I approached the walls to a point where I could clearly distinguish bowmen peering at me from between the battered merlons. What transpired next was wholly unexpected.

I'd completed my inspection of the damage wrought on the stonework and was about to turn Scimitar toward our siege lines when the south gate of the city swung partially open. A single rider emerged and moved toward me. My first thought was that the Sung warlord had chosen a champion to sally forth and challenge me to single-handed combat. I reined in and waited to see what would develop.

As the mounted rider neared, I identified him by his trappings as a Sung general. Combat appeared unlikely. The more probable explanation was that the general wanted to discuss surrender terms. Perfectly willing to accommodate him if that was his intention—or to accept a challenge to do battle, should that be what he had in mind—I waited patiently.

When he'd closed the distance to about twenty paces, the general reined in and dismounted. He sank to his knees on the stubbled soil of a paddy field and kowtowed. Rising up, he drew his sword and, holding it with its hilt extended toward me, he advanced with measured tread.

I raised my visor and stared at the approaching figure incredulously. God's blood! Was this some kind of stratagem, or was the general actually surrendering the city?

When he came alongside my stirrup, the general said something in a dialect I couldn't understand. Noting my frown of bewilderment, he handed his sword up to me and indicated the city with a sweeping wave of his hand to make his meaning abundantly clear.

Without losing a man the Army of the Blue Dragon had taken Linchow.

The city could have withstood a lengthy siege. The encircling cavalry could have starved Linchow into submission only by laying waste to the surrounding countryside. Mindful of the havoc created by Mangatei's massacre at Hengyang, I'd expressly prohibited such scorched-earth tactics. The cavalry had acted solely as a containing force. They had not been in sufficient strength to seal off the city, and in consequence the city had been resupplied by stealth during the dark hours. Only with the arrival of the main body of the army had it been possible to put in place what amounted to an impenetrable barrier.

When we entered the city, we found the rice stocks in the granaries but little depleted and week-old produce still being sold in the marketplaces. Why then had Linchow capitulated?

I believe the answer to that question was, in part, that word had reached Linchow of the generosity of my terms of surrender at Kochow. But the deciding factor appears to have been that neither the general commanding the defending force, nor the governor, was very deeply committed to the Sung cause. It had taken but token pressure to make them shift allegiance to the Yuan. The ease with which we'd achieved our objective caused me some concern.

I presented the same surrender terms to Linchow as I had to Kochow, with but one difference. I withheld judgment on the governor and the military commander.

"Are men of such shallow convictions to be trusted? Should the tide swing against the khan, where would they stand? There seems little point in making them swear allegiance to Kubilai," I commented to Brother Demetrios.

The friar laughed. "They'll go with whichever side is winning. Their only true loyalty is to the land. They're realists. Here, in Kwangsi Province, they are a long way from the Sung seat of authority in Lin-an. I doubt that the residents of Linchow care very much one way or the other who governs them. As for the governor and the general, the question to ask yourself is whether or not they were popular figures on the local scene."

"They both seem to enjoy popularity."

"Then don't question their loyalty. Use them to advantage."

I accepted the friar's advice. When I installed General Wu as Linchow's military governor, I saw to it that both the former governor and erstwhile military commander had prominent positions on Wu's advisory council. Both appointments were well-received by the townspeople.

Linchow showed little evidence of having been subjected to a siege. Damage had been inflicted on its southern battlements. Explosive-headed rockets had caused fires in some sections of the city. Within a few days of the city's surrender laborers were hard at work restoring the defenses, and a latticework of bamboo scaffolding betokened repairs to fire-damaged residences.

Neither in appearance nor in the attitudes of the city-dwellers did Linchow strike one as a conquered city. There was nothing subdued about the city or its inhabitants. Life, with all its noise and bustle, went on as usual. The troopers and foot soldiers of the Army of the Blue Dragon mingled freely with the townspeople and were treated more as guests than as conquerors.

My staff and I directed the transfer of authority from a residential compound pressed on us by a wealthy merchant. Spoils of war! Gifts had been presented to me at Kochow, but in Linchow I was showered with expensive presents to the point of embarrassment. As Brother Demetrios pointed out when I suggested rejecting some of the more expensive gifts, to do so would cause the donor to lose face. When I protested that the donors would expect favors in return, he commented dryly that I'd already returned the favor by granting them their lives and allowing them to retain their property. He suggested that I graciously accept whatever was given me. After all, if my objective was the acquisition of wealth to defray the expenses I anticipated, I should not complain when expensive gifts were thrust upon me. It was sage advice.

The spoils of war, however, aren't confined to material

benefactions. The favors embrace wider spectra, such as the provision of female companionship.

While I'm a man of lusty sexual appetites, my taste runs more to European than Asiatic standards of beauty. The young women presented for my selection were courtesans skilled in erotic practices. I found no fault with them in that respect. Where I encountered problems was that almost invariably they had bound feet—a barbaric fetish I found repugnant. When my aversion to footbinding became known, the supply of lissome lovelies dropped off dramatically; yet it was still more than adequate for my needs. The only remaining drawback was that, by comparison with Gentle Breeze, they lacked the ability to bring fire to my loins. They satisfied my physical desires but left me emotionally far from satisfied.

The lunar New Year was upon us. Linchow was in festive mood. We joined in the festivities as the Year of the Rat gave way to the Year of the Ox.

Early in February, on the ninth day of the Month of the Tiger in the new lunar year, word came to me from Kweilin. A month earlier Marshal Sögatü had moved his headquarters to that location. The message I received from him was that my siege engines were required at Kweilin without delay.

There were a number of reasons that led me to welcome the marshal's directive. It indicated tacit acknowledgment of the effectiveness of the devices in siege warfare. A second reason was that my stocks of iron projectiles and black powder were being depleted more rapidly than I'd anticipated. Consideration should be given to establishing a foundry and black-powder factory in South China, preferably Changsha. I had intended to have a scribe prepare a scroll outlining the necessity for these facilities in the south. Now I could present my case to the marshal in person. Not only would I send the siege engines to Kweilin, but I would accompany them in order to advise Sögatü of their limitations and how they could be used to best effect.

The mortars, rocket launchers, rockets, projectiles, and kegs of black powder were loaded on wagons. When I'd appointed General Wu as military governor of Linchow, I'd given a dual responsibility to Toghu. Not only was he the commander of cavalry, but my acting second in command. I turned over temporary command of the army to him and set off for Kweilin with the wagon train of siege devices.

I had an escort of two troops of cavalry and was accompanied by Brother Demetrios. Although I'd not told him of it as yet, I had in mind for him a specific mission.

Chapter Six

Although we could move at a faster pace than an army slowed by its baggage train, the two-wheeled *mappa*s on which the siege equipment was loaded governed our speed of advance. It took us five days to reach Kweilin.

As we neared the city the rounded hills gave way to terraced paddy fields and flatland bordering the Kwei River. Ahead, masked by folds in the hills, lay the walled city. We were still some li from our destination, yet I could see that the dusty roadway was lined on both sides with what appeared to be an honor guard. I found this surprising. Why should Marshal Sögatü welcome us in this manner? He'd displayed little by way of affection at our previous meeting.

It wasn't an honor guard. Far from it. As we came up to the men that had looked to be lining the route at rigid attention, what we found were corpses impaled on bamboo stakes. The sharpened bamboo had been inserted into their rectums with the lethal points scant inches from vital organs. When the poor wretches could no longer support their weight on tiptoe, the points had penetrated ever deeper as the impaled victims settled lower on the stakes. It was an agonizingly slow and painful way to die. I wondered what had brought this fate upon them.

All the corpses were naked below the waist and there was nothing by way of clothing clinging to their upper bodies by which they could be identified. Most of them were in a state of decomposition, yet some appeared to have been impaled more recently. All of them faced inward toward the roadway. Where flesh still masked the skull beneath, the lips were drawn back from the teeth in silent screams of agony. These phalanxes of cadavers were staked at intervals of about ten paces. They extended, hundreds upon hundreds of them, over the last four li of the southward approach to the city. It was a macabre and unnerving spectacle.

Marshal Sögatü received me in his command pavilion. He was abrupt to the point of rudeness. "Why are you here? It wasn't necessary for you to accompany the siege engines. You belong with your army."

I explained as best I could that what we'd learned through trial and error I felt should not be left to a subordinate to explain. Moreover, there were matters pertaining to the siege devices and their continued and expanded usage that I thought should be discussed between us. Though they'd proven their worth at Kochow and Linchow, in themselves they didn't guarantee a quick end to any siege. At best they merely speeded up the breaching of fortifications with the added advantage of instilling fear in those manning such defenses.

"I intend to evaluate their usefulness," Sögatü said tersely. Following a pause he added, "I don't consider them to have played a dominant part in your recent successes."

"They were a contributing factor."

"I'll judge that for myself. In my estimation you had the singular good fortune to encounter forces which had no stomach for further resistance."

The implication was that my army would have faltered if faced with stiff resistance. It was an imputation that I deeply resented, yet I withheld comment.

"That," Sögatü continued caustically, "has not been the case at Yungchow, or here at Kweilin. The Army of the Jade Panther has faced stubborn resistance. Last month, in fact, its cavalry routed a strong Sung force attempting to lift the siege of Kweilin."

That explained, I thought, the corpse-fringed approaches to the city. They were Sung survivors unlucky enough to have been captured. Again, I made no response.

"I strongly disapprove of the surrender terms you presented at Kochow and Linchow," the marshal observed acerbically. "Such leniency will be interpreted as softness."

"I received no direction with respect to surrender terms," I countered heatedly. "At first glance the terms might seem overly generous but the penalties for noncompliance should discourage continuing resistance. My reasons for this approach are twofold. They are designed to improve the khan's image and, by the same token, encourage recruitment."

Sögatü glowered at me from beneath his beetling brows. His next comment caught me completely off guard. "You were unconventionally garbed at the battle of Hengyang. I've heard comment on that score. But at Kochow, and again at Linchow, you saw fit to parade yourself conspicuously in gilded finery. What purpose did that ostentatious display serve?"

The tone of his question left no doubt concerning his disapproval. Why? Why was he making no effort to mask his animosity? Why was he belittling the performance of the Army of the Blue Dragon and leveling criticism against me personally? Was he trying to provoke me?

With an effort I held my temper in check. "The armor wasn't gilded. It was bronze, copied from my steel plate-armor at the khan's order. It might seem unconventional in Cathay, but it's the customary battle garb of European knights-at-arms."

"Then why didn't you wear it at Hengyang? Why wait until this campaign to honor us with such grandeur?"

I fought to keep annoyance from my voice. "At Hengyang the action was of lengthy duration. My stallion was protected by armor. Lacking the stamina of a Flemish war-horse, he'd soon have buckled under the added weight had I worn full armor. So, I wore chain mail, which is much lighter. At Kochow and Linchow my horse could sustain the weight for the short period involved and *I* needed the protection of plate armor in order to get close enough to the battlements to ascertain the damage inflicted by the siege engines."

Sögatü accepted my explanation with a curt nod which I took to be a gesture of dismissal. I wasn't prepared to accept it as such, since I'd yet to advance my proposal concerning the siege engines. "Sir," I said, "there is another matter I would like to bring to your attention."

"What matter?" he growled ungraciously.

"I will soon need additional supplies of black powder for the mortars. Resupply from Cambulac will take many months. We could save a good deal of time by setting up a factory at Changsha. I would like, sir, to request a six-week leave of absence to attend to the project."

"Why Changsha? Why not Linchow?"

"Two reasons. Materials needed to make the black powder can be transported to Changsha by river craft. The second reason is that the khan has expressed the wish that I take a wife. I'm betrothed to Governor Wang's niece. He will ensure that the project receives priority attention."

Sögatü's brows drew together in a scowl and a muscle twitched on his cheek. I was sure that he was going to refuse my request and was surprised when he gave it his grudging approval. "Four weeks," he grated. "A cavalry troop is scheduled to join your army in the Month of the Hare. The officer commanding the troop is Kubilai's grandson, Prince Timur."

I left the marshal's command pavilion seething inwardly. The performance of the Army of the Blue Dragon hadn't warranted criticism. Since my army would have to stay encamped at Linchow until the fall of Kweilin and Yungchow, I could see no reason for Sögatü to have reduced my leave of absence from six weeks to four.

I was still fuming when I reached my tent. It wasn't until I was pushing aside the tent flap that it came to me. God's teeth! Timur! Patently, it was not to the marshal's liking that Kubilai's grandson had been posted to the Army of the Blue Dragon to undergo field training.

Brother Demetrios put down his chopsticks, belched, and eyed me owlishly. "What other choice does he have?" the friar queried in Greek.

I replied in the same tongue. "When the Sung force failed to lift the siege, precious little. I'd hate to stand in his shoes as Kweilin's military commander. Every time he looks down from the battlements his gaze falls on the decomposing corpses lining the approaches to his city. A grisly reminder of the fate in store for him. So, unless he can find a way to make good an escape, his only option is to hold out as long as possible and pray for a miracle.''

"It's little wonder Sögatü has called on your siege engines . . . and I'm not at all surprised that he granted you leave to set up a black powder factory in Changsha. Regardless of what he might say of an uncomplimentary nature, you've demonstrated the effectiveness of the devices in siege tactics. Sögatü needs them.''

"But not me. He made that painfully obvious.''

The friar nodded. "True, but think on it, Edmund. Like Sögatü, the commanding generals of the armies of the Jade Panther and Golden Boar, generals Toktai and Bayntu, are Mongols, and both armies are bogged down in protracted sieges. Only the army commanded by a 'foreign devil' is enjoying success. Yours would have been Sögatü's *last* choice had he been asked to recommend an army for Prince Timur's introduction to conditions in the field. Manifestly, Sögatü wasn't consulted—which has added to his resentment.''

"His antagonism seems to go deeper than resentment.''

Brother Demetrios chuckled. "Of course it does. His spies have informed him of your growing popularity with the rank and file of the Army of the Blue Dragon. Sögatü views that with suspicion. He sees you as a possible threat to his authority. Only a *possible* threat, mark you, otherwise he'd not have shown his anger openly. Walk softly, lad. If he comes to look on you as an active threat, he could destroy you, Kubilai's favor notwithstanding.''

I'd regretted my pointed references to Kubilai's patronage during my conversation with Sögatü. In retrospect they seemed pointlessly stupid. Sögatü hadn't needed any reminders about my privileged position. It had been like rubbing salt into an open wound. I vowed to keep a tight rein on my temper and guard my tongue in any future dealings with the marshal.

Brother Demetrios leaned back against the cushions and rubbed his paunch contentedly. "Tell me, Edmund,'' he said, "why did you want me along on this trip? So far I can't see how I've been of any assistance."

"I wanted you in case Sögatü rejected my request for a leave of absence. Had that happened, I'd have asked you to supervise the setting up of the factory at Changsha."

"Then I'm beholden to the marshal for granting you leave. The idea of sharing your hard ride north doesn't have much appeal for me."

"That's a shame, little father, because you're coming with me when we ride out at dawn tomorrow."

His look of complacency was replaced by one of bewilderment. "Whatever for?"

"There's something else to be attended to in Changsha that I can't do myself without attracting unwanted attention. I want you to make discreet inquiries among merchants to determine how we can convert the paper money and strings of cash we're acquiring into precious stones."

The friar's brow cleared. "You shouldn't need too many gemstones. Your passage can be paid in Chinese specie. Chinese currency is negotiable in any Arab port that trades with China."

"I appreciate that, but Hormuz, or Siraf, or whatever port we reach in the Persian Gulf, still leaves us a long way from England."

"But not too far from Acre. I thought that Roccenti was supposed to have your swollen share of the caravan profits waiting for you in Acre."

"I've a dark suspicion that I won't find Roccenti in Acre. In truth, I know not if Acre still remains in Christian hands."

"Hmmm. I see what you mean."

I smiled. "I thought you would. More wine?"

The friar shook his head. "No, Edmund. If ride forth at dawn I must, sleep beckons."

When Brother Demetrios had taken leave of me, I added a few more lumps of charcoal to the brazier and stood gazing into the glowing coals reflectively.

It was ironic. I'd been raised to believe that tradespeople and commercial activities were beneath contempt. To an enfeoffed nobleman in Europe the mere thought of trade was anathema. Yet here I was immersed to my ears in financial planning. Who would have thought that I'd be brought to this?

I'd come by my attitude toward the merchant class naturally. In England the tenant farmers of estates paid rents in produce or in specie. The collection of these levies was left to stewards and chamberlains. Any delinquencies in payment fell within the purviews of the constables of castles or the sheriffs and bailiffs of the shires. Feudal lords, such as my father, were responsible to church and state for everything, and everyone, within the confines of their fiefdoms, yet they were shielded from petty fiscal concerns. This left them free to devote themselves to weightier matters, such as safeguarding the public weal.

I must confess that this attitude had colored my reaction to the Polos, who judged everything in terms of profit and loss. Marco, some two years my junior, I could tolerate even though I found him singularly lacking in humor, but his uncle and father I found well nigh unbearable. Nor could I bring myself to think of them more charitably now that my own thoughts were gravitating toward mercantile activities.

I had no choice. If I wanted to escape from the khan's silken web, I had to adjust my thinking accordingly. It was a simple matter of survival. Praise be to God I had Brother Demetrios assisting me, but his support was transient at best. Once quit of Cathay, I'd be cast on my own devices.

Though I'd confidently asserted to Brother Demetrios that King Edward would restore my rightful lands and title once I reached England, I was not sure that this would happen in whole, or in part. The king might well bestow on me a title, yet withhold land. I could face the prospect of being an impoverished knight-at-arms. For myself that caused me little concern. I could sell my sword to the highest bidder. But I had Gentle Breeze to consider.

I stirred the coals with a bronze poker and watched the sparks dance upward, hang for a moment in the still air, then, one by one, wink out. Life, I thought, was something like those briefly glowing points of light. The upward path was erratic—the inevitable end, oblivion. Ashes to ashes!

I chided myself for such morbidity. Gentle Breeze and I were but on the threshold of life. It was ours for the shaping, regardless of her abiding faith in karma.

Chapter Seven

We were a party of eight, I, Brother Demetrios, and six escorting cavalrymen. We traveled lightly laden with naught but saddlebags. No banners or pennants proclaimed the presence of one of rank. In garb, if not in stature, I was indistinguishable from a cavalry trooper. I was not riding Scimitar. Our intention was to average better than ten leagues per day. To do that we'd have to change horses along the way at Chuanhsien, Yungchow, and Hengshan. A hard ride lay ahead of us.

We'd left in the half-light of dawn. Even now, as the daylight strengthened, it was a gray and somber day. A thin fog hugged the ground, hiding the walled city from view and obscuring the roadway. As we gained higher ground in the surrounding mountains, the clutching tendrils of mist grew more tenuous, then gave way entirely to naught but haze and low-pressing clouds.

We were in the waning days of February. For the past few weeks the weather had been undergoing a change. No longer were the winds from the north. They'd grown light and undecided as to direction. The nights were still raw and cold but the days were growing warmer and decidedly more humid.

February! Some two weeks gone Thomas de Beauchamps would have celebrated his seventh birthday. I could not but wonder what manner of lad he was now. Did he still favor me in coloring and appearance?

I'd fantasized about his mother only the previous night, something I'd done frequently in years gone by but only rarely of late, yet had devoted not so much as a passing thought to her bastard son.

Why had Ethelwyn of Hebb intruded unbidden into my innermost thoughts? It was because my deliberations had turned on the difficulties I undoubtedly would face on my return to England. God's teeth, was she not the root cause of all my problems—the very reason I now found myself in the Middle Kingdom?

The memory of her had sent the blood surging to my groin. I did not often resort to masturbation to find sexual release, but had done so last night. I thought wryly of the term crusading knights applied to such self-gratification: "flogging the gauntlet." To the Chinese it was known as "massaging the one-eyed monk."

I considered the subtle differences in the terminology applied to the onanistic act. In a sense it illustrated the wide gulf that separated European from Asiatic thinking. The crusaders' analogy conjured up visions of self-flagellation in expiation for some real or imagined sin. The Chinese expression presented imagery of an entirely different nature, of pleasurable, unhurried self-indulgence.

It mattered not what term I applied to the act. The fact was that Ethelwyn of Hebb had occupied my inflamed thoughts to the exclusion of all else as I'd coaxed my rigid shaft toward ejaculation. If not for the act, at least for the fevered fantasy, I experienced a compelling sense of guilt. It brought sharply into focus an episode from my youth I'd lief forget. Some events, however, refuse to lie decently buried.

As I rode along over the stone-smoothed roadway winding through the rearing pinnacles and weathered mountains to the northeast of Kweilin, my thoughts disconcertingly bridged time and distance. Once again I found myself reliving the events that had transpired in the spring months of 1269, events that were to affect me profoundly and do much to shape my future.

I was going on eighteen, an undergraduate at Oxford's Merton College reading classical Latin and Greek. Studies were not to my liking. I would much have preferred to have been knighted at sixteen to take my father's place in the ranks of England's tourneyers. I was at Oxford owing to the insistence of Brother Bartholomew, the Dominican monk who had been my mentor, tutor, and confessor since childhood. Reluctantly, my father had acceded to the good monk's wishes.

In early April my father had written advising me of his remarriage to someone named Ethelwyn of Hebb. His news came as a surprise. My father, then a widower of nine years' standing and left partially crippled by a jousting accident, had evinced little interest in the opposite sex. Quite naturally I was curious as to what manner of woman could have rekindled desire in my father sufficiently for him to have taken her to wife and in so doing made of her my stepmother.

In late April word reached Oxford of an event of such magnitude that all thought of further education fled my mind. England's Henry III had joined forces with his longtime foe, Louis IX of France. Setting aside their differences, the two monarchs had agreed to make common cause in a holy crusade directed against the forces of Islam.

We were visited at Oxford by the preceptor and knights from the Hounslowe Preceptory, a commandery of the Knights Templar. The purpose of their visit had been to persuade upperclassmen and undergraduates to take the cross in this holiest of causes. Though fired with crusading zeal, the idea of taking vows in a militant religious order held little appeal. I wished to be knighted by my father's hand, then take the cross. Surely Brother Bartholomew would raise no objection to this course of action.

Early in May I bade farewell to Merton College and pointed my horse's head toward our family seat on the Welsh border, Ravenscrest Castle.

Two surprises awaited me at Ravenscrest. My father had journeyed to the court at Windsor and wasn't expected to return for some weeks. Since his presence was required for my investiture, I was keenly disappointed.

It was, however, the second surprise that proved to be the most unsettling. My stepmother was scarcely two years my senior, a woman of hauntingly surpassing beauty.

A goodly company dined that evening, but I had eyes only

for Ethelwyn of Hebb, though I tried not to make it obvious.
She must have known how she affected me. To mask my
disquietude I drank more wine and mead than was my wont
and stumbled off early to my bedchamber.

Some hours later I awoke to find Ethelwyn disrobed at my
bedside. In seducing me she took the initiative, but that
doesn't absolve me from blame. I was a more than willing
partner to the act.

Never before had I encountered anything remotely approaching the unbridled passion exhibited by Ethelwyn of
Hebb. Orgasm followed orgasm, and when I had tried to
disengage, she had held me firmly sheathed by constricting
her vaginal muscles while she coaxed my flagging phallus to
renewed rigidity.

Now, thinking back on it, I shifted my weight in my saddle
and smiled self-deprecatingly. At that time I had thought
Ethelwyn to be unique in that erotic dexterity. Subsequently I
had been proved wrong. I'd told Gentle Breeze of the
experience, attributing the competence not to Ethelwyn but to
a Syrian slave girl. Practicing in secret, Gentle Breeze had
mastered the art to a point where, if anything, she surpassed
Ethelwyn's expertise.

Once more memory winged me back to Ravenscrest, to the
disquieting aftermath of Ethelwyn's seduction. When leaving
my bedchamber, her parting remark had been an invitation to
a further assignation. It was only then that the enormity of
what I'd done struck me with chilling force. Unable to sleep,
I'd paced the castle battlements steeped in guilt and remorse.
Patently, my stepmother didn't intend our coupling to be an
isolated incident.

I'd cuckolded my own father! I'd dishonored him. If my
immortal soul wasn't already beyond redemption, but one
course was open to me. I doubted that I had the strength to
resist temptation, therefore I must not stay so much as another
day under the same roof as my stepmother.

It presented me with a dilemma. My investiture called for
my father's participation, but I couldn't remain at Ravenscrest
awaiting his return. I could follow him to Windsor, but I
dreaded the thought of facing him.

It was daybreak before the obvious solution struck me.

There *was* a means by which I could attain knighthood and take the cross without involving my father—a militant religious order.

I rode to nearby Coombs Abbey to apprise Brother Bartholomew of my decision and to seek his advice concerning the whereabouts of the closest preceptory of the Knights Templar. To my astonishment Brother Bartholomew would not hear of my taking such a path to knighthood. He tartly pointed out that, apart from my not being temperamentally suited to such a calling, as heir to the Hartleigh earldom and estates I had an obligation to continue the bloodline. Any religious order demanding vows of celibacy was out of the question.

I could not dispute the monk's logic. I had no choice but to seek out my father. That very morning I rode forth toward Windsor and then, since the king and court had moved temporarily to that location, to Nottingham.

That I was resolved to take the cross delighted my father, who forthwith arranged for my investiture. Of a truth, Prince Edward, who would lead the English crusading force, was sorely in need of knights.

It was a proud moment for my father when I, together with fourteen other aspirants, was knighted by King Henry's hand.

His business at court concluded, my father tarried at Nottingham only long enough to witness my participation in my first royal tourney. I did not accompany him on his return to Ravenscrest. It would have been folly for me to have done so.

When I bade him farewell at Nottingham, it was the last I was to see of my father.

Chapter Eight

It had rained intermittently for the better part of our journey, but from Hengshan onward it rained without letup. Heaven and earth seemed joined by an opaque curtain of somber gray. The roadway became a quagmire. Soaked to the skin, we rode in single file, hunched forward in our saddles, keeping wherever possible to the sodden verge skirting the mud-bogged road. The final twenty-four-league leg of our journey took three and a half days to negotiate.

When we reached Changsha, I arranged for my cavalry escort to be billeted with the city's garrison, following which Brother Demetrios and I rode directly to my residence. How word of our coming reached the compound ahead of us, I know not, but when, mud-splattered and weary, we rounded the spirit screen and emerged into the outer courtyard it was to find Gentle Breeze and the entire household staff assembled before the Hall of Ancestors to make us welcome.

We were greeted effusively. To an accompaniment of chatter and laughter the friar was led off to one of the compound's many residential pavilions. With Gentle Breeze skipping ahead of me, peppering me with questions, I proceeded to our quarters in the dwelling once occupied by the former occupant of the compound, the patriarch of the venerable House of Soong. As we wound our way through inner courtyards and along covered walkways, I did my best to satisfy her curiosity.

Yes, it was quite true that the Army of the Blue Dragon

had been victorious at Kochow and Linchow, though the stories that had reached Changsha had been greatly exaggerated. No, the campaign was far from at an end. Then why was I here? I explained that I'd used our shortage of powder and projectiles as an excuse to visit her, albeit briefly. Well, it wasn't an excuse without a basis in fact. I would have to devote *some* time to military duties. Yes, I'd missed her. And yes, I could do with a hot bath, a hearty meal and, providing it fell in with her plans, a good night's sleep.

In the bathing chamber she'd seen to it that the sunken bath was filled with hot scented water. I stripped off my soggy outer garments, damp underclothing, and, naked and shivering, sank gratefully into the steaming bath. I stretched out full length and let the warmth seep into my very bones and leach the fatigue from my aching muscles. Then, when I sat up, Gentle Breeze soaped my back, neck, shoulders, and chest. I attended to rubbing soap into my hair and beard. When I was thoroughly lathered, Gentle Breeze cascaded water over me from ewers filled with hot water and laughed as I spluttered protestingly.

When I rose dripping from the bath, she toweled me vigorously and draped a robe over my shoulders. Then she pressed herself against me and murmured innocently, "Shall I order the food served in the bedchamber or the salon, my lord?"

I drew her close and laughed softly. "My appetite seems to have deserted me. It is my one-eyed monk who hungers most at this particular moment."

Gentle Breeze laughed throatily and slid her hand up the inside of my thigh until her fingers met and curled around my swelling phallus.

Brother Demetrios joined us in the salon for our evening meal. He'd replaced his customary cassock with a flowing gown of brocaded silk and his sandals with soft slippers of embroidered felt. The graying fringe of hair above his ears had been neatly trimmed. Freshly scrubbed, his face literally glowed, though how much of that could be attributed to the flush imparted by the hot rice wine he was consuming in liberal quantities, and how much to good health and high spirits, was a matter for speculation.

The friar selected a tender morsel of duck, dipped it in soy sauce, then added it to the contents of his rice bowl. He sighed contentedly and observed, "Delicious! A most welcome change from the rough fare to which we've been subjected for the past ten days."

"Rough, but substantial," I said. "Wherever we stopped along the way, folks went out of their way to entertain us royally."

"That they did, Edmund, lad . . . but our stops were confined to small farming communities. It's good to be back in a city untouched by war."

"Make the best of it, little father," I said. "Within the week we'll be on our way back to beleaguered Kweilin. There's much to be done in the few days at our disposal."

Brother Demetrios chuckled. "True . . . not the least of which, I imagine, will be plans for your forthcoming wedding. Tell me, has it been decided just which of the governor's nieces is to be the blushing bride?"

The friar's sally was not to my liking. I scowled. Gentle Breeze and I had been far too occupied to discuss that painful subject. I shot her an inquiring glance.

She smiled sweetly. "Wang Mei-ling. Actually there never was a question of which we'd choose. Yü-huan is too shrewish to make a suitable wife for my lord. I included her in the negotiations solely to prolong the process. Governor Wang submitted Mei-ling's name to Cambulac for the khan's approval more than a month ago. The answer should be forthcoming within a matter of weeks."

The following morning I called on Governor Wang to discuss my plans for the establishment of a black-powder factory and to invite his suggestions concerning the selection of a local foundry to cast both iron projectiles and bronze mortars of a modified design. I was warmly received.

Having disposed of the business at hand, our conversation turned to other matters of a military nature. The governor had received word that the envoy sent by Kubilai to treat with the Nipponese emperor had been put to death. Kubilai, from all accounts, was beside himself with rage. He'd issued orders for the raising of an expeditionary force in Southeast China to augment the armies already assembled in the Kingdom of Korea and had commissioned the construction of a fleet of transport vessels to ferry Yuan forces to Nippon. Manifestly, Kubilai's intention was to launch an all-out invasion against the eastern island kingdom.

This news disturbed me, even though it didn't come as a surprise. When he'd been banished to an army command in Korea, General Hsü Ch'ien had predicted that this might be the shape of things to come if Kubilai's envoy met with Nipponese intransigence. What troubled me was that the raising of an expeditionary force in Southeast China could only mean that Kubilai would have to draw on the Yuan forces now engaged in the campaign against the Sung. As commanding general of the Army of the Blue Dragon, this was a matter which directly concerned me. I shouldn't have had to learn of the khan's intentions from the governor of Changsha. I concluded that, even though nothing had been said to me about it, Marshal Sögatü must be alive to the developing situation.

Governor Wang appeared to be remarkably well informed. I questioned him concerning the expeditionary force in the far west, the campaign to which Marco Polo was attached as an observer. Wang told me that the Yuan force from Tali was enjoying conspicuous success. It had pushed into the princely state of Kaungai, had inflicted a decisive defeat on the Burmese at Ngasaunggyan, and was said to be in hot pursuit of the Burmese now fleeing westward into Pagan.

If Governor Wang's information was accurate, it was encouraging insofar as the campaign against the Burmese was concerned. It struck me, however, that the Yuan forces were becoming overextended. Kubilai had too many irons in the fire. It was obvious that he had in mind conquest extending well beyond the borders of the Middle Kingdom, but such plans would have to be held in abeyance until he'd completed the subjugation of the recalcitrant Sung. Until the Sung were crushed, I didn't see how he could turn his attention to further military adventures. And, as far as I could see, the campaign against the Sung was far from completion.

I left the governor's palace deep in thought. I was confident that Sögatü eventually would conclude his campaign successfully. It was only a question of time. Yet, when

finally the Sung had been driven into the sea, the conquered
territory would have to be garrisoned. From which army, or
armies, did Kubilai mean to draw the garrison force? What
did he have in mind for the Army of the Blue Dragon? More
to the point, what did he have in mind for me?

I shrugged. At the moment those questions were pointless.
All I hoped was that I'd be long gone before they were
answered.

Over the next four days the weather improved. Fleecy
clouds floated lazily in the sky. The sun-warmed cobbled
streets of the city dried. Birds sang in the blossom-bedecked
peach and cherry trees. I was thankful for the change, since it
made my task much easier. I had to spend most of my waking
hours absent from the residence.

The site I selected for the powder factory was outside the
city walls located on the bank of the Siang River. It was far
enough from the city that an accidental explosion would cause
no damage to the metropolis, nor do any harm to the city-
dwellers, yet close enough so that the factory workers wouldn't
have too far to walk. I found workers familiar with black
powder and recruited a work force from the various small
shops that made and sold firecrackers. With Brother Demetrios
acting as a go-between, I arranged for supplies of sulfur and
saltpeter to be delivered to a quay close to the factory site on a
regular basis. Charcoal was readily available locally. The
friar negotiated a contract with a Changsha cooper for a
steady supply of kegs. We drew up plans, and construction
got under way on the sheds and warehouse needed to house
the factory. I was assured that the factory would be in at least
limited production within a matter of weeks and full production no later than the end of the Month of the Hare.

I next turned my attention to the foundry recommended by
Governor Wang. The iron projectiles presented no difficulties,
but the urn-shaped mortars were a somewhat different
proposition. I presented drawings illustrating what I had in
mind. I wanted the bronze castings to be thicker in the base
and walls than the devices I'd originally procured from the
armory in Cambulac. In addition I wanted iron straps secured
to the outer walls to strengthen them. The foundry's chief

artisan studied my drawings carefully. He finally agreed to produce one mortar so that I could subject it to a field test. If that prototype proved satisfactory, he would turn out more of the devices as required. The only drawback was that it would take him at least two weeks to make the prototype.

Attention to all these details absorbed much more of my time than I'd anticipated. In consequence the time I could devote to Gentle Breeze was less than I'd expected. Nor did it help that my preoccupation with these vexing details left me short of temper. I fear that I was less attentive to her than I should have been.

Her infectious good humor didn't desert her entirely, but on the fifth day of my brief homecoming, she became noticeably quiet and withdrawn. I should have taken heed of this as a warning signal, but put it down to the approach of the time of her red tide. She was wont to grow irritable at such times. Any wrong word or gesture on my part could have sparked an explosion, yet I can't recall having said or done anything to make her react as she did.

We had dined with Brother Demetrios. All through the meal Gentle Breeze had taken no part in the conversation. When the friar had taken leave of us, we retired to our bedchamber. When I took her in my arms, she stiffened and moved from my embrace.

"Do you recall when first we met in Turfan?" she asked.

I was perplexed, both by her avoidance of my attention and by the unexpected nature of her question. "Ye-es. What makes you ask?"

"You acted strangely, both in Turfan and when I was sent to your tent in Shangtu. It was as though the sight of me reminded you of someone else. Was that so?"

"In face and form you put me in mind of my stepmother, Ethelwyn of Hebb. I've spoken of her to you."

"Rarely. If I reminded you of her, she must have been much younger than your father. You didn't mention that."

I didn't like the direction of the conversation. "She was my senior by several years," I responded cautiously.

"Since you profess to find me attractive, she also must have found favor in your eyes. Is that not so?"

I frowned. "I don't wish to discuss it."

"Why not?" she snapped. "Is her memory sacred?"

I suppressed my annoyance with difficulty. "There was an incident between us I'd fain put from my mind."

"Without success," Gentle Breeze observed acidly. "Upon occasion you've used her name when making love to me. I can only assume from those slips of your tongue that not only did you bed her, but that she's still in your thoughts."

God's blood! Had I used Ethelwyn's name in the heat of passion? I must have done so—and recently. I should have started with a clean slate by telling Gentle Breeze about Ethelwyn. Now I was left with no choice but to explain myself as best I could.

Chivalry, and pride, dictated that I not disclose the fact that it had been Ethelwyn who had taken the initiative. Omitting that aspect, and certain other intimate details, I recounted the illicit encounter at Ravenscrest. I blamed myself; youthful passion inflamed by wine was my excuse. In particular I stressed the shame I'd felt following the rash act.

Gentle Breeze's eyes flashed. "You hunger for her still. That is what draws you toward your homeland."

"Not so," I retorted angrily. "It was a fleeting infatuation . . . nothing more."

"This son of hers who now holds your title . . . he is of your spilled seed, is he not?"

Gentle Breeze's intuitive perceptiveness astonished me. "She claims not. She alone knows for certain."

"And so you fled, knowing that if you stayed the act would be repeated. . . . Is *that* not so?"

"I . . . ah—" There was no answer I could give without inviting further recrimination.

Her eyes sparkling with unshed tears of anger, Gentle Breeze tugged at her robe to straighten it. "The memory of her continues to inflame your blood," she snapped. "Then let that memory warm your bed . . . until Mei-ling can take its place." Then, with an angry toss of her head, she swept from my bedchamber.

My mind in turmoil, I watched the swaying curtain till it stilled. What had prompted the tirade? If she'd harbored those disconcertingly accurate suspicions about Ethelwyn of Hebb, why had she waited until now to throw them in my face? And that parting thrust about Mei-ling was sheer nonsense. No one knew that better than Gentle Breeze. It was she who had supported the khan's contention that I should take a wife, and Mei-ling had been her choice, not mine.

"God's blood!" I groaned aloud. "If I outlive Methuselah, I'll never understand women."

The gray light of waxing dawn was brushing aside the shadows of night when Gentle Breeze crept into my bedchamber and crawled in beside me. Her face was wet with tears; her shoulders shook with sobs. I held her close and stroked her hair gently until her sobs subsided and she slept encircled in my arms.

I never did learn what had prompted her to force the issue. Strangely, though, it served to clear the air. It swept away the cobwebs of uncertainty that had been slowly abuilding in my mind. Never again did I fantasize about Ethelwyn of Hebb. Nor did I ask myself again the question whether or not she'd have paid my ransom. I think I'd always known the answer, but had been reluctant to face it. Her son, Thomas, notwithstanding, my rejection of her invitation to continue the illicit relationship had been an intolerable blow to her pride and she'd not have come forward with the ransom.

The confrontation Gentle Breeze had precipitated had acted as a catharsis. Perhaps *that* had been her purpose.

Chapter Nine

Before going on to Linchow we stopped at Kweilin long enough for me to issue instructions to the officer in charge of my siege engines, and to render a report to Marshal Sögatü concerning the progress made at Changsha.

The bombardment of Kweilin's defenses was still under way, but there was every indication that a breach in the walls was imminent. My orders were that the engines were to continue the bombardment until the walls were breached and the city capitulated. By that time the prototype mortar should have been delivered from the foundry in Changsha. If not, however, the officer was not to wait for delivery, but was to bring his equipment and rejoin the Army of the Blue Dragon at best speed.

General Toghu reported to me on my return to Linchow. There had been little change during my absence. There had been fewer disciplinary infractions than I'd anticipated. Another welcome piece of news was that recruitment had exceeded my expectations. The Army of the Blue Dragon now stood at a strength of slightly better than twenty thousand.

I advised Toghu that we should be ready in all respects to break camp and move out on short notice. Our next objectives were to be the cities of Pinglo and Kweiping. At Pinglo, the northernmost of those cities, we would be assisted by units of the Army of the Jade Panther acting under my command.

Somewhat to my surprise word had not yet reached Toghu

that a cavalry troop under the command of Prince Ye-su Timur would soon be joining our force. The only order I gave Toghu was that under no circumstances was the prince to be given preferential treatment.

My siege-engine company rejoined the army later that same week in late April. The officer in charge reported that Yangchow had fallen, and after four days of bloody fighting within its breached walls, Kweilin had capitulated. In retaliation for Kweilin's obdurate resistance Marshal Sögatü had exacted a grim price. All officers above the rank of captain and all civic officials, together with their families, had been sentenced to death. It had been nothing short of a bloodbath. Most of the public executions had been by decapitation, but more lingering deaths had been meted out to the Sung military commander, the governor, and senior members of their respective staffs. These executions had been carried out by the use of devices referred to by my officer as the "birdcage" and the "board cage."

From having seen a number of corpses in varying stages of decomposition, I was familiar with the Mongol refinement of protracted execution known familiarly as the birdcage. The condemned culprit was stripped naked and placed in a bamboo cage of such dimensions that he could neither stand nor lie down. In that cramped confinement the victim simply starved to death. The body remained on display, suspended in a public place for all to view, until the flesh rotted from the bones and the skeleton was bleached by the elements.

The device he'd referred to as a "board cage" was something I'd yet to encounter. Not wanting to display ignorance, I said nothing. Later in the day I questioned Brother Demetrios about this form of execution.

"It's reserved for only those of the highest rank," the friar explained. "You've seen it used in Cambulac's Square of Celestial Serenity."

"When? I don't recall seeing anyone executed there."

"You didn't recognize it as an execution . . . and I didn't draw it to your attention. The condemned man was suspended in a cage in an upright position clad in his full regalia of rank as a minister of the court."

"Oh. I recall that spectacle. He didn't appear to be suffering.

I thought he was simply being subjected to public ridicule, a punishment similar to England's pillory.''

"I know nothing of this pillory you mention, but the official certainly was being exposed to scorn and pity until death released him from his agony. If you'd looked closely you would have noticed that his head protruded through a hole in the top of the cage. A circular wooden collar, called a 'cangue,' was fastened around his neck preventing the withdrawal of his head. The cangue was about two and a half feet in diameter, so even though he could reach up through the cage, he couldn't reach his mouth.''

"He looked well fed to me.''

"I imagine he was. Relatives and friends give him food and drink.''

"Then what causes his death?''

"The cage had another feature which escaped your attention. The condemned man's feet were resting on a wide board elevated a foot or so from the bottom of the cage. The board fits into slots spaced one inch apart. The normal procedure is for the board to be lowered one set of slots each day. By the eighth or ninth day the poor wretch is standing on his toes. Very soon there comes a point where he can no longer remain on tiptoe and his entire body weight is on the unyielding cangue. His neck stretches and slow death by strangulation follows. His relatives can do nothing but stand by and watch him die. Moreover, the board need not be lowered on a daily basis. The agony of life can be prolonged almost indefinitely.''

The Fourteenth Cavalry Troop, Prince Ye-su Timur commanding, joined the cavalry of the Army of the Blue Dragon early in May. A few days later, when the Month of the Dragon gave way to the Month of the Snake, we broke camp and advanced eastward. When we reached the village of Loyung, I sent a cavalry detachment north to Changsha to fetch a resupply of powder, projectiles, and the prototype mortar that should be awaiting pickup at the foundry.

I must admit I toyed with the idea of detailing the Fourteenth Troop as part of the northbound detachment. It would remove Prince Timur from whatever danger confronted us. I put that idea behind me as smacking of favoritism, the very condition I'd instructed Toghu to avoid at all cost. The Four-teenth Troop stayed with the main body of the cavalry.

At Loyung I broke the force into two sections. The smaller section, under Toghu's command, struck out in a northeast-erly direction to rendezvous with units of the Army of the Jade Panther and place the fortified city of Pinglo under siege. The larger section, under my command, swung south toward the walled city of Kweiping. Timur's cavalry troop was with my section.

After a three-day march we came to the Hungshui River and followed it downstream for a further three days until we reached Kweiping, situated at the confluence of the Yu and Hungshui rivers. We encountered no opposition of any conse-quence along the way. Kweiping, however, was a different matter. Its gates were closed and its defenses fully manned.

I'd divided my siege engines equally between the two sections of the army. It made little difference, since my dwin-dling supply of rockets, powder, and projectiles allowed only token employment of the devices. Our reliance would have to be on catapults.

On the seventh day of the siege Major Chang and Brother Demetrios visited my tent at an early hour. Chang did the talking. The friar stood to one side grinning like a court jester savoring a clever witticism.

"Sir," Chang said diffidently, "the unit commanders have expressed a wish they wanted brought to your attention."

Wiping soapsuds from my face and beard, I said, "Just what do they have in mind?"

"If you were planning to ride forth today to inspect the city's defenses, they respectfully request that you postpone the inspection until tomorrow, or the next day."

I was nonplused. I didn't think that the catapults had inflicted enough damage to warrant an inspection. "If they are that anxious to storm the walls," I said tersely, "I'll have a look at them. But why tomorrow? Why not today?"

"Today is an unlucky day."

When Chang left, I turned to Brother Demetrios. I hit my forehead with the heel of my palm. "God's bonnet, how am I supposed to remember which are unlucky days? I don't even know what day it is by the Christian calendar . . . how am I supposed to keep track of theirs? Does today happen to be the fifth day of their lunar month?''

A chuckle welled up from the friar's chest. ''Same thing. It happens to be the fourteenth. One and four add up to five. You should be flattered, lad. When the Chinese warn you about lucky and unlucky days, it means they hold you in esteem . . . a rare privilege for a foreign devil. They've taken it upon themselves to guide your barbaric footsteps in the path of wisdom as dictated by the ordered passage of the stars in the heavens.''

''Hmmph!'' I snorted. ''Why do they want me to assess the damage to the defenses? They know as well as I that it will take at least another week of pounding to breach the walls.''

''It isn't the state of the battlements they have in mind. They want you to put in an appearance in full armor. They firmly believe that the spectacle strikes abject fear in the hearts of our enemies.''

''Am I supposed to perform on cue like a trained dog?''

''Come now, Edmund. As you well know, the Chinese are a superstitious lot. Your troops, both officers and men, are convinced you lead a charmed life, that your armor imparts some mystical power. The enemy appears to share that opinion. Think on it. The armies of the Jade Panther and Golden Boar have experienced heavy casualties. They are emptying the prisons in North China to find replacements. We, on the other hand, have had relatively few casualties . . . since Kochow, virtually none. Your policy of leniency has not been interpreted as weakness. More recruits than are actually needed are being attracted to your banner. It is considered an honor to serve under you. If donning armor adds to your luster as a military commander, take advantage of it.''

''God's teeth,'' I groaned. ''Sögatü considers my knightly accoutrements an affront. My troops are offended if I don't make a display of myself so garbed. I'm damned if I do, and damned if I don't.''

There must have been some truth to the friar's assertions. On the fifteenth day of the lunar month I sallied forth in full trappings to check on the state of Kweiping's west-facing battlements. No arrows greeted me. That evening the city surrendered.

Leaving a garrison at Kweiping, we marched north to join Toghu in the siege of Pinglo. That action, as well, was speedily concluded. Then we had to cool our heels while we waited for the Army of the Jade Panther to take Shiukwan. It was well into September before we marched to the southeast. I celebrated my twenty-sixth birthday before the gates of Wuchow.

I had reason to celebrate. The detachment I'd sent north to procure more projectiles and black powder caught up with us at Wuchow. The snaking column of bullock-drawn carts was a most welcome sight.

Once again the rolling thunder of our mortars, the clouds of drifting smoke, and the flare of exploding rockets were an integral part of our siege tactics. The beleaguered city surrendered after only four days of bombardment.

All through the months of October and November my army sat encamped on the fertile plain outside Wuchow. For all the action we saw we might just as well have been back at Changsha. While we were enjoying the freedom of the conquered city, the less fortunate troops of our sister armies were fighting to bring the defended towns of Yingtak, Sinfeng, and Waichow to their knees.

If Kubilai had wanted Prince Ye-su Timur to gain battle experience, the Army of the Blue Dragon had been a poor choice. In the seven months Timur commanded a cavalry troop with my army, the sieges we undertook were of short duration and not once were we called upon to storm a city's walls and engage in hand-to-hand combat. All he was exposed to was along the lines of garrisoning cities that had surrendered peaceably and the maintenance of order so that neither planting nor harvesting nor the collection of taxes was seriously disrupted. In my estimation those were lessons of more lasting value than learning to kill efficiently.

Late in October, Marshal Sögatü moved his headquarters from Kweilin to the more central location of Shiukwan. Shortly thereafter I received a disquieting directive. It stated bluntly that, owing to increasing Sung intransigence, the governors and military commanders of all towns and cities captured by Yuan forces were to be sentenced to lingering deaths. Additionally, their senior staffs and the immediate families of all concerned were to be publicly executed.

The armies of the Jade Panther and the Golden Boar had followed this practice since the outset of the campaign. Manifestly, the directive was aimed at me personally. It caused me a good deal of concern. It was diametrically opposed to the policy I had adopted. It seemed to be more than coincidence that the directive hadn't reached me until after the departure of Prince Ye-su Timur to take up a new posting in Nanking.

The directive left me no option but compliance. While the former Sung military commander had no official position, I'd appointed the erstwhile governor to serve on the advisory council assisting General Liu, my designated military governor. I summoned the former Sung governor.

When he stood before my desk in private audience, I handed Sögatü's directive to the venerable mandarin. The white-bearded oldster unrolled the scroll and squinted myopically at its contents. Slowly, with obvious difficulty, the old man scanned the brushstroked characters, his wispy beard waggling as he formed words with his lips. It was clear from his reaction that he understood what he was reading. His face paled, his hands trembled, and his shoulders sagged.

When he finished reading, he slowly rerolled the scroll. By the time he handed it to me, he had regained his composure. His posture straightened. His hands no longer trembled. He returned my gaze unflinchingly. "I understand, honored General," he said softly. "I only hope that my unworthy life, and that of General Chu-tse, will satisfy the demands made of you. I will advise the general of the contents of this directive. Rest assured, he will not shirk his duty."

"You need not trouble the general," I said evenly. "You, the general, and your staffs . . . all have sworn allegiance to the khan. He is not a vengeful man. It would not be his wish that loyal subjects lose face—or their lives."

A look of bewilderment clouded the oldster's face. "Then why did you send for me, noble lord?"

"Soon, my army resumes its march toward Canton. In our path lie cities that must be subjugated. I speak specifically now of Koyiu and Samshui. In their cases I would have to comply with what you have just read, would I not?"

"No other course appears open to you, noble lord."

"But I wonder," I said musingly, as though thinking aloud, "what I would do if we reached those cities and found that their gates were flung wide and that the Sung officials, together with their staffs and families, had fled the scene well in advance of our arrival?"

We broke camp and moved out late in December. Our route followed the downstream course of the Si Kiang. On the fifth day of the march we arrived at Koyiu.

Imagine our surprise to find the gates opened wide and the battlements bedecked with flags and banners. A delegation of citizens met us before the gates. They told us that the military and civic officials, together with their families, had disappeared mysteriously and bade us consider the city ours.

While I went about the business of setting up civil administration, I sent a scouting party the two days' march downstream to reconnoiter Samshui. It was my hope that they would report that that city was prepared to make us welcome in similar fashion to Koyiu. That hope proved groundless.

I cannot explain it. Samshui must have been forewarned. The military commander, or the governor, or both, must have been fanatics. They paid for their obstinacy a month later when they starved to death in cages suspended in the market square.

Chapter Ten

The armies converged on Canton. We were the first to arrive.
We took up a position in the hills to the northwest of the city.
Twelve days later the Army of the Golden Boar entrenched
itself on the eastern approaches. A week later the Army of the
Jade Panther, fanned out over a wide front, emerged from the
hills just north of the port city. In February 1278, as the Year
of the Ox was drawing to a close, we placed Canton under
siege.

Under siege it may have been, but sealed off from the
outside world it was not. Sealing off Canton would have
called for a much larger Yuan force than Marshal Sögatü had
at his disposal, the cooperation of the Yuan navy, and putting
to the torch what amounted to a city outside a city.

Just as, in North China, Ch'ang-an was the eastern terminus of the caravan routes, so, in South China, did Canton
perform a similar function with respect to maritime trade. It
was ideally situated to serve this purpose. It was built on the
Chu Kiang at the northern extremity of an estuary that probed
inland some twenty-three leagues from the open sea. Apart
from the Chu Kiang—the Pearl River—four other rivers,
through myriad mouths, emptied into the estuary, the Si
Kiang, Peh Kiang, Tseng Kiang, and Tung Kiang. East,
south, and west of Canton the land was flat and interlaced
with a bewildering network of natural and manmade waterways.
To have brought to a halt the waterborne traffic that pulsed

endlessly through that intricate web was a task well beyond our capabilities, even though naval units had been placed at Sögatü's disposal.

The city's defenses were formidable. The centuries-old moss-blackened walls were massive. The population was such that the battlements could be repaired from within almost as fast as they could be pulverized by outside bombardment. And to starve the city into submission looked to be out of the question.

The city was located on the north bank of the Pearl River. The ground between the wooden quays and storage sheds fronting the river and the rearing fortifications was occupied by a welter of rude thatch-roofed shacks and shanties. A sand spit projecting into the river southwest of the walled city boasted a motley collection of food stalls, wineshops, and doss houses catering to seafarers. Since the crude dwellings crowded right up to the south-facing battlements, it was relatively easy to smuggle produce into the city by means of ropes and ladders let down from the wall. By the same token men could slip in and out of the city under cover of darkness. But the shantytown hugging the southern battlements was not the only quandary facing Marshal Sögatü.

Thousands of small boats clustered along the quays and in the fingering waterways. The families who lived on these craft often lived out their entire lives without once setting foot on dry land. This floating population, called *tankia,* had to be dislodged if the city was to be encircled effectively.

Had the khan not directed that Canton was to be preserved as a focal point of waterborne commerce, Sögatü's dilemma could have been resolved by setting fire to the shantytown and by dispersing the *tankia* by burning or sinking their frail craft. But to do so would have destroyed the wharves and warehouses along the river and damaged, or destroyed, merchantmen tied alongside the quays or anchored in the stream. Once word of such a disaster spread, both river craft and oceangoing vessels would avoid Canton like the plague.

We had no recourse but to breach the walls and take the city by force of arms. In my opinion Canton would not yield readily, nor fall quickly.

*   *   *

Brother Demetrios set out on his journey north, accompanied by a troop of cavalry, on the eighth day of the Month of the Tiger in the Year of the Tiger. The distance from Canton to Changsha, by the shortest route, is approximately one hundred twenty leagues. I didn't expect to see the friar back at Canton until well into May. It might not take him even two weeks to reach Changsha—and the tasks I had given him to perform there should not take long—but on his return he would bring with him Gentle Breeze and his speed would be slowed to that of a sedan chair.

There was nothing I could do to hurry the process. I was resigned to the fact that it would be a minimum of two months, and probably longer, before I once again held Gentle Breeze in my arms. But she was much in my thoughts.

It had been well nigh a year since last I'd enjoyed the company of Gentle Breeze. As before, I hadn't practiced celibacy during those months. Bed companions were thrust upon me as one of the rewards of conquest. I'd have been lacking in manly juices had I spurned such generous offers. Yet, regardless of the skills in the art of lovemaking displayed by these surrogates, I found them capable only of bringing me physical release.

I'd made mention of this to Brother Demetrios. His response had been that my relationship with Gentle Breeze had deepened into an abiding love that beggared comparison. My objection to this observation stemmed from my interpretation of the word "love."

When poets wrote of love, or troubadors sang of it, the image evoked in my mind was of an ethereal emotion divorced from reality. Adjectives such as "lost," "unattainable," or "unrequited" seemed applicable. The knights and maidens-fair of minstrels' ballads seemed always to be pining for something that remained tantalizingly beyond their reach. Yearning, not fulfillment. I couldn't visualize those knights and their dreamlike maidens lying naked and sweat-slicked in each other's arms as they coupled with abandon. The relationship I shared with Gentle Breeze was too vibrant, too earthy, to be labeled by so pale a word as "love."

But if love wasn't applicable, how could my feelings be

expressed? Forsooth, I knew not. All I knew was that I'd met no one who could take Gentle Breeze's place. I had need of her.

Together with elements of the Army of the Golden Boar, the Army of the Blue Dragon interdicted the western approaches to the city and patrolled the flank fronting on the river. Instituting searches in the rabbit warren of huts and hutches—even had we known who or what we were looking for—would have been an exercise in futility. Our efforts were concentrated on keeping merchant vessels under close surveillance.

The latter activity provided me with an opportunity to learn something about the centuries-old trade between the Arab world and Cathay, or "Al Sin," as China was known to the Arabs. Using the periodic searches of ships as an excuse, I had the sailing masters of a number of ocean-going dhows brought to my command tent for questioning. Imagine their slack-jawed surprise to find not only a flaxen-haired general in command of a Mongol army, but one who addressed them in Arabic.

I learned much about the perilous sea passage between Canton—or Khanfu, as they called it—and Arab ports such as Basra, Siraf, Hormuz, Sohar, and Sur. I'm sure that many of their tales were grossly exaggerated, or were pure fabrications. Who could believe that waves rose higher than the tallest minaret, or that monsters lurked in the ocean depths of such size that they could swallow a fully rigged ship in a single gulp? Who would credit there being lands where natives hunted to collect human heads as trophies?

Woven into the fancy were threads of fact. I had it confirmed that ports in the Persian Gulf could be reached from Khanfu in eight months—if the weather was favorable. I was told that the northeast winds which favored the westward passage blew more or less steadily from October through May. This meant that any merchantman now in Canton intent on a westward voyage must set sail ere many weeks had passed. The alternative was an eastward voyage to Nippon, or to remain in Canton for the next five or six months.

*   *   *

Major Chang brought me the news later in the afternoon. Since it was only the third week in April, I hadn't expected to be advised of Brother Demetrios' return. Unless—

"Less than two hours' ride to the north," I said, echoing Chang's statement. "If they'd been slowed by a planaquin, or sedan chair, they couldn't have made such time. With a horse-drawn cart . . . perhaps. Was there any mention of a wheeled conveyance?"

"All that was reported, sir," he replied tactfully, "was that the holy man and his mounted escort were approaching. Nothing was said about carts, or a sedan chair . . . but that doesn't mean that some such conveyance couldn't be following at a distance."

"Of course," I said, affecting a lack of concern. "The friar probably rode on ahead for some reason. Thank you, Chang."

I was on tenterhooks. Resisting the temptation to ride out to meet the incoming party, I paced my command tent restlessly. If she wasn't with Brother Demetrios, there must be some good reason. There was nothing to be gained by torturing myself with wild conjecture. I would know the answer soon enough.

When a soldier came in to light the oil lamps, I told him not to bother and went directly to my private quarters in the gathering dusk. I had time only to pour myself a cup of wine before I heard hoofbeats and the jingle of harness. I took a swallow of wine to compose myself before pulling aside the tent flap and stepping out beneath the overhead canopy.

There were four horses before my tent. Only one of them showed much liveliness—the steed on which Major Chang was mounted. He must have ridden out to meet Brother Demetrios. The other horses looked well-nigh spent. In the waning light—though I had no difficulty identifying Chang, or the cassock-clad friar—I didn't recognize immediately the other two mounted figures. One of them I assumed to be the commander of the escorting cavalry troop. The other, a slight, turbaned figure wearing a sleeveless jacket over a tuniclike loose shirt, I took, at first glance, to be a boy. While I was wondering why a young lad should be of that company, the youth's lips parted in a flashing smile.

God's bonnet! My heart vaulted upward like a grouse breaking from cover. The fourth dust-filmed rider was Gentle Breeze. The anxiety that had gripped me fled. I laughed aloud as I strode toward the mounted figures, evoking an answering laugh from Brother Demetrios and a broad smile from Chang.

I lifted Gentle Breeze down from the saddle. When her face came level with mine, I hugged her close and, oblivious to the onlookers, kissed her hungrily. Her arms encircled my neck as she returned the kiss with equal fervor. Just how long we would have stood there, our lips glued together, is hard to say. I lost track of time and place, then was brought back to reality by Brother Demetrios pointedly clearing his throat. As I eased her to the ground, a gurgling sound something like the purring of a contented cat issued from between her lips as she slid her fingers down my bearded cheeks.

I turned toward the friar. "Thank you," I said.

Brother Demetrios beamed down at me. "My pleasure. Unless you have questions that need immediate answers, I'll leave my report on the trip until tomorrow morning."

I grinned. "If you value your life, little father . . . not before noon."

They didn't linger. Chang seized the reins of the weary mare Gentle Breeze had ridden and led it off. I had one of my servants carry Gentle Breeze's saddlebags into the tent and ordered the servants to fetch a bathing tub and buckets of hot water. When the tub and water were brought, I told the servants that I would order food later and didn't want to be disturbed until I called for them.

While Gentle Breeze disrobed, I filled the tub with hot water. She stepped naked into the tub and stood there in the steaming calf-deep water while she deftly piled her hair atop her head. Then she sank down in the wooden tub, drew her knees up, leaned back, and sighed gratefully as the warmth seeped in to dispel the stiffness of tired and aching muscles. I watching her admiringly, marveling anew at the perfection of her pert-breasted body. God's teeth, was it really two and a half years since she first had appeared in my tent at Shangtu? She didn't look a day older now than she had then.

Stripped down to my undershirt, I knelt beside the tub and gently soaped her breasts, arms, shoulders, and back. The

muscles at the back of her neck and across her shoulders were
tense from fatigue. I kneaded the stiffness from the muscles.
She sighed contentedly.

Her forearms, neck, and face were reddened from exposure
to wind and sun. "Much more weathering," I said jokingly,
"and you'll end up looking like one of my cavalrymen. I
thought that ladies were wont not only to shield themselves
from unseemly scrutiny but from the elements, as well."

It was said lightly. In no way was criticism intended, but I
seemed to have touched an exposed nerve. "I am *not* a
simpering Chinese bitch," she flared, glaring at me. A note
of bitterness crept into her tone, as she added, "If my conduct is considered lacking in decorum, surely it can be excused.
I am a barbarian, am I not?" Then her sense of humor
overrode her indignation. Her features softened and she
chuckled."But I hope I don't look to you like a cavalryman
. . . unless, that is, your tastes have changed during your
absence."

I cupped her breasts in my hands and laughed. "Don't
worry, little one, they have not altered."

She rose to her feet. I rinsed her with warm water. She
stepped dripping from the tub onto the straw mat. I toweled
her dry. When I came to her pubis I noted with inner amusement that it was pink and puffy from recent depilation. "I
hope," I observed, "that your barbaric lack of restraint did
not prevent you from effecting this cosmetic toilet in private."

She giggled. "Have a care, my lord, lest your half-blind
monk find the gate closed to him."

Chapter Eleven

A thin beam of early-morning sunlight slanted flatly through the opening in the peak of the tent. I stretched lazily and breathed in the faint scent of musk and jasmine that still clung to Gentle Breeze's warm body at my side.

"Mmmm," I murmured contentedly, then added as an afterthought, "I'm starved. Should have ordered us at least a couple of dishes last night."

Gentle Breeze laughed. "Food didn't seem important at the time." She untwined her legs from mine and pushed herself up to a sitting position. Brushing her tousled hair back from her brow, she observed, "But before you order breakfast, hadn't you better let me cloak my nakedness? I don't want you chiding me again for my lack of propriety."

"I wasn't chiding you."

"Well," she said, pushing back the covers and rising to her feet, "that's what it sounded like."

She went over to the basin, splashed water on her face, then walked lightly over to her saddlebags and rummaged through their contents until she found what she wanted. She donned a sheathlike garment of silk that rustled seductively as it slid down over her hips. Over this she put on a brocade robe secured at the waist by a wide sash. She slid her feet into embroidered slippers, then reached again into one of the bags and brought forth a hairbrush. Seating herself on a low blackwood stool, she addressed herself to the serious business of grooming her rebelliously tangled hair. Smiling at me, she said sweetly, "Now, my lord, you may summon your manservant."

I paused in the act of donning underdrawers and pointed at her saddlebags. "Is that all you brought?"

"With me, yes. Wong Sin and the servants are following with our clothing and possessions . . . but I fear it will be some weeks before they get here."

The portent of her answer took a moment to register. I was shrugging into my undershirt before the full significance struck me. "Everything!" I exclaimed. "All the servants? *All* our possessions?"

She stopped brushing her hair and looked at me questioningly. "Yes. Isn't that what you wanted?"

"No. Why should I?"

She looked bewildered. "Won't you have to set up a new household once you become governor of Canton?"

Brother Demetrios was ushered into my command tent. I greeted him with a question. "Where did Gentle Breeze get the idea that I was going to be named military governor of Canton once the city falls to us?"

"She must have heard that from Governor Wang."

"So she said . . . but where did *he* get the idea?"

"From the khan. Wang showed me the scroll. It advised the governor that your army would not return to its former base camp at Changsha. Once Canton is taken, the Army of the Blue Dragon is to take over the administration and policing of the newly conquered territories . . . and you are to become military governor of the city and prefecture of Canton. That's common knowledge in Changsha. Is your concern because you wanted it kept secret?"

"Secret!" I exploded. "God's blood, it seems I'm the last to be informed. I heard naught of this until it came from her lips this morning."

The friar's countenance was a study in confusion. "But you should have been the first to know. Good Lord, Meiling's father is preparing to journey here with his daughter and a wedding party. He but awaits word of the city's surrender."

"Gentle Breeze told me that, as well," I said glumly. "Of *course* I should have been the first to be advised of the khan's intentions . . . either directly, or through Marshal Sögatü, who has to know of this. Why he has kept it from me I can't imagine. I thought his attitude toward me had softened since Prince Timur's departure. Apparently not." I stroked my beard, then added grimly, "I'll demand an answer."

"Now, now, lad," Brother Demetrios interjected hastily, "don't act rashly in anger."

"I've every right to be angry. The troopers of your escort returned from Changsha with this knowledge. By now the news has swept through the army like a plague. I have legitimate cause to lodge a strong complaint, but don't concern yourself, I'll keep a tight rein on my temper. I hold no brief against being installed as the military governor. My objection is to the way I've learned of this."

"I can't say that I blame you. When do you think the city will fall?"

"A hard question to answer. The Sung defense is resolute. Nonetheless, I think we'll be in a position to storm the walls within three to four weeks. After that it will depend on the degree of resistance we meet within the city. Frankly, I think that the Sung forces will simply melt into the local populace and that resistance will be minimal. I would say that Canton will be in Yuan hands by no later than June."

"Mmmm. Sooner than I thought. Your marriage is not far off . . . an event, I wot, little to the liking of Gentle Breeze."

"Nor to mine," I observed tartly. "What prompted you to raise the subject? Has she voiced complaint?"

"None at all," the friar assured me hastily. "Neither in Changsha nor on our journey south, despite the fact that she has ample grounds for grievance."

"God's teeth," I snorted irritably, "what grounds? She knows we must bow to the khan's wishes. It was she who narrowed the choice down to Mei-ling. It's a little late in the day for her to be having second thoughts. I—"

Brother Demetrios stopped me with an upheld hand. "It isn't your taking a wife that concerns her . . . at least not directly. After all, Edmund, she has been raised in a social structure that accepts polygamy as a natural state. Indirectly, however, your betrothal affected her adversely. Women she had thought were friends started to avoid her. Changsha society treated her as an outcast."

I frowned. "She said nothing of this to me."

"I doubt that she will. I learned of this not from her but from Wong Sin. He's devoted to her. The treatment accorded her angered him."

I shrugged helplessly. "What can *I* do about it?"

Brother Demetrios laughed. "Without knowing it, you've already done much just by sending for her. It's astonishing how rapidly the local attitude changed once that fact became known in Changsha."

I had all but lost sight of the fact that both Gentle Breeze and I were looked upon as barbarians. I owed my social acceptance to the khan's patronage. In turn Gentle Breeze had been accepted by association. Without me to protect her, how would she fare in a society that considered even its own women of little worth? What if I fell from favor? It was a possibility I did not care to contemplate.

Changing the subject, I queried, "And what of your other task? Did you have any difficulty converting our paper money and strings of cash to gemstones?"

"None. I did better than I'd expected. Cut and uncut rubies, sapphires and cat's eyes, some magnificent pearls, and several truly beautiful pieces of gemstone-quality jade. A small fortune. If you were of a mind, you could purchase a sea-going vessel and have gems to spare."

"Would that I could, but it would soon come to Kubilai's attention. I wouldn't get out of sight of the coast before a warship overtook me. Do you think he'll get wind of your purchases in Changsha?"

"Undoubtedly, but I doubt he'll learn of their extent. I spread the buying over a number of gem dealers. When it reaches his ears, he'll suspect that I've made the purchases without your knowledge."

"Let us hope so . . . but any thoughts of passage by sea will have to await the fall of Canton. The last westbound Arab merchantman sailed a week ago. It will be at least six months before any dhows arriving during the summer months proceed again toward Persian ports."

"Why is that?"

"I'm told it's due to a reversal in the direction of seasonal winds. I'll have Gentle Breeze sew the jewels into the hems of our garments against the day when they will be needed . . . a precautionary measure I learned from Niccolò Polo. Speaking of the Polos, what news of Marco?"

"When the expeditionary force returned to Tali from its Burma campaign, Marco was summoned to Cambulac. Kubilai appointed him to a ministerial position, but it is rumored that he is to be named governor of either Foochow or Yangchow." A smile played around the corners of the friar's mouth as he added, "Isn't it remarkable, Edmund, how closely Marco's career in Cathay parallels your own?"

That I intended to take Gentle Breeze with me when I left Cathay was something I accepted. I appreciated that her well-being was my responsibility and that leaving her behind would place her in an untenable position. Now, I had something else to consider. Ere long I'd be saddled with yet another responsibility—Mei-ling. That obligation notwithstanding, in no wise did I contemplate taking Mei-ling with me.

The khan's chop and gyrfalcon seal identified the com-appearance of a tangled skein.

Marshal Sögatü advanced no explanation. Handing me a scroll, he turned his attention to a map he'd been studying when his adjutant had ushered me into the command pavilion.

The khan's chop and gyrfalcon seal indentified the communication. Following a formal salutation addressed to the marshal, the communication came directly to the point.

Kubilai concurred with the marshal's assertion that, once Canton had been secured, only two of the three armies involved in the siege would be required to conduct follow-up operations. However, the khan disagreed with Sögatü's proposal that the Army of the Golden Boar be assigned the task of policing the newly subjugated territories. Kubilai observed that reports received from Prince Ye-su Timur, and other sources, indicated that the Army of the Blue Dragon was

the force best suited to undertake these administrative
duties.

Once the city fell and the marshal was satisfied that resistance within its walls had been quelled, the marshal was
directed to promote me to general of the first rank. Relieved
of my army command, I was to be installed as the military
governor of Canton and its prefecture. A garrison drawn from
the ranks of the Army of the Jade Panther was to be detailed
to assist me in maintaining order.

To take over the command of the Army of the Blue Dragon,
General Toghu was to be promoted to general of the second
rank. The army was to establish its headquarters and base of
operations north of Canton at the centrally located city of
Shiukwan.

Rerolling the scroll on its spindle, I handed it to Sögatü.
He accepted it, and dismissed me with a curt nod.

Outside the pavilion I paused a moment before stepping
forth into a thin rain that had started to sift down from a
lowering leaden sky. The weather was well suited to my
somber mood.

I was perplexed. Marshal Sögatü must have had the khan's
directive in his possession for some time. It was inconceivable that Kubilai would have advised Governor Wang of my
forthcoming assignment prior to informing Sögatü of the
posting. Why had Sögatü withheld the information? For that
matter, though he hadn't been advised of matters of a purely
military nature as now had been revealed through his directive
to Sögatü, why had Governor Wang been notified at all
concerning my prospective employment as military governor
of Canton?

I thought I could discern the answer to the latter question.
Having approved of Mei-ling as my bride-to-be, Kubilai had
placed me in a position where there was no necessity for the
campaign to be concluded before the wedding could take
place. Governor Wang had wasted no time in taking advantage of the situation.

What troubled me more, however, was the fact that I'd
been isolated from contact with my former comrades-in-arms
in an army I'd directed and shaped for more than two years.

Why had Kubilai considered it necessary to draw the projected garrison force from within the ranks of the Army of the Jade Panther?

I pushed that question to the back of my mind. For the moment its answer eluded me.

Chapter Twelve

The walls were breached in mid-May—on the third day of the Month of the Snake. The fighting raged in the western quarter of the city for two days and nights. On the third day, quiet reigned. The Sung defenders either had slipped over the southern wall and fled, or had blended in with the populace within the city and in the jumble of ramshackle huts and myriad small craft along the northern bank of the river.

What infuriated Marshal Sögatü was that the Sung warlord and his officers had evaded the tightening Yuan net. Had he not been prohibited from damaging the quays and storage sheds fringing the river, I'm sure that the marshal would have had the sprawling shantytown and every living creature within it reduced to smoking ashes. What he did to vent his frustration was to sink and torch all the *tankia* craft unable to escape downstream, and to slaughter every man, woman, and child on the boats unable to flee his wrath.

Within the city neither the governor nor senior mandarins were anywhere to be found. They must have fled along with the escaping Sung forces. Sögatü had those administrative officials remaining in the city—down to even minor functionaries—rounded up. To pay lip service to legality the hapless officialdom were subjected to mass trials for treason, judged guilty, and publicly beheaded as fast as the weary executioners could wield their swords. A few of the more senior of these officials were singled out to serve as gruesome

examples of what could be anticipated for any defiance of
Yuan authority. Cages containing these wretched petty officials festooned the square fronting the governor's palace. The
city echoed to the wails of grieving kinfolk and reeked of the
sickly stench of death.

The orgy of vindictive bloodletting continued for the better part of a week before Sögatü grudgingly conceded that
resistance had been rooted out and quelled. Only then was I
installed as military governor.

I was expected to exercise authority over a city and prefecture steeped in fear, smoldering with resentment, and virtually denuded of civil servants. An unenviable task. Moreover,
the troops assigned to garrison my newly acquired fiefdom
were drawn from the ranks of the very army which had
carried out the marshal's punitive mandate—and had been
given a good deal of license in its performance of those grisly
duties. To restore order in Canton I first would have to instill
strict discipline in my enforcing troops.

Fortunately, it was not as gloomy a prospect as I'm making
it out to be. My task was lightened by Gentle Breeze, my
companion and confidante, by Brother Demetrios with his
wise counsel, and by Chang—now promoted to the rank of
colonel—whom I could trust to relay my orders accurately to
the garrison force commander. Actually, that I had been
allowed to retain the services of Chang as an aide rather
surprised me. He represented my sole link with my former
command and I had more than half expected Marshal Sögatü
to reject my request for Chang's retention. The marshal's
preoccupation with plans for his continuing campaign must
have given rise to this oversight. I did not question my good
fortune.

I took office at the end of May in the Year of our Lord
1278—on the fifteenth day of the Month of the Snake in the
Year of the Tiger. I found temporary quarters in an unpretentious hostelry pompously named the Inn of Celestial Happiness.

The reason I'd selected this inn was that it was located
close to the Huisheng Mosque. The mosque's soaring minaret
dominated the skyline and served as a landmark for me in
these unfamiliar surroundings of a maze of narrow twisting

streets. There was also, I suppose, a deeper reason. I was told that the mosque had been built by an uncle of Mohammed's during the early years of the T'ang dynasty, some six centuries back in time. It was a legend I found hard to credit but I would not have disputed the fact that the Islamic faith had a long-established regional toehold. I drew comfort from the mosque's symbolic proof of a lengthy foreign presence.

Prior to establishing myself in the governor's palace, I conducted the affairs of my office from the nearby Heavenly Hall of Records. We did not take up residence in the palace until mid-June, following Wong Sin's arrival with our personal effects and household staff.

The palace was an imposing structure. To be more accurate, it was a complex of interconnected wings, outbuildings such as stables, storehouses, kitchens, and quarters for the guards and servants. There were secluded nooks and formal gardens. One of the latter boasted a seven-tiered pagoda of carved marble. In effect it was a self-contained community in miniature, sealed off from the city by a high wall. This fact, however, did not manifest itself readily. When one entered the compound through the massive main gate, all one saw was a large expanse of marble-flagged courtyard and the majestic building that hid all else from view.

It was similar in structure to palaces I had seen in Cambulac's Forbidden City. Five wide marble steps led up to a covered veranda extending the full length of the palace façade. At the courtyard level these steps were flanked by a pair of grotesquely grinning, stiffly erect marble lions. Rising from the front edge of the veranda were six red-lacquered pillars that supported the overhang of the lower section of a three-tiered roof of green-glazed tile. The outer corners of these roofs flared upward gracefully. Except where the steps gave access to the veranda, the pillars were connected by a low balustrade of ornately worked marble.

The interior was equally impressive. To the left of the entranceway was a high-ceilinged audience chamber of vast proportions; to the right, a banquet hall almost as big. To the rear of these cavernous chambers, the doorways leading to it hidden behind carved wooden screens, a corridor ran the entire length of the building. Opening off this corridor were private salons and cubicles where scribes labored diligently with brush and inkpot. From each end of the corridor, passageways led off to the residential wings.

Restoration of order was a consideration demanding immediate attention. It called for the imposition of iron discipline on both the arrogant garrison forces and on the unruly civilian population. To this end I issued and had widely promulgated a proclamation. This edict specified that looting, murder, rape, and unprovoked assault were punishable by public execution, and that lesser crimes would draw prison sentences with, or without, publicly administered corporal punishment. I had Chang make it abundantly clear to the garrison commander that these regulations applied equally and without favor to the officers and men under his command.

In the first five weeks from the time I took office eleven decapitations were carried out in the central square. Four of these were civilian offenders, six were Yuan soldiers, and one a junior cavalry officer. Thereafter, though petty crimes persisted, capital crime dropped off dramatically.

Other major problems confronting me were the restoration of the city's defenses, the provision of food and shelter for those dislocated by the conflict, the restructuring of civil administration, the continuing collection of taxes, and the reestablishment of mercantile confidence in Canton as a commercial port. In the latter three of those tasks I had good cause to curse Marshal Sögatü. By his vengeful acts he had succeeded in all but dismantling the machinery through which the city and prefecture were governed and the port made to function. In the latter case the *tankia* performed an essential function. Their sampans scurried back and forth like water beetles in the loading and offloading of cargo and in the transportation of passengers to and from ships anchored in the stream. Without the boat dwellers that Sögatü had driven off, the efficiency of the port would be seriously impaired. The suspicion grew in me that Sögatü's actions had not been inspired by Mongol ferocity as much as they had been by malice directed toward me.

I let it be known that the *tankia* would not be molested if they returned to Canton's riverfront. In the same manner I had the word spread that civil servants would be made welcome if they returned to their former employment.

The response was not immediate, yet better—and more rapid—than I had expected. By late July the *tankia* had drifted back in sufficient numbers to cope adequately with the seasonal influx of merchantmen. By early August enough mandarins had emerged from hiding to enable me to appoint an advisory council. Through the council, functionaries were persuaded to return to their former administrative duties.

Throughout the complex negotiations, bargaining, and maneuvering involved in stablizing the economy and the administrative infrastructure, Brother Demetrios proved to be of inestimable worth. He now served me in the capacity of chamberlain. His demonstrated shrewdness—particularly in the realm of finance—made him well suited for the role. I turned over to him my most vexing problem—tax collection.

Tax collectors, looked upon as extortioners, are not popular figures under any regime. Deprived of their Sung military support, Canton's tax collectors seemed to have evaporated into thin air. Along with them most of the tax records also had disappeared.

Revenues were derived from a number of sources. Commercial shipping paid harbor dues. Merchants, shopkeepers, and artisans were assessed taxes on their declared volume of trade. Farmers were levied a percentage of their crops and produce. Without reliable records to guide him Brother Demetrios would have to set tax rates arbitrarily. And therein was my dilemma. I needed funds and produce to support the garrison forces, the labor force engaged in public works, the administrative structure, and to finance ongoing projects. At the same time I didn't want to impose a tax burden that would discourage trade or stifle economic recovery. I left it to Brother Demetrios to arrive at a workable compromise.

It is small wonder, then, that I saw little of the friar for weeks on end. In late July he returned from a visit to the hamlets, villages, and military outposts of the prefecture. He was the bearer of welcome news.

During the siege we had seen nothing but old men, women, and children working the fields in the vicinity of the city. The early rice harvest had been discouraging. Now Brother

Demetrios reported that young men were helping with the farm chores and everything indicated that, if the weather held, a bumper crop was in the offing. And, since the young men must be local conscripts who had deserted from the fleeing Sung forces, the news boded well for Sögatü's continuing campaign. The forces opposing him were dwindling.

In August, when the pressure of my administrative duties eased, I accompanied the friar on a tour of the rural communities. I doubt that to have been a practice of my Sung predecessor, but I wanted to familiarize myself with the prefecture. I encountered suspicion, but little in the way of hostility. On the friar's advice I had eased the taxes imposed on the countryfolk. He had offset the loss of revenue in produce by increased assessments on the city's merchant class.

Brother Demetrios sighed contentedly, put down his chopsticks, and wiped his mouth with a damp towel provided by the innkeeper. "Yes," he said, "I agree with you, but only to a point. Kubilai pushed you into the political arena to broaden your experience, yet I don't believe that to have been his sole reason for divorcing you from the Army of the Blue Dragon."

"Oh. What other reason could he have had?"

"You were becoming too popular a figure. Not just with your army, but with the inhabitants of the region you subjugated, as well. You have a talent for administration and are a born leader. I don't think that Kubilai counted on your achieving popular support so readily. As a 'foreign devil' you *should* have remained isolated to a greater degree. Kubilai didn't expect you to acquire a loyal following. I venture to say that there have been quite a few developments he didn't foresee. It's caused him concern."

"I may have earned a measure of respect, but that hardly constitutes a 'loyal following.' Even if it did, why should that worry him?"

The friar shook his head irritably. "Look," he said, ticking off each point on his fingers. "You introduce weapons that prove their worth under both field and siege conditions. In this southern campaign, you pile one success on top of another with few casualties. Not only do you pacify the regions you conquered, but you actually attract recruits to the Blue Dragon banner. Morale ran high in the army you commanded. Even though it was reduced in cavalry strength, it was a fighting force superior to either of the two armies under Sögatü's command. Put yourself in Sögatü's place. How would you look on the Army of the Blue Dragon?''

I saw it. I was annoyed with myself for not having seen it sooner. ''Mmmm. He saw me as an ambitious upstart. He viewed my army and its tactics as a threat to his position of authority as long as I retained command. I put his attitude down to personal animosity.''

Brother Demetrios nodded. ''That entered into the picture. He's jealous of your success . . . and the favor shown you by the khan . . . but he is far too seasoned a campaigner to have attacked you openly in his reports to the khan. He knew full well that Kubilai had other sources of information. His more likely approach would have been to damn you with excessive praise. I've heard it rumored that he advanced a recommendation that the Army of the Jade Panther be detached from his overall command to administer the conquered territories, that you be promoted to general of the first rank, and that the armies of the Blue Dragon and Golden Boar be combined under your command to conclude the campaign. If that is what he did, it was damnably clever. It served to reinforce suspicions already growing in Kubilai's mind.''

''What suspicions?''

''That a taste of power was going to your head. That you were building a power base from which you could launch a bid to become an independent warlord in South China. It is not as farfetched as you might imagine, Edmund. You could have done it. I have it on good authority that the commanding generals of the armies of the Jade Panther and Golden Boar would have sided with you if you had chosen to oust Marshal Sögatü. I imagine that it was fear of how you might react that caused the marshal to withhold the terms of the khan's directive from you until circumstances forced him to reveal its contents.''

I laughed bitterly. ''Absurd . . . when all I really want is to leave China. Doesn't the khan suspect that? Surely, by now, he must know that—with your help—I'm well on my way to becoming financially independent.''

"Of course he knows about your financial activities. And he is well aware that by making you governor he's put you in a position where you'd have to be a half-wit not to increase your wealth substantially. If financial dependence was a factor in his planning, I doubt it is now. He must believe that you've acquired an appetite for power that will hold you here. Without a military power base on which to build, wealth by itself poses little threat to Kubilai. So he simply severed all connection between you and your army—which, in his estimation, nullified any threat you might have posed."

I smiled. "A clean cut . . . with but one loose end. Through some oversight I'm left with Colonel Chang as the sole surviving member of my once proud army.''

Brother Demetrios regarded me speculatively. "Are you sure it was an oversight?''

Sobering, I replied with candor, "My initial reaction was that Sögatü slipped up in approving my request. But probably it was no error. It doesn't matter. Whoever else he serves, Chang has always served me well. I like him. At the moment I don't know what I'd do without him.''

That night, in the private sleeping chamber I occupied in the village inn, I gave thought to what the friar and I had discussed—and some of the things we had *not* talked about. Since Brother Demetrios knew it to be a touchy subject, he had avoided any mention of my forthcoming marriage. And, though I had introduced it into the conversation, we hadn't pursued the subject of my escaping the khan's entrapment through flight.

By now I'd put aside enough to cover sea passage for me and Gentle Breeze, but I needed a good deal more negotiable valuables to finance our onward journey and an extended period in England when I might well be bereft of funds. As I saw it, it would take me many more months to accumulate what I considered an adequate hedge against contingency expenses that might arise. The flaw in my projections was obvious. If, before I could acquire the necessary additional

funds, marriage was forced upon me, the situation would call
for rethinking.

I didn't subscribe entirely to the reasoning advanced by
Brother Demetrios. If, however, he was close to the truth, it
shed light on some features that had puzzled me. Did Kubilai
suspect that I was hatching a plan to leave the Middle Kingdom by sea? Did he know that no vessel could embark on a
westbound voyage until the seasonal change of wind which
should occur sometime in October? Was his introducing a
Chinese wife into my life a means of forestalling my departure?

On my return to Canton I was greeted with unwelcome
tidings. My intended bride had departed from Changsha,
together with a sizable wedding party, in July. She and her
party were expected to reach Canton by mid-September.

Whether by accident or by design Kubilai's move had
partially blocked my intended gambit.

Chapter Thirteen

Having ridden fortune's floodtide for some time I must have come to think of it as a permanent condition. When the tide changed, I was slow to recognize or accept the fact.

Mei-ling and I were joined in matrimony by Buddhist ceremony early in October. By Chinese computation it was deemed to be an auspicious day and hour for the rites. It may be that such auguries do not apply to Norman-Saxons. I now believe that to have been the moment when my fortunes started to ebb. The reversal, however, was so gradual that I did not detect it for some months.

I think what misled me was that I had expected a greater disruption in my way of life than actually came to pass. As Brother Demetrios had pointed out, the Chinese character for "trouble" is depicted by a pictogram of two women under one roof.

In this case the roof in question extended its cover over the governor's palace, which included two widely separated residential wings. Gentle Breeze had arranged it so that the accommodation reserved for Mei-ling and her attendants was in the western wing—well removed from my apartment and Gentle Breeze's adjoining chambers in the eastern wing. In effect what was established for Mei-ling was a household within a household—a domain she ruled with petty tyranny. It was a realm I visited infrequently.

Raised to a life of pampered seclusion, Mei-ling seemed

not to mind that I spent so little time with her. Moreover, since she had bound feet, her movements were confined to a comparatively restricted area. She seldom ventured beyond the confines of her chambers and the formal garden to which her quarters gave access. Her handmaidens and seamstress were her eyes, ears, and purveyors of titillating tidbits of palace gossip. Since she had virtually no direct contact with Gentle Breeze, friction between the two women beneath my roof was practically nonexistent.

What was she like? Of a truth I have difficulty in bringing Mei-ling's face to mind. It was round and childlike, framed in an abundance of raven tresses. Her dark eyes were almond-shaped, her nose was buttonlike and flat-bridged, her mouth full-lipped but small. By Chinese standards she was considered a beauty. I found her singularly unattractive.

In body she was short, plump, and soft. Her small-nippled breasts were somewhat larger than those sported by most of the Chinese I had bedded.

In neither face nor figure did Mei-ling stir me to passionate response. In all fairness, however, she must have found me coarse-featured and grotesque—a hairy monstrosity that had materialized in the flesh from the dark stories told to frighten her as a child. At eighteen, in many ways she was still a child.

In disposition—except when some minor annoyance moved her to passing petulance—she was placidly amiable. She was, however, incredibly vain and inordinately proud of her tiny "golden lotus" feet. Most of her waking hours were spent in having her hair groomed, in having herself bathed and massaged with scented oils, in being fitted for new gowns, in lavishing cooing affection on her peevish pug-nosed miniature dog, or in eating. Her only productive activity was needlework.

Mei-ling knew nothing of, nor evinced the slightest interest in, anything happening beyond the confines of her proscribed world. Her conversational range was limited to topics such as food, drink, wearing apparel, and the odd snippet of scullery gossip. Yet I could not fault her for being featherbrained. She was unlettered and had been confined since early childhood to the inner apartments of the women's quarters. By Confucian standards she epitomized the perfect wife—an unobtrusive broodmare.

I considered coupling with Mei-ling a duty rather than a pleasure. Nor did she appear to derive much pleasure from the act. She submitted to, rather than participated in, sex. We indulged in intercourse sparingly, which seemed not to displease her, though she would not have dreamed of denying me my conjugal rights.

The fact was that Mei-ling's introduction into the household made very little difference to the pattern of life to which I'd grown accustomed. The major departure was that the plans I had made for quitting China had to be revised radically.

Mei-ling presented me with an enigma. I could not think of taking her with us. On the other hand it was not her fault that the marriage had been arranged between us. If I returned her to her family, both she and her kinfolk would lose unconscionable face. I needed to devise some scheme whereby I could free myself without bringing loss of face to Mei-ling. I did not think there was anything dishonorable in this course of action. I didn't feel myself to be bound by Buddhist vows. Nonetheless, by those vows, I had assumed an obligation to Mei-ling.

Simple. Her world must believe me dead. As a widow she could return to the bosom of her family without shame or stigma. I would make adequate provision for her future while still retaining enough to finance my and Gentle Breeze's defection.

The plan I hit upon looked to be foolproof. Come late April I would arrange secretly for passage aboard an Arab dhow.

A day or so before the designated sailing date I would invite a few friends and officials to join me in a picnic on the riverbank. At dusk I'd take Gentle Breeze for a boat ride on the river.

At a predetermined point screened from the picnic party's view, we would rendezvous with Brother Demetrios sculling a second sampan. We would transfer to the friar's craft. With his help we would capsize the sampan in which Gentle Breeze and I had been sailing and scatter a few readily identifiable articles of clothing on the water. That done, Brother Demetrios would take us to the offshore side of the Arab vessel, where,

under cover of darkness, we would board the ship. We would
remain hidden belowdecks until the vessel sailed and was
well clear of the Pearl River estuary.

Once darkness fell with no sign of our return, the picnick-
ers would grow concerned. When we failed to put in an
appearance by morning, a full-scale search would be instituted.
Sooner or later our overturned sampan and clothing would be
found and it would be assumed that we had drowned. That
fact established, Brother Demetrios would turn over to Mei-
ling the funds I had put aside for her and arrange for her
return to Changsha.

It was a stratagem that should work. That I didn't divulge it
to either Gentle Breeze or Brother Demetrios was because it
would not be executed for some months and I still had some
of the details to work out.

Why wait until late April? One reason was that it would
give me time to make financial provision for Mei-ling. Another was that the Arab merchantman I would select would be
one of the last to set sail before the seasonal shift of prevailing winds. Even if Kubilai suspected me of deception, by the
time the word reached him it would be far too late for him to
order naval pursuit.

In February, during the festivities ushering in the Year of
the Dragon, my plan was a dealt a heavy, if not mortal, blow.
It was then that Mei-ling informed me proudly that she was
with child.

"God's blood," I snapped angrily, "I followed your
instructions. How could it happen?"

Gentle Breeze's face wore a worried frown. "It might not
have happened. Sometimes the wish to bear a child . . . or
some minor affliction . . . stops the red tide temporarily. The
flow might start again."

"I doubt it. So do you."

Her gaze averted, Gentle Breeze traced the pattern on the
sleeve of her brocaded gown with one finger. "I warned you
it was not infallible," she said defensively.

"True . . . but the method has been so effective for you
that I felt it foolproof. I . . . well . . ."

Gentle Breeze looked up, a chastened expression on her

face. "No two women are exactly alike, Emun. Our fertile periods are not governed solely by the moon. The sun exerts an influence . . . as do the stars. In Shangtu the court astrologer worked out a chart to guide me. Here, I employed an astrologer recommended by Wong Sin. He might not have been as gifted in such matters . . . or it may be that we erred concerning the exact hour of Mei-ling's birth. A safety factor was supposed to have been included to compensate for error. I don't know what went wrong. I . . . am sorry that I failed you."

The Chinese concept of yin and yang! Auspicious and inauspicious hours! The pervasive influence of celestial orbs! Mysteries beyond my comprehension. "The fault is not yours," I said gruffly. "Recrimination will not repair the damage."

I slumped dejectedly in my chair and stared fixedly at a bronze replica of a reclining water buffalo atop the table. It seemed to leer at me malevolently.

God's teeth, I thought morosely, it is one thing to walk away from a woman to whom I did not consider myself bound; quite another to abandon one carrying my unborn child. She would have to go to term and the baby be old enough to travel before I could consider putting my escape plan into effect. I sighed heavily. It meant a delay of about one year. Much could happen in a year.

In the khan's game of chess, what piece was Mei-ling? Queen, or pawn? It didn't really matter which. The move I had planned had been blocked effectively. If I wanted to stay in the game I'd no option but to retreat from my threatened position and wait for an opening that would allow me to regain an advantage.

Chapter Fourteen

It would take another twelve years for the cycle to repeat itself and bring another Year of the Dragon onto the scene. If 1279 was any example of evils that could be wrought by the mythical monster, I dreaded the thought of what 1291 might bring upon us.

Though I used her pregnancy as an excuse for not sharing her couch, I didn't neglect her. Except for those periods when I was visiting the rural communities of the prefecture, I made it a practice to visit Mei-ling daily, if only for a few minutes. I listened with feigned interest to her banal chatter, murmured sympathetic responses to her questions, then left to engage in more rewarding pursuits. We had nothing in common but the life that stirred within her womb.

I suppose I was expecting to see some physical change in her. I'm sure there was, but any swelling of her belly or enlargement of her breasts was concealed beneath the flowing robes she affected. It was not until May, when she was entering the fifth month of her pregnancy, that I noticed anything different about her appearance—a puffiness of face. It was sometime during that month that she complained of pains in her feet and ankles and took to spending most of her time abed.

One afternoon, entering her bedchamber unannounced, I came upon her soaking her tiny misshapen feet in a basin of

cold water in an attempt to reduce the swelling of her ankles.
I normally avoided looking at her feet. The sight offended
me. How, if they practiced such disfigurement, could the
Chinese lay claim to being civilized?

On this occasion it was difficult to avert my gaze without
offending Mei-ling. She lifted one foot from the water in
order to bring the swelling of her ankle to my attention in a
childish bid for sympathy. Her querulous observation was that
the added weight of her swollen belly was too much for her
poor feet to bear.

Stripped of its shielding bandage, the dead-white append-
age was a grotesque parody of a foot. It was not just that the
ubiquitous binding had stunted the foot's growth. The shape
of the foot had been altered to conform to the dictates of
fashion. It had been shortened by compressing it until the ball
of the foot was separated from the heel by an arch reduced to
no more than a deep crease. To make the foot look narrower,
the big toe had been left in its normal position but the rest of
her toes had been bound beneath the foot. They had atrophied
through disuse to withered stumps.

"Did it hurt?" I questioned before I could check myself.

"Of course it hurts," Mei-ling replied petulantly. "Aren't
you listening? That's what I've been telling you."

I smiled apologetically. "I mean when your feet were first
bound."

"Oh. No, I don't recall any discomfort. My nurse was
skilled in footbinding."

"How old were you when this took place?"

"Six," she responded proudly, then added smugly, "With
most girls, it starts when they are seven or eight."

To take pride in having been crippled at an early age
seemed to me to be the height of imbecility. "But why? What
purpose does it serve?"

She looked at me pityingly—as one would regard a re-
tarded child. "You make it sound like some sort of punishment.
It is a mark of gentility. It sets us apart from our inferiors . . .
the laboring classes who do our bidding and till the fields.
Are no such distinctions made in *your* country?"

In England we did so without maiming our children, but
I refrained from making that comment. Nor did I point out

that I had met few bawds or courtesans in China who did not
have bound feet. Far from being a mark of gentility, the
"golden lotus" feet appeared to set apart those women who
relied on their jade gates to attain financial security—a
category, evidently, that applied equally to prostitutes, and
wives and concubines of gentler station. As far as I could see,
lotus feet signified an admission of male dominance. A woman
with bound feet cannot stray *too* far from the bedchamber.

I did not dignify Mei-ling's question with an answer.

In the weeks that followed, Mei-ling grew listless and less
concerned about her appearance. The weather was a contributing factor.

I had found the summer months in South China to be
excessively hot and humid, yet given to intermittent rather
than continuous rainfall. That June was an exception. From
the end of the first week onward we scarcely caught a glimpse
of the sun. Rain fell almost without letup. The clouds pressed
down, obscuring the hills to the north of the city. The tops of
the city's two prominent pagodas and the minaret of the
Moslem mosque seemed to scrape the bloated underbellies of
the lowering cloud mass. Even when it was not raining, the
air was heavy with the threat of yet more rain to come.

In the palace the walls were beaded with moisture. Dampness was everywhere. Anything of leather was furred with
mildew. Everything of cloth was clammy to the touch and
smelled faintly of mold. It was depressing. Tempers grew
short.

Venturing beyond the palace compound did nothing to lift
my spirits. The streets were puddled or, wherever there was a
slight depression, had become miniature lakes. The narrow
side streets that were not cobbled or paved with flagstones
were impassable quagmires. Everywhere, the drainage ditches
were clogged with refuse and overflowing. The sodden city
stank.

I received daily reports reflecting concern. All the rivers
flowing into the estuary had risen to dangerous levels.
Fortunately, the early rice crop had been harvested. Farm
labor was diverted from planting to bolstering the protective

earthworks. The fear was, however, that if the rain persisted the dikes would not hold.

It was as though God had relented. At the beginning of July the rain stopped. For the next four days the sun beamed down from a practically cloudless sky. The puddles dried; the drains were cleared of offal. The city was bedecked with drying laundry and airing bedclothes. The peasants returned to their temporarily suspended chores in the paddy fields. Smiles replaced the worried frowns that had graced most faces for the better part of a month.

On the fifth day disaster struck.

The day dawned hot and sultry—and ominously still. The voice of the city was strangely muted. The loudest sound seemed to be the insistent buzzing of flies. There wasn't a breath of air; not a leaf stirred.

By midmorning—when I was down at the docks checking on the level of the swollen river—the sky had taken on a brassy sheen. I noted that there appeared to be a good deal of activity aboard the craft tied up alongside the quay.

Lines were being doubled up. No cargo was being worked. Sailors were busy battening hatches and securing everything movable. I walked over to a high-pooped oceangoing junk and questioned a sailor concerning the cause of this frantic activity. He answered tersely, *"Tai-fung!"*

I had heard much about the destructive force of the Great Wind which periodically struck the coastal regions and roared inland. I had not yet experienced this awesome phenomenon. I hurried back to the palace not at all sure what needed to be done to prepare for its onslaught. I didn't question the sailor's grim prognosis. Seafarers, I have found, have an uncanny knack of reading the weather in advance of the gathering storm.

At midday, when I reached the palace, there was a more positive indication of the coming storm. A line of ragged dark clouds had put in an appearance to the southeast. The clouds advanced rapidly toward the city.

Our distraught Cantonese servants knew what was coming. They cautioned us against venturing into open spaces as they scurried about shifting everything deemed of value into the inner salons. It was our Cantonese chef who directed this activity. Both Wong Sin and I were more than happy to accept the chef's advice.

A few soughing gusts of wind and a spatter of fat raindrops, the storm's outriders, reached us before the afternoon had progressed much more than midway into the hours of the horse. Then the dread *tai-fung* struck with unrelenting fury.

The wind shrieked. It was as though all the tortured shades of hell had been unleashed upon us. The heavens flung wide their floodgates to release a torrential downpour.

Though the wind gradually shifted toward the northwest, the storm raged with unabated fury through the afternoon and night into the following day. Even when the scream of the wind subsided to a wail in the afternoon of the second day, the rain did not diminish. By the morning of the third day the wind had dropped to blustery gusts and the rain slackened. The storm had passed—leaving havoc in its wake.

The Great Wind was an infrequent visitor, but its unwelcome visitations came often enough to inspire precautions. The governor's palace had been built to withstand such storms. Notwithstanding this fact the damage was substantial.

Large sections of tiles had been stripped from the roofs. Furniture inadvertently left in outer chambers had been reduced to matchwood. The gardens were ankle-deep in water and strewn with broken branches and uprooted shrubs. One of the stone lions had been toppled by the wind and lay on its side partially blocking the entranceway steps.

What had befallen the palace was as nothing when compared to the havoc wreaked in the city. The pagodas, mosque, and many of the more solidly constructed residences had weathered the storm with comparatively little damage, but crowded poorer districts were a shambles. Roofs were gone, walls had collapsed, and the flooded streets were littered with wreckage.

Canton's woes, however, paled into insignificance by comparison with the calamitous state of affairs outside the city's walls. The shantytown had been flattened and left in ruins by the battering winds. Few had escaped death's clutching hand. The doss houses, wineshops, and food stalls on the sand-strip first had been leveled by the wind, then submerged beneath the rising river. Warehouses had been smashed and their contents scattered. The motley collection of *tankia* craft largely had sunk or had been left as kindling spread along the high ground. Oceangoing vessels and large river craft had fared little better and lay at crazy angles stranded on the foreshore. The stench of death was everywhere. Those who had survived wandered dazedly in search of food and shelter.

All that was bad enough, but was not the worst of it. The deluge had gorged the rivers already swollen by the June rains. They had overflowed their banks, inundating the deltaic lowlands for leagues around us. Entire villages had been swept away. In the hills to the north, mudslides had obliterated terraced fields and buried whole hamlets.

Canton stood like a forlorn island in a windswept sea.

Having vented her spleen, Mother Nature now smiled on us contritely. The sun shone down benignly for extended periods. Clouds gathered during the heat of the day but no rain, other than evening showers, fell to plague us. Cooling southwesterly winds fanned us.

Gradually the waters receded from the silt-mantled flatlands. It was gratifying that the weather favored us, since we were faced with monumental tasks.

Temporary shelter had to be provided for the homeless. Ships had to be repaired and refloated. Wharves and storehouses had to be patched up and returned to service. The city had to be cleared of debris and refuse. Canals and irrigation ditches had to be freed of clogging silt. Roadways leading from the city had to be made passable. To these ends every man, woman, and child capable of labor—and most of the garrison forces—was pressed into service and fell to with a will.

Bringing order out of chaos involved backbreaking labor and maximum effort from all concerned. Reconstruction was a Herculean labor that taxed our strained resources to the utmost. It was work, however, that the Cantonese and the garrison troops accepted and bent to uncomplainingly. In an astonishingly short space of time the port city was functioning with some semblance of its former entrepreneurial verve and the countryside was greening with seedbed planting. Things had not returned to normal, but they were headed in that direction.

Two major problems confronted me. Building materials were in short supply. Even worse, stocks of rice in the city's granaries were being depleted at an alarming rate. I sent an urgent appeal for assistance to General Toghu in Shiukwan.

Toghu's response was prompt and even better than I had hoped. He sent a courier to advise me that a wagon train loaded with rough-cut timber and bagged rice was on its way south. He added that a labor battalion had been recruited and was accompanying the wagon train.

The news relieved me of a good deal of pressure. With assured relief on its way I breathed easier.

It was then, in the third week of July, that disaster struck for a second time. Without warning, pestilence descended on the city, then spread to its environs with the speed of a grass fire fanned by a high wind.

They called it the "rice-water illness." The affliction was no stranger to the Cantonese, but it had been some years since the grim visitor had put in an appearance.

It manifested itself initially in the teeming western part of the city. From there it raged throughout the rest of the city and beyond its walls. In less than three days it had assumed epidemic proportions.

The palace compound did not escape the ravages of the pestilence, though some of us were touched but lightly by the affliction while others suffered not at all. Why the spectral visitor struck some down while leaving others untouched remains a mystery I cannot explain. Few of those stricken with the virulent disease survived. Some died quickly. Others lingered on in agony for days.

Rice-water illness! It was aptly named. The onset of the affliction was marked by gut-wrenching diarrhea. The next stage was when the stool became watery, white-flecked, and colorless—resembling liquid drained from cooking rice. Next came raging thirst and uncontrolled vomiting. In the final stages the body grew outwardly cold to the touch and the skin became wrinkled and grayish in hue as the flesh beneath melted from the bones. When the disease progressed to that stage, death was a merciful release.

I suffered nothing but a mild attack of diarrhea. Gentle Breeze was stricken with a more acute attack of loose bowels that stayed with her for several days—but did not develop into the "rice-water" stage. Mei-ling was less fortunate.

Five days after the onslaught of the epidemic the dread infection was visited upon Mei-ling. It might have been that her delicate condition had weakened her defenses, since, in her case, the disease ran its course with terrifying swiftness.

It began in mid-morning with diarrhea. By noon she was voiding the thin colorless stool characteristic of the disease and complaining of an insatiable thirst.

The palace physician already had told me that he knew of no cure for the ailment. All that could be done was to make the patient as comfortable as possible and hope and pray that he or she would survive the ordeal. From the frown on his face I didn't think he held out much hope for Mei-ling in this advanced stage of her pregnancy.

All through the afternoon the physician attended Mei-ling to the exclusion of other patients. He did all that he could. He forced watered wine spiced with honey and cinnamon between her parched lips. The honey, he explained, would bolster her strength; the cinnamon would serve to calm her rebellious stomach, and the watered wine should help restore the liquids streaming from her body. Had she been able to keep it down for anything more than a few seconds, the potion might have performed the functions he claimed for it.

Toward evening she complained of chills. The physician sighed resignedly. He must have interpreted this as a sign of the approaching end. He sent one of her handmaidens to fetch a fur-lined robe. When the servant returned, the physician had Mei-ling's upper body wrapped in the robe. He instructed me to ensure that she was kept as warm and comfortable as possible, then took his leave of me. He had, he explained wearily, to look in on other patients.

I kept solitary vigil well into the night. I watched her cheeks and eyes sink slowly into her ashen face. About midnight she heaved a final shuddering sigh. As her karma had ordained it, her life on this earth was at an end.

I gave instructions for her Buddhist priest to be advised of her death and that her corpse be prepared for cremation in accordance with Buddhist rites. I ordered that her bedclothes and garments be taken to the inner courtyard and burned. That attended to, I took myself to the garden to breathe some cleansing air—and to give myself over to sober thought.

I cannot pretend that I mourned Mei-ling's passing, nor the life within her that had been snuffed out without ever having seen the light of day. Nonetheless, her demise saddened me. She had not deserved death at such an early age. Guiltily, I admitted to myself that I hadn't prayed for her life to be spared. Still, had she lived, I would have accepted that as a manifestation of God's will and done everything within my power to speed her recovery.

The inescapable fact was, however, that her passing had relieved me of a tremendous burden.

Chapter Fifteen

The dying went on apace. Day and night the crackling of exploding firecrackers echoed through the all but deserted streets. The noise did little to deter the evil spirits. The scent of burning joss sticks mingled with the stench of death. A pall of smoke from bonfires consuming the clothes and bedding of the deceased hung over the city like a black haze. At night the squealing of ungreased *mappa* axles announced the grisly traffic as cartloads of corpses were trundled from the city to be dumped without ceremony into the river.

There was nothing I could do to allay the city's grief. The council meetings had been discontinued by common consent. The work undertaken to repair the damage wrought by the *tai-fung* was at a standstill. At the outset of the epidemic I had sent Colonel Chang north to intercept the southbound wagon train. His orders were to detain the column until he received word from me that the plague had run its course. There was nothing to do but wait.

In the second week of August, to add to our misery, the weather turned exceedingly hot and dry. It brought with it swarms of flies. Nightfall witnessed myriad flying insects drawn to the flames of oil lamps and candles. Yet, oddly enough, while this weather favored insects it seemed to have the reverse effect on the plague that afflicted us. As that week drew to a close, deaths from the pestilence lessened markedly.

A week later I was able to send word to Chang that I

considered it safe for the wagons and laborers to resume their southward trek. The dying continued, but the incidence of new cases had dropped to a level that indicated the epidemic had spent itself. I prayed that I was not misreading the signs. In my view Canton had endured more than its fair share of disasters and deserved a respite.

I did not have accurate figures for the prefecture, but it was estimated that the pestilence alone had claimed more than one third of the city's population.

The resiliency of the Chinese never ceased to amaze me. By the end of August work on the restoration projects had resumed; the streets once more bustled with frenetic activity. The voice of the city, muted during the onslaught of the plague, had regained its former stridency. I commented on these things to Brother Demetrios.

"Not fatalism, exactly," the friar opined. "They are realists. They have mourned their loss and now must get on with the business of living."

"But the horrors of the past two months seem to have faded from memory as though they had never occurred."

"Not at all, Edmund, not at all. It's just that they view things differently. Floods may claim lives, but they restore the soil's fertility. Plague and famine take a heavy toll—but, generally, claim the weakest. The race is renewed through childbearing." Brother Demetrios chuckled dryly before adding, "I can assure you that they are applying themselves to the latter process enthusiastically. Do you know what they're saying in the streets?"

I looked at him admiringly. Since the onset of the plague I'd had little chance to spend much time beyond the confines of the palace compound. The friar, on the other hand, had worked heroically, assisting the harried physicians in attending the sick and dying in all quarters of the city. "No," I answered, "I have no idea."

"They are saying that the pestilence was a blessing in disguise. By reducing the number of mouths that had to be fed, it averted the famine that normally follows flooding."

"Hmmph," I snorted derisively. "Had Toghu not responded

to my plea for assistance, they would still face famine. Our stocks of rice were all but exhausted."

"As are our stocks of wine and spirits," Brother Demetrios observed sourly. "You could have included those commodities in your plea."

I laughed. "I might have, had I known you would consume such prodigious quantities of both."

"They ward off chills and fever," Brother Demetrios said defensively.

"Undoubtedly. Is it to that you attribute your immunity?"

"By no means," the friar snapped sententiously. "I live a godly life and placed my fate in His hands."

I did not have the heart to dispute his claim to Holy Grace.

In September I discharged my last obligation to Mei-ling. I sent those of her servants who had survived the plague on a journey back to Changsha. With them they carried a funerary urn containing Mei-ling's ashes, a sandalwood box containing a substantial sum in paper currency, and a scroll to be delivered into the hand of their master, Mei-ling's father. In the scroll I extolled Mei-ling's virtues, expressed my sorrow over her untimely death, and suggested that the money I was sending might be used to erect a shrine to her memory. I made no mention of the circumstances surrounding her death, confident that her handmaiden would give a vivid account of the event and make mention of the fact that I had been with her mistress until the end. That taken care of, I dismissed all further thought of Mei-ling and our unborn child from my mind and turned my attention to more pressing matters.

News had just reached me that Marshal Sögatü, at long last, had concluded his campaign successfully. E'en though they must have known the struggle to be futile, the remnants of the Sung had resisted stubbornly to the end. The previous year, with their backs to the sea, they'd fled the mainland to the sanctuary of some rugged offshore islands. There, the young pretender, their so-called Emperor Shi, had died on the island of Kiang-chou. The Sung warlord had wasted no time in declaring a youthful cousin, Ping, the rightful heir to the Dragon Throne. Finally, the last act of this absurd drama had been acted out in a day-long naval battle. It would have taken

place sooner, my informant assured me, had not a *tai-fung*
scattered the Yuan squadrons and forced a delay. At the end
of the sea battle the Sung flagship was at bay, but its commander refused to strike its colors. Knowing he faced execution if captured, the Sung commander chose a dramatic
alternative. He had his wife and children thrown overboard;
then, clutching the struggling young pretender to his chest,
the commander, bellowing defiance, flung himself and his
bewildered charge into the sea.

Three centuries of Sung overlordship came to an end.
Kubilai Khan had reunited the Middle Kingdom.

The collapse of Sung resistance brought about a number of
radical changes. Internal opposition suppressed, Kubilai was
free to pursue long-standing plans he had been forced by
circumstances to hold in abeyance. One of these—as we all
knew—was to wreak vengeance on the Island Kingdom,
Nippon.

The garrison forces policing the newly subjugated regions
of South China were reduced in strength. These duties were
taken over by units of the Army of the Golden Boar. The
balance of that army, plus the Army of the Jade Panther in its
entirety, were redeployed to the deltaic region of the Yangtze
Kiang. That came as no surprise. What was less readily
understood was why the Army of the Blue Dragon was
ordered to proceed to the west to join up with Mangatei's
Army of the Silver Ram based at Tali.

It would take many months to effect this massive redeploy-
ment of forces. It would give rise to much confusion in the
regions affected. As far as Canton was concerned, we would
experience but little of this disarray. It made its presence felt
in mid-September when units of the Army of the Golden Boar
arrived to relieve those of the Army of the Jade Panther. The
disruption caused by the changeover was annoying but no
serious dislocation. Actually, the regional confusion gener-
ated by troop movements—and the fact that Marshal Sögatü
had returned to Cambulac—suited my purpose.

Now that Mei-ling had been removed from the picture,
there was no reason for me to delay my clandestine departure.
As soon as the winds favored the enterprise, in late October
or early November, I would put my plan in motion. Then all

that remained would be to select an appropriate Arab vessel, arrive at an agreement on the amount of baksheesh needed to ensure her captain's full cooperation, and to brief Brother Demetrios and Gentle Breeze on their respective roles in the deception. In my estimation Sögatü might have suspected my defection and was the only officer who'd had the authority to order naval interception and search of outgoing merchant ships. It was just as well that he was no longer in the area. And garrison troops new to Canton should take longer to conduct a downriver search, which would give Gentle Breeze and me more time to make good our escape.

From earlier conversations, and his acquisition of gems on my behalf, Brother Demetrios knew roughly what I had in mind. Gentle Breeze, as well, had been told that the stones were for our use if it became necessary for us to flee the country. I'd told her that when I had asked her to sew the gemstones into the hems of our traveling cloaks. Neither of them, however, knew the details of the scheme I'd devised. It would be time enough to tell them once I had concluded the arrangements for our passage. Until then, for their peace of mind, it was better for them to remain in ignorance.

As things turned out, it was providential that I had exercised that restraint.

Bedecked with flags and pennants, a Yuan warship came to anchor off an island in midriver. Accompanied by his staff captain, Admiral Kwan Tse-wen paid me an official visit. I received him in the audience chamber of the palace.

When we had dispensed with the courtesies demanded by the occasion, the admiral asked to have a word with me in private. I had him conducted to a small pavilion in the garden.

When jasmine tea had been served and the servant had withdrawn, the admiral brought out a scroll and handed it to me without comment. No introductory remarks were called for. The gyrfalcon seal impressed into the wax blob that covered the knot of the tying ribbons attested to the origin of the communication.

I read the scroll with mounting dismay. It required a considerable effort to keep my features from betraying my consternation.

It began innocently enough with a salutation followed by a commendation. The khan praised me for having restored the city to commercial prominence following the lengthy siege and for the measure I had adopted to ameliorate the tragic consequences of both storm and flood. I had justified his faith in my abilities; he declared himself well pleased. In recognition of my services—over and above my military rank—he conferred on me the title of Mandarin of the Second Grade.

He had raised me high indeed. As a mandarin of that grade I would defer only to mandarins of the first grade, or marshals of the army. It bestowed on me the right to wear the yellow robes, a residence in the Imperial City, and a place at court; it was flattering in the extreme. It was what followed that disturbed me.

In my new civilian rank I was charged with a mission of trust. To execute this mission the admiral's flagship had been placed at my disposal and the admiral and his staff were mine to command.

What was my mission? With all possible haste, while the winds favored the passage, I was to make my way by sea to the Kingdom of Korea, notably to the ports of Inchon and Pusan. There I would find a Korean-Chinese army assembled and a fleet held in readiness against the day when a seaborne invasion could be directed at Nippon. That army numbered some sixty thousand, but was not considered large enough to undertake the conquest of the Island Kingdom.

From Korea I was to return to Southeast China, first to the seaport of Chuanchow, then to Nanking and Yangchow. At Chuanchow and the port of Yangchow on the Grand Canal, additional troop transports were under construction. The end result was to be an immense fleet of vessels. Near Nanking, now that the Sung resistance had been crushed, a military force of approximately one hundred thousand was being gathered together. Chiefly composed of veterans of the Sung campaigns, and including forty thousand Mongol cavalrymen, this force would serve as the main body of the invasion.

Specifically, my mandate was to determine the fitness of the military commanders and the readiness and morale of the troops under their command and to advance recommendations that would improve the caliber of either, or both. A secondary task was to do everything possible to speed up ship construction. In the latter I would find Admiral Kwan Tse-wen's naval knowledge of invaluable assistance. The admiral had been ordered to cooperate with me to the fullest.

When I had concluded my inspection of the Yangchow shipyards, Admiral Kwan's commitment would be at an end. I was to commandeer a suitable river craft and proceed north via the Grand Canal to Tientsin and thence to Cambulac, where I would report my findings and the recommendations based thereon directly to the khan.

Since I would not be returning to Canton, the khan would appoint a governor to replace me. However, since it might be some months before my replacement would arrive, I was to select a Cantonese mandarin to take over as acting governor prior to my departure.

With respect to my personal responsibilities, I was to arrange for an escort to conduct my women, household staff, and personal effects on an overland journey to Nanking. There, the governor would provide river transport and an onward escort to take them safely to Cambulac. There they would be installed in the residence assigned to me and have everything in readiness to welcome me at the conclusion of my mission.

I gazed meditatively at the khan's chop. Patently, when he had dictated this directive, news of the pestilence had yet to reach him. He had not known of Mei-ling's death.

Significantly, he had made reference to the seasonal winds. No longer could I cherish the hope that he was ignorant about their pattern.

I was being bribed by flattery, titles, and honors—none of which I wanted. It was now October, less than a month from the anticipated shift in wind direction. Was I to be thwarted once again? It looked very much as though, whether by accident or design, Kubilai had forestalled me yet again. He had, that is, unless—

As I rerolled the scroll on its spindle, I shifted my gaze to the admiral. His gaze was politely averted. He seemed totally absorbed in the mating antics of the silk moths that fluttered among the leaves of the Chinese oak that shielded the open-sided pavilion from the glare of the sun. I cleared my throat to attract his attention. His leathery face expressionless, he turned toward me.

I tapped the scroll against the palm of my left hand. "Have you been advised concerning the text of this directive?" I inquired.

"No, but I presume that it contains confirmation, sire, of the direction I received from the Lord High Admiral."

"Which was?"

"That I and my ship are yours to command until you complete a mission entrusted you by the emperor."

"Were you informed about my destinations?" I queried as I placed the scroll within the left sleeve of my robe.

"Yes, sire. You go first to the Korean port of Inchon, then to Pusan. After that you return to several ports in Southeast China. Those ports were not disclosed to me."

"Mmmm. How much time would you say I have before we should leave Canton?"

"The Month of the Cock is already well advanced. At the beginning of next month the winds will be uncertain until they steady onto a northerly heading. I would say we have no time to lose. At the most we should up anchor three days hence if we are to fetch Inchon this year."

I cursed inwardly. Three days! God's blood, I needed that many weeks, or more, before I could have set my plan to defect into motion. I'd been robbed of the chance to make good an escape. God alone knew when, or if, the opportunity would come my way again.

The glittering threads of Kubilai's entrapment grew ever tighter.

Chapter Sixteen

The flagship was due to sail at midday. Early that morning I walked in the palace garden with Brother Demetrios.

"No matter what I recommend," I observed acidly, "the invasion will be launched. Nothing I say will stay his hand."

The friar inclined his head in agreement. "Knowing that should lighten your task. Tell him only what he wants to hear . . . that the launching of the invasion but waits for the court astrologers to name a propitious day."

"Were I a diplomat, that might be my approach. Alas, I have no skill at dissembling. Whether he heeds it or not, he expects from me an honest appraisal."

"So be it, but guile might serve you better. Bluntness could be your undoing."

I smiled wryly. "I won't be *that* blunt."

"Well, if nothing else, it should prove to be an interesting journey. It's too bad that Gentle Breeze isn't going with you."

"Indeed it is, but she cannot. It wasn't a suggestion that I move my family to Cambulac. . . . It was a command. She is a hostage guaranteeing my return."

Brother Demetrios pursed his lips. "Had Mei-ling lived and borne you a child, he would have considered them hostages. I don't think he views a concubine as such."

"Then the more fool he. I'm glad that you are going north with her. Take good care of her."

"Rest assured, lad, I will . . . and see to it that she gets safely installed in the new residence."

"I shall miss her." Placing my arm affectionately across the friar's shoulders, I added, "And you as well, you lecherous old tosspot. I'll count the days till next we meet in Cambulac."

Brother Demetrios stopped and turned to face me. "Your mission should occupy the better part of a year. I doubt I'll be on hand to greet you when you return. It shouldn't take me more than five or six months to put together a caravan."

"That's still your intention?"

"It has never changed. My goal is to settle in Constantinople ere old age o'ertakes me. Hiring out my services as a caravan guide was but a means to that end. Three years ago purchasing a modest share of a westbound caravan was the height of my ambition. Now, thanks to our mutually profitable association, I'm in a position to outfit an entire caravan on my own and set my face toward Byzantium. Thanks to you, Edmund, my dream has become reality."

"No thanks is due me. It is through your efforts that we've prospered." I paused and regarded him speculatively before venturing into an area that, until now, I had avoided but that long had puzzled me: "In fact, your grasp of financial matters, and your—er—proclivities in other directions, have sometimes made me wonder if . . ."

When I hesitated, Brother Demetrios laughed and finished the sentence for me, ". . . if I truly was a man of the cloth . . . or merely a merchant masquerading as a monk? I've expected this question from you for so long, lad, that I'd concluded you could not bring yourself to broach so sensitive a subject."

I grinned weakly. "You've yet to answer it."

"Quite so. I'll try to satisfy your curiosity. I entered a Nestorian monastery at an early age. I first took monastic vows and later was ordained as a priest. As I matured, I became increasingly aware of compelling appetites of the flesh that defied gainsaying."

"Was not wenching denied you by your vows? Do Nestorian prohibitions differ from those of Catholic orders?"

Brother Demetrios smiled. "The vows do not differ overly

much, but I fear my vows of chastity sat not well with me and soon fell by the wayside. However, nowhere in Holy Writ will you find it specified that priests *must* be celibate. I have known many who profess to be good Catholics who hold that Christ was wedded to the Magdalen . . . and sired sons.''

I couldn't refute that. I'd heard such heresies voiced by Knights Templar. I refrained from comment.

The friar continued, "Fearing my excesses would not long escape notice and could lead to defrockment, I decided to make myself scarce by becoming an itinerant mendicant. I undertook a pilgrimage to the Holy Land. On my return to Turfan some six years later I did not tarry long. I struck out for Cathay. I spent several years in Ch'ang-an and Kaifeng learning the language and familiarizing myself with Chinese ways and customs. On my return to Turfan I found that my services were in demand . . . as a caravan guide rather than as a cleric. I then became what I was when first we met . . . friar, caravan guide, and, in a small way, a merchant."

"In the latter, without much success," I said dryly.

"Sad, but true. A friar's habit can be an asset in that it opens doors that might otherwise remain closed. It confers on the wearer an aura of probity. On the other hand a cassock has drawbacks. One is that it's assumed that a mendicant friar, having turned his back on Mammon, puts little store in money. I was rarely paid more than a pittance for my services. Orsini, God rest his soul, was an exception. He paid me well because he had dire need of me. Your party was stranded without the vaguest idea of what confronted you."

I laughed softly. "Had Orsini been granted a glimpse of the future, he might well have turned back."

"Ah, but he didn't. His death marked a turning point in our fortunes. We've shared many an adventure over the past six years. They have been good years, have they not?"

I don't think it truly came home to me until that moment that we were not just parting . . . our lives were diverging. This was the last I was likely to see of the old reprobate. I stopped and grasped him firmly by the forearm. Clearing my throat, I said gruffly, "They *have* been good years. It grieves me, little father, that we have come to the parting of the ways. May fortune smile on you, old friend."

He brought his free hand to rest lightly on the sleeve of my robe. "I, too, am saddened, but it was inevitable that one day our paths must separate. That day has come. And, Edmund . . ."

"Yes?"

"May God protect you . . . and cause His blessings to shine on you and yours."

It was a new experience for me. Heretofore, my exposure to the sea had been confined to the Mediterranean aboard Venetian and Genoese vessels. Those voyages did not compare with my passage aboard the Yuan warship.

The flagship was a high-pooped junk more than a hundred feet in length. She was wide of beam and of shallow draught. Her lack of keel facilitated her negotiation of river estuaries but made her prone to roll alarmingly in the open sea. In lieu of a keel, leeboards were dropped from the offwind gunwale and the rudder could be extended downward in order to reduce leeway. Her batten-extended, red-dyed lugsails pushed her along at good speed in conditions of following or beam winds, but I thought she did not work as well to windward as the lateen-rigged Arab dhows I'd seen in the eastern waters of the Mediterranean or maneuvering in the river off Canton.

We cleared the mouth of the Pearl River estuary at dawn of the day following our departure from Canton. The water changed from muddy brown to sea-green. A fresh breeze blew from the southwest. The warship rolled heavily in response to the ocean swell while the seamen, with practiced ease, went about their tasks of lowering a leeboard and trimming the lugsails. From a vantage point on the poop I watched them at their labors, then gazed astern and watched the landmark peak of Dawanshan recede and dwindle as we set an easterly course. When Dawanshan was but a faint blur in the distance, I descended from the poop and walked unsteadily across the canted deck to a hatch leading downward.

Belowdecks, I found Colonel Chang already there ahead of me seeing to it that his horse and Scimitar were secure and comfortable in their stalls.

*   *   *

For the most part it was an uneventful voyage. The offshore islands in those waters teemed with pirates, but none ventured forth to challenge a warship.

The southwesterly winds held more or less steady until the end of the first week in November, by which time we were well to the northeast in the Yellow Sea. Then the winds became capricious, variable both as to strength and direction. For four days, in fact, we had no wind at all and sat becalmed on a glassy sea. In the predawn hours of the fifth day we were hit by violent squalls that ripped great holes in our main and mizzen sails, snapped our foremast like a rotten twig, and carried away our foresail. These seemed to be matters of no great concern to the naval personnel. Repairs were soon effected and we continued eastward buffeted by northerly gale-force winds.

We arrived off Inchon late in November. Flags and pennants fluttering gaily, we entered the harbor and tied alongside the quay.

It had been my hope that I would find my former commanding officer, General Hsü Ch'ien, soon after my arrival. As chance would have it, he was the general commanding the combined Chinese-Korean forces based at and near Inchon.

I was happy to see the scarred old warrior—all the more so since he was in a position to answer most, if not all, of my questions concerning the morale and fighting preparedness of the forces in Korea. Leaving Admiral Kwan to assess the naval situation, I spent most of my time in Hsü Ch'ien's company at his command headquarters and on visits to the various encampments in the area.

By late December I had concluded my inspection of the troops under Hsü Ch'ien's command. On the morrow the flagship would set sail for Pusan, where Admiral Kwan and I would conduct a similar investigation. The evening before our departure Hsü Ch'ien dined with me aboard the warship.

Hsü Ch'ien put down his chopsticks and wiped his mouth with a damp towel. "If they're half as good at fighting the Nipponese as they are at fighting each other, they'll do well enough. Keeping Manchu Tartars, Mongol horsemen, and Koreans from each other's throats is a battle in itself. If we don't move soon against *some* common enemy, I won't have enough troops left to mount a skirmish. It's bad joss to keep fighting men inactive this long.''

"I agree," I responded, "but it's not as bad as you're making it out to be." Grinning broadly, I added, "They aren't exactly the Army of the Blue Dragon, that I'll have to concede, but they look fit enough. My one complaint is that, except for the Mongol cavalry units, there are too few seasoned soldiers in the ranks.''

"I know," Hsü Ch'ien said, "yet that is not the drawback you imagine. Those among them who are battle-tested are chiefly veterans of the disastrous campaign conducted in the Island Kingdom five years ago. Defeat doesn't inspire confidence.''

"Pusan," I said. "How would you rate the forces there?"

"I would say the situation there is much as it is here. The difference is that General Kim has more Koreans and fewer Mongol and Chinese units in his command. I think you'll find his complaint the same as mine. Lack of action. Can you give us *any* idea about when we might expect the launching of the invasion?''

In my view, Kubilai already had decided on a date for the launching of the invasion. It was highly unlikely that anything I could report or recommend at the conclusion of my mission would alter his predetermined decision. That, however, was not something I wished to tell Hsü Ch'ien. "I can but hazard a guess," I replied. "It will depend on how soon the ships will be ready to embark troops and supplies in the Yangtze estuary. I would say that the invasion will get under way, wind and weather permitting, about this time next year.''

Hsü Ch'ien's one eye widened in shocked disbelief. "Oh, no," he groaned. "Another year in this misbegotten kingdom. I had hoped your coming signaled an early reprieve.''

"It can't be *that* bad," I said consolingly.

"You have no idea how bad it is. The summers are insufferably hot and humid; the winters raw, damp, chillingly cold, and we are often snowbound for weeks on end. Korean food is terrible, their language is an abomination, and their customs primitive beyond belief. My wives have not let a day go by without voicing a steady stream of complaint. And *that* is not the worst of it. Last year I stupidly committed a grave tactical blunder.''

''Oh! What?''

''I met a young woman I found captivating. So much so, in fact, that I brought her under my roof as a concubine. It was a grievous error. Korean women are not like the Chinese. Once installed in my residence, she proved to be ill-tempered, stubborn, and bone-lazy. She paid not the slightest heed to the legitimate demands of my principal wife, or my *ying*. She simply would not accept her proper place and has made impossible demands of me. I have not enjoyed a moment of peace under my roof since her arrival. My wives berate me and squabble endlessly among themselves. My concubine screams at me shrewishly. I spend as little time as possible in my official residence. Believe me, Barbarian, I would find facing the enemy on the field of conflict infinitely preferable to spending another week—let alone a whole year—caught up in the battle that rages beneath my roof.''

Chapter Seventeen

In spite of a delay in Chuanchow owing to tardiness in the change of prevailing winds, I had completed my assessments of the military situation in Nanking and the naval picture in Yangchow by early May. Parting company with Admiral Kwan, Chang and I boarded a river craft for our northbound transit of the Grand Canal. We arrived in Cambulac in mid-June—on the last day of the Month of the Snake in the Year of the Dragon.

I made my way at once to the Forbidden City to make my return known to Kubilai, only to learn that the royal family and the court had left for the summer capital. The khan had not accompanied his court. He had joined a hunting party and was not expected to take up residence at the summer palace in Shangtu for at least another ten days.

I welcomed this news. It meant that I could spend a week with Gentle Breeze in our new abode in the Imperial City without having to worry about appointments, affairs of state, or court intrigue.

It was an idyllic week given over to idle conversation, leisurely meals, bathing in the pool in the secluded garden off our sleeping quarters—and to lovemaking whenever the spirit moved us.

As the day neared when I would have to ride north to Shangtu, I debated taking Gentle Breeze with me. I decided against it. If the khan wished me to stay close to the court in Shangtu, I could always send for Gentle Breeze.

On the warm morning in late June when Chang and I rode forth from Cambulac, I was in excellent spirits. Fortunately for my peace of mind I had no inkling of what awaited me in Shangtu.

Kubilai was five days longer on the hunt than had been indicated to me; then, on his return, a week went by before I was summoned to his presence. I don't know whether or not the intent of the delay was to disconcert me but it certainly was a clear indication of one thing: my report didn't enjoy much by way of priority.

For the private audience I wore the distinctive headgear and yellow robe betokening my rank as a mandarin of the second grade. I was received by Kubilai in the pavilion by the lake familiar to me from previous meetings. On this occasion, however, there were a number of differences. One was that the khan was seated in a blackwood chair heavily inlaid with mother-of-pearl that stood on a carpeted dais at the far end of the pavilion. Another was that the khan was more formally attired than he had been for our last meeting some four years earlier; the hands resting in his lap were adorned with tapering gold finger extensions and his brocade gown was resplendent with gold and silver threads and glittering jewels. But the most marked difference was the presence of two guards flanking his chair. They stood a pace or two to the rear of the seated emperor. Sunlight reflected from the placid surface of the lake glanced in dancing shards off their spiked helms and the blades of their vertically held halberds.

There were other differences I noted as I rose from my kowtow. Where formerly it had been of ebon hue, the khan's moustache, scant beard, and the hair that showed from beneath his cap were silvery gray. I reflected absently on this change in his appearance and concluded that, since he was now in his mid-sixties, he had, in accordance with Chinese custom, given off dyeing his hair. There was yet another, more subtle, difference; it was one of attitude.

True, Kubilai had never received me as an equal or a friend—yet, in our previous meetings, he had seemed well disposed toward me. There had been, I thought, a measure of rapport between us. There was none now. I sensed a coldness in him. A chill of apprehension coursed through me as I stood before the dais awaiting his command to speak.

His eyes mere slits, Kubilai regarded me steadily for close to a full minute before initiating a dialogue. His opening remark indicated that he had noted the questioning glance I had directed at the Imperial Guards flanking him. "The guards are deaf. Their tongues have been removed. Whatever you have to report will be for my ears alone. Well, what thought you of our armies in the south and east?"

Believing him to be already well informed, I confined my answers to those aspects that would have bearing on the recommendations I intended to advance. "As you know, my lord, the forces massed in Korea are composed largely of unblooded conscripts. Inactivity has magnified differences and eroded morale. Their commanders are anxious for them to face combat with as little delay as possible. As for the transports and warships based on Inchon and Pusan, sire, Admiral Kwan Tse-wen considers them adequate—but no more than adequate—for the task assigned to them."

"And in the south?" Kubilai prompted.

"The armies encamped near Nanking are up to strength. All are seasoned veterans of the Sung campaigns. Provisions and supplies are plentiful. Morale runs high. The problem lies not with the military posture but with the naval side of the picture."

"How so?"

"At Chuanchow, my lord, the program of ship construction is almost on schedule. Admiral Kwan estimates that they will have achieved their assigned quota no later than by the end of the Month of the Ox. In Yangchow, however, it is a different story. At the present rate of construction they barely will have reached two thirds of their quota by the end of this year."

"I was aware of the lag in construction," Kubilai said tersely. "I have sent Marco Polo to relieve the governor. I'm sure the situation will improve under Marco's direction. So, now that you have reviewed things at first hand, what would you recommend?"

"In view of the deteriorating morale of the armies in

Korea, sire, I would recommend that the invasion be launched no later than the end of this year. This, of course, means accepting the limitations imposed by the availability of shipping. In my estimation, however, the advantages outweigh the disadvantages. The alternative would be to postpone the invasion until the waning months of next year when once again the winds favor the crossing of the Inland Sea.''

The khan inclined his head slightly. ''Your suggestion has merit. I will give it due consideration. Have you any other suggestions?''

''Yes, sire. One other which I feel is crucial to the success of the undertaking. The enterprise calls for a high degree of coordination. Not counting reinforcing elements, four armies and two navies make up the invasion force. At the command level, jealousy and rivalry are rife. I submit that one man be placed in overall command.''

''Oh. Do you have anyone in mind as supreme commander?''

''Yes, my lord. Marshal Sögatü . . . or, failing him, the most senior and ablest of the military commanders involved, General Hsü Ch'ien.''

Kubilai paused briefly before responding gratingly. ''I have other plans for Sögatü. As for Hsü Ch'ien, he is no longer with us. Four months ago, on my orders, he was subjected to a lingering death as befits a traitor. His sons and women were disposed of more mercifully . . . by decapitation and strangulation. Manifestly, this is news to you.''

I was so stunned by this revelation that, momentarily, I was speechless. When I regained my tongue, I blurted out, ''*Traitor!* What did he do? How could this be? When I saw him last, some seven months back, his one ambition was to come to grips with the foe. He voiced dislike of Korea . . . but no word against you, sire, passed his lips. What—?''

I wasn't given a chance to complete the question. The khan cut into my tirade. ''His treachery was not in Korea. It took place at Hengyang when you served under his command, but I learned of this perfidy only recently.''

''Treachery! How so, sire? He was in the thick of the fray and fought with valor. Thanks to his brilliant generalship we inflicted a crushing defeat on an army considerably superior in numbers to our own. Wherein lay his treachery?''

"I have learned that, had he known of my instructions to General Mangatei, Hsü Ch'ien would have defected to the Sung. Does that not constitute treason in your eyes, Chin Man-tze?"

"If he gave passing thought to defection," I countered hotly, "it is understandable. He had kinfolk among those slaughtered in the town. But he did *not* defect . . . and has served you loyally, my lord. I do not consider a fleeting thought born of anguish an act of treason."

"The act," Kubilai observed dryly, "grows from the thought. I was well aware of the presence of his blood relatives at Hengyang and throughout the region. Did he tell you that the *chün fa* commanding the Sung forces at Hengyang was his cousin?"

That he had blood ties with the Sung warlord was something Hsü Ch'ien had *not* told me. Did that have bearing on the relative ease with which the warlord and his staff officers had made good their escape following the battle? Was there substance to Kubilai's charge of treachery? If so, why had it taken some four years to have the fact confirmed?

The questions running through my thoughts were stilled by Kubilai's small gesture of impatience. He lifted one hand slightly. Reflected sunlight glinted off his golden extensions. I noted that the guards tensed and did not become less rigid until the khan's hand dropped again to his lap.

"The Hsü Ch'ien incident is closed," Kubilai said coldly. "The issue before us now is your conduct, not his."

I looked at him blankly. I knew not to what he referred, so held my tongue.

"Some months ago," Kubilai continued, "it came to my ears that you had entrusted your Nestorian confidant with a mission in Changsha. On your behalf he secretly purchased gemstones of considerable value. To what purpose, *Chin man-tze*?"

I was convinced he suspected, or even knew, my reason for the acquisition. That word of the friar's activities in Changsha had come to Kubilai's attention did not surprise me particularly. What did surprise me was the time it had taken to reach his ears. Even so, I did not feel inclined to adopt a defensive posture.

"I had need of them, sire," I replied forthrightly, "against the day when I would be homeward bound and find myself in lands where Chinese specie is not accepted."

I don't think that Kubilai had expected such candor. His eyes widened. "You contemplated leaving China without seeking my permission to do so?"

I feigned surprise. "I didn't consider that a prerequisite, my lord. I am properly grateful for the titles bestowed upon me and the responsibilities entrusted to me, yet at no time have I pledged myself to a lifetime in your service."

"Acceptance of the titles and responsibilities was an unspoken pledge of fealty," Kubilai retorted sharply. "If you believe this not so, why have you made no attempt to leave? Surely, since procuring the gems, opportunities to leave China have presented themselves aplenty."

He was baiting me. He knew as well as I did that his adroit maneuvering had robbed me of the opportunities he spoke of so glibly. "I was of a mind to do so, sire, but was overtaken by events. In good conscience I could not leave Canton until I had discharged my obligation to restore the city and prefecture to order and stability. Then I assumed new responsibilities with my marriage vows. When the region was devastated by storm, flood, and pestilence . . . even though the plague claimed Mei-ling and her unborn child, releasing me from my marriage vows . . . I could not leave the city in its hour of direst need. Then, when everything was restored to normal, Admiral Kwan arrived to advise me of the mission you had entrusted to me. By my acceptance of the exalted civilian rank with which you had honored me—and the task that went with it—I had assumed yet another obligation that took precedence over my personal wishes."

"Word of the pestilence did not reach me in enough time for me to abort your mission. Had I known that your wife had died . . . or that you covertly had amassed a small fortune in gems . . . you would not have the mandarin rank to which the robes you now wear attest nor the task of trust that went with it."

No, I thought, not for a moment would he have considered a concubine a hostage of sufficient worth to ensure my return

to Cambulac. A wife—maybe. A wife and child—undoubtedly.
A mere concubine—never.

"Do you know why you were entrusted with that mission?"
Kubilai questioned.

"No. Frankly I could see no sense in having me confirm
information readily available to you from other sources."

"The information was for your benefit, not mine. In line
with the recommendation you advanced a moment ago, my
intention was to promote you to the military rank of marshal
and place you in overall command of the invasion forces."

The image that sprang unbidden to my mind was that of a
chessboard. The khan *had* planned a knight attack; the king I
was to have toppled being the emperor of Nippon and—

Kubilai's words cut short my fanciful musing: ". . . a
great disappointment. You had proved yourself a born leader
with a flair for administration. I was well pleased with your
performance. Once the conquest of the Island Kingdom was
successfully concluded under your direction, I had in mind
for you a position of great trust. Then, when word reached
me indicating your intended defection, my initial inclination
was to have you executed. It occurred to me, however, that
considerable time had elapsed since your acquisition of the
gems. You could have had a change of heart about leaving
China. If this was so, I would learn of it when you reached
Chuanchow, a port also much used by Arab traders. You
would arrive there during the season when winds favor westbound voyages. When you failed to avail yourself of that
opportunity, I was glad that I had exercised forbearance.
Now, however, you make bold to say that the desire to leave
China has not lessened. Why did you not seek passage from
Chuanchow?"

I had looked wistfully at the Arab merchantmen loading
cargo at Chuanchow. Had Gentle Breeze been with me I most
certainly would have secured passage on one of them. That it
was due to her that I had been drawn back to Cambulac was
not something I wanted brought to Kubilai's attention. "I was
duty-bound to complete the mission I had undertaken," I
replied evenly.

A suspicion of a smile touched Kubilai's lips. "It is well
that your sense of duty restrained you. I have sent word to my

nephew Abaqa, the Ilkhan of Persia, that should you set foot in his domain you were to be returned to Cambulac shackled as befits a runaway slave.''

Despite the heat of the July morning a chill went through me. I did my best to preserve outward calm in the face of this revelation—and all that it implied.

''Now,'' Kubilai said matter-of-factly, ''we must consider what is to be done with you. You have tried my patience and destroyed much of the confidence I had in you. Nonetheless, *Chin man-tze*, in view of your past services . . . and the fact that you did return to the capital . . . I am disposed toward leniency. Tomorrow, escorted by a detachment of the Imperial Guard, you will return to Cambulac. There, you will join a cavalry *touman* being sent to reinforce the cavalry of the Army of the Blue Dragon at Tali. The armies of the Blue Dragon and Silver Ram have been placed under the overall command of Marshal Sögatü. In your capacity as a general of the first rank, you will be Sögatü's second-in-command.''

I could hardly believe my ears. The posting was by way of being a promotion.

''Do not consider this a mark of favor, *Chin man-tze*. The combined force will launch a campaign against the Kingdom of Champa. On the successful conclusion of that campaign, I will reassess your future position. It may be that I will look with favor on a request from you to return to your homeland. However, should that campaign falter, you, not Sögatü, will bear the blame and pay the price of failure.''

Chapter Eighteen

On our ride south toward Cambulac I paid scant heed to the passing scene of neat villages and fields of grain yellowing beneath the summer sun. I sat slumped in my saddle, prey to dark thoughts and grim conclusions.

Kubilai had been uncommonly direct of speech. I had escaped the fate meted out to Hsü Ch'ien by the narrowest of margins. And still I lived on borrowed time subject to the khan's whim. It had been no empty threat. If Sögatü bungled the conquest of Champa, I would be the scapegoat. My life, not his, would be forfeit.

By design Kubilai had thrust me among Mongol commanders, most of whom would gladly see me dead. Sögatü was hostile. Mangatei hated me.

All that, of course, was in the future. What troubled me was in the past.

How had Kubilai known the gemstones had been purchased on my behalf? Only two people, Brother Demetrios and Gentle Breeze, had known that to be the case. And Kubilai had not learned of it until comparatively recently. It seemed more than coincidence that this knowledge had come to him about the time that Gentle Breeze and the friar had returned to the capital. Had one of them let something slip that had aroused Kubilai's suspicions? If so, the likely culprit was the friar, whose tongue wagged freely when he was in his cups.

It was not accurate to say that Kubilai's suspicions had

been aroused. They simply had been confirmed. From the beginning, appreciating I was no common adventurer, he had known my heart lay in my homeland. He had set about weakening those ties by substituting links that would bind me ever closer to China—high military rank, challenging employment, a concubine, a wife, wealth within my grasp, exalted civilian rank, and a promise of even greater honors and wealth to follow. A beguiling web designed to enmesh me. Now, frustrated in these efforts, Kubilai had revealed the silken strands for what they really were: encircling filaments of steel. He had held out yet another lure—a vague promise that he would consider releasing me from bondage at some unspecified future date. This, I was convinced, he would never do. Did my only avenue of escape lie in death?

Why was I indulging in such morbid reflections? I can think of but one answer. It was an attempt on my part to avoid facing a dread fact confronting me.

Kubilai might have suspected Hsü Ch'ien of harboring treasonous thoughts at Hengyang, but until recently the khan had had no proof of this. In a moment of sorrow Hsü Ch'ien had revealed his innermost thoughts to me in confidence. I had spoken of this to but one person, Gentle Breeze, and in the telling had sworn her to secrecy.

There was but one inescapable conclusion. Sometime following her return to Cambulac, Gentle Breeze had betrayed my trust.

I dreaded a confrontation with Gentle Breeze. When I reached my residence, word of my coming had not preceded me. Gentle Breeze was not on hand to greet me. I was told that she had gone to dine with friends. So be it. It was my hope that I could gather together those possessions I would need for my journey and be gone before her return.

I was in my bedchamber supervising the stowing of arms and battle raiment in my teak traveling chest when I heard her voice in the outer chamber. My heart sank. I turned to face the screened doorway.

She entered the chamber and ran lightly toward me. I had never seen her look so radiantly beautiful. I made no move toward her. She took in the activity in which the servants were engaged, and stopped a few paces from me in confusion. "Emun," she questioned, "what are they doing?" Turning toward me, she must have noted the grim set of my visage. "Wha—" she said falteringly. "What is wrong?"

I dismissed the servants brusquely. When they left the room, I swallowed the bile that was rising in my throat and addressed Gentle Breeze "Five years ago, when the khan sent you to me, did he impose conditions?"

"Ye-es."

"What were they?"

"I was to do whatever was needed to bring you happiness."

"Was that *all*?"

She stood before me, eyes downcast, her hands clenched tightly to her breast. "No-o. I was to encourage you to take a wife . . . and I was expressly forbidden to bear you any child until your principal wife had presented you with a son and heir and—"

"And what?" I barked.

Her voice sank almost to a whisper. "And I was to report to the khan all that was said and done beneath your roof."

"How could you do that?" I asked incredulously. "Soon after you joined me, we were on our way to Changsha. You can neither read nor write. How could you forward these confidential reports on my domestic activities . . . and the confidences I shared with you?"

"Through Wong Sin, my lord. He is versed in Chinese characters."

Wong Sin! I had never suspected that he was literate! God's teeth, I had been surrounded by spies in my household and my very bed for five long years without ever suspecting what was going on. She had played her role to perfection. No wonder she had encouraged me to marry Mei-ling. No wonder she had seen to it that Mei-ling got with child. That had been no accident—as Gentle Breeze had claimed.

"So," I rasped, "you reported on my every word and deed."

She looked up, her eyes wide with anguish, her cheeks tearstained. "No, Emun. No. I *had* to send reports, but they were few in number . . . and never from my lips did the khan learn anything to bring you injury."

"And since your return to Cambulac," I asked, "has Kubilai summoned you to his presence to report in person?"

"Yes. He did so soon after my arrival."

"Did you tell him of the gems Brother Demetrios brought back from Changsha . . . the ones you stitched into our traveling cloaks a couple of years ago?"

Gentle Breeze looked at me blankly for a moment, then shook her head. "No. I wouldn't have mentioned that. I've told no one about those precious stones. I thought you wanted that kept a secret."

I believed her, but that left one important question to be asked—and answered. "Do you recall another secret, something told to me in confidence by General Hsü Ch'ien four years ago?"

Her eyes widened. She paled slightly. "Ye-es," she breathed falteringly. "I remember."

"Did you discuss that with Kubilai?

"No."

"Did you talk about it with anyone . . . either in Canton, or since coming here?"

Her cheeks colored slightly. She ran the tip of her tongue across her lower lip. "No. . . . That is, I . . . I . . ." Her voice trailed off into embarrassed silence.

She needed to say no more. I suddenly felt weak in the knees and a wave of nausea swept over me. She had betrayed my confidence—and in the betrayal, unwittingly, she had condemned Hsü Ch'ien and his family to execution.

Sick with revulsion I brushed past her. I had reached the carved rosewood screen by the doorway before she found her voice. "But—but," she stammered, "my lord, I—"

Without turning I interrupted her with a grating comment. "*I* am not your lord, Wei-feng. Your lord and master, as of now, holds court in Shangtu."

Pride blinded me to reason. For the first week of my southwestward journey prideful anger overrode the hurt within me. By the code of ethics instilled in me since boyhood, a vow was an inviolable covenant. That Gentle Breeze had broken her vow of silence I considered to be an unforgivable breach of trust. Yet, try as I might, I could not bring myself to despise her for her conduct.

When the anger finally ebbed from me, it left me empty, drained of emotion. Only then, with Cambulac some three-score leagues behind me—and growing more distant by the hour—was I able to review the circumstances rationally.

In all fairness, could I blame her for her conduct? After all, she had not come to me of her own free will. It had been arranged by Kubilai to suit his purpose. To him she was but a tool—a pawn. That he had attached a number of provisos and imposed restrictions on her was understandable. Why had I thought it would be otherwise?

She'd admitted freely that one of the khan's stipulations had been that she report regularly all that was said and done within my household. I should have guessed that. I should have been more circumspect in my dealings with her. Yet I had believed her when she'd said that never had she reported anything that would harm me in Kubilai's eyes. Was she so different in the role she had been called upon to play than Wong Sin—or my trusted aide, Colonel Chang?

With each day that passed, I missed her more and regretted that, in anger, I had condemned her unjustly. She had as much as admitted betrayal of my confidence, yet claimed not to have made this disclosure directly to the khan. In my self-righteous arrogance I'd given her no chance either to explain or to defend her action.

Gradually, one salient fact emerged. It mattered little what Gentle Breeze had done; I loved her and must make amends for my stupid behavior in Cambulac.

Chapter Nineteen

From Cambulac to Tali, in the extreme southwest corner of the Middle Kingdom, is a goodly journey. By the route we followed, I estimated the total distance to be in excess of six hundred leagues.

For the first third of our journey we traveled the reverse of the route I had followed five years earlier on entering fabled Cathay. At Ch'ang-an, the ancient capital of the Han dynasty and onetime eastern terminus of the caravan routes, we left the much-traveled thoroughfare and continued due west for five days until we reached Fengsiang. At Fengsiang we cut south between the Tsin and Ch'in ranges. We came to the headwaters of the Kialin Kiang and followed the river southwest into the fertile Red Basin of Szechwan.

It was well into September when we entered the red-soiled uplands of Szechwan. All through that month and into October we traveled south through that prosperous part of the realm. The days were gloriously warm, the nights pleasantly cool. Fleecy clouds floated lazily in a cerulean sky. On our right were the terraced flanks and forested slopes of the foothill ranges—the marches of Szechwan—beyond which, blued by distance, majestic peaks fretted the skyline. To our left tree-bordered fields and vineyards stretched to the far horizon. The roadway that we followed was dotted with pagodas, wayside shrines, and neat tree-shaded villages. It was an appealing countryside which I would have enjoyed the more had I not been preyed upon by bleak reflections and somber speculation concerning my uncertain future.

At Chengtu we faced a choice. The track leading off to the southwest was said to be the shortest route but I was informed it was a mountain road fraught with many treacherous stretches. I opted for the longer southbound roadway.

Three days later, in Ipin, we were ferried across the Yangtze Kiang and entered immediately into rugged and forbidding terrain. We threaded our way through confined mountain passes, descended into thicket-choked gorges, and snaked along narrow valleys, only to be confronted with more steep-sided mountains, yawning chasms, and rock-strewn hills. The rutted roadway was little more than a goat track. As the days extended into weeks, I wondered why we'd been cautioned against the shorter southwestern route.

It wasn't until the first of November that we started our steep descent into a broad mountain-ringed valley. A placid lake smiled up at us from the valley floor. Midway along the western shoreline of that lake lay our destination, the huddled city of Tali.

Tali was the royal seat of the former Kingdom of Nan Chao. Although overrun by Chinese armies during periods of military expansion in the Han and T'ang dynasties, Nan Chao had slumbered through many centuries virtually unmolested until annexed by the Mongols in the middle years of the present century. Considering the difficulties we'd experienced in reaching Tali, it required no great stretch of imagination to appreciate why this landlocked realm had remained isolated for centuries on end. Yet I could see what had attracted the Mongols to this remote region. It provided an ideal staging area, a secure base from which Kubilai could launch Yuan forces in attacks against unsuspecting neighbors to both west and south.

I gazed pensively down at the panorama spread out below me. The far end of the valley was still shrouded in morning mist. Jagged encircling peaks rose like ghostly sentinels trapped in a clutching sea of white. I'd never seen such grotesque rock formations. I could well appreciate why Brother Demetrios had found this starkly forbidding region little to his liking. Forsooth, it *did* seem peopled by malevolent wraiths.

As I turned Scimitar's head back from the lip of the escarpment, a presentiment gripped me. This place, I felt, boded ill for me.

A shout of welcome echoed through the ranks as I rode toward the Army of the Blue Dragon's encampment. A solitary rider detached himself from the assembled troops and approached me at a gallop. As he neared me, I recognized Toghu and reined in. When he was a few paces from me, Toghu brought his war-horse to a skidding stop and leaped from the saddle. I dismounted, strode toward him, and embraced him warmly. As I did so, a cheer went up from the officers and men-at-arms.

Smiling broadly, Toghu said, "Welcome, Chin Man-tze! News of your coming winged ahead of you."

I laughed. "You know, then, of my posting?"

"That you are to become the marshal's second-in-command. It was not news welcomed by General Mangatei."

"Nor by the marshal, I warrant. Would that his welcome could be as warm as yours. Still, it's good to know that you and I will ride once more together."

The smile left Toghu's face. "I fear that is not to be, Chin Man-tze. When the expeditionary force marches south, I ride north. The khan has honored me beyond my due. I am to be promoted to general of the first rank and assume command of the Imperial Guard. General Liu is to take over command of the Army of the Blue Dragon."

Marshal Sögatü received me with frigid formality. He briefed me cursorily on the forthcoming campaign, then assigned me a number of administrative duties that could have been performed just as well by his adjutant, army quartermasters, or civilian contractors. Fortunately, the expeditionary force was due to move out in mid-December—on the first day of the Month of the Rat. I had but five weeks to endure this petty administrative tyranny.

Inexcusable as it was, I suppose Mangatei's truculence was understandable. Prior to my arrival he'd acted in the dual capacity of commanding general of the Army of the Silver Ram and second in command of the expeditionary force. The strutting bandy-legged Mongol's thinly veiled antagonism came perilously close to open insubordination. Lest he be tempted to step over the line and provoke me into combat, I avoided Mangatei as much as possible.

In making reference to the Kingdom of Champa, Sögatü used its Chinese name, Linyi—Savage Forest. As he presented it to me, the campaign to be launched against Linyi posed few major problems.

The casus belli was rooted in indignities. Emissaries sent by Kubilai to demand tribute from India had been intercepted and put to the sword in the Gulf of Tonkin by Cham naval forces. Claiming infirmity, the Cham king had rejected an invitation to journey to Cambulac in order to pay personal homage to the khan. These were affronts that Kubilai could not tolerate.

My attention was directed to maps of the region. Champa's northern frontier was approximately two hundred fifty leagues southeast of Tali. It would take the expeditionary force two full months to cover that distance and, to do so, it first would have to march the entire length of an intervening state, Annam.

Annam! In Chinese that meant "Pacified South." I asked Sögatü if the Annamites might oppose our trespassing on their realm. He brushed my question aside with a disdainful answer. Since the Annamites and Chams were age-old enemies, the Annamites should welcome, not oppose, our passage through their realm. Moreover, twenty-three years ago a Mongol army had sacked Hanoi, the Annamite capital. With that still fresh in their memories, they would be loath to incur Mongol wrath.

With the exception of a handful of coastal locations, Sögatü's terrain map of Champa was distressingly lacking in detail. The kingdom areed southward along a lengthy stretch of east-facing coastline, but neither its southern limits nor its extension inland were delineated. When I questioned Sögatü concerning these omissions, he answered curtly that the interior was mountainous and not suited to habitation. His equally vague answers to other questions led me to the conclusion that the Mongols were woefully ignorant about Champa's geographical features and manpower resources.

Sögatü's plan of attack was deceptively simple. We would take the northernmost stronghold, Mu Cheng, then march south along the coast to overrun, in turn, Indrapura, Vijaya, and Panduranga. Once the capital, Vijaya, fell to us, further resistance should collapse, making the conquest of the southernmost provinces simply a matter of occupation. Between Indrapura and Vijaya there was a small trading port called Faifo which he would capture and use to our advantage. Since, by that time, our supply lines would be overextended, we would use the river port of Indrapura and the seaport of Faifo to receive supplies sent by sea from Canton.

I left Sögatü's briefing with a distinctly uneasy feeling. It seemed to me that he was taking too much for granted and counting too heavily on the invincibility of our cavalry. His expeditionary force numbered some sixty thousand, almost half of which were cavalry units. If the conquest proceeded as he'd planned it, he would be the one to get the credit. But, if not . . .

Toghu's views were considerably less sanguine than those expressed to me by Sögatü.

"Annam!" Toghu said with a grimace. "To have termed it the 'Pacified South' was an example of Chinese wishful thinking. True, the Chinese exercised dominion over the Annamites for close to a millennium, yet they were anything but docile vassals. Some three centuries ago, when the T'ang dynasty was in decline, the Annamites threw off the yoke of Chinese thralldom and have resisted successfully all attempts since then to reestablish the overlordship of the Middle Kingdom."

"Sögatü told me that their capital, Hanoi, was overrun and sacked by a Mongol army two decades ago."

"Yes . . . but did he mention that the Annamites retook the city and forced that army to retreat northward?"

"No-o, he said nothing of that. Then you don't think we'll have an easy time of it in transiting their realm?"

Toghu shrugged expressively. "I do not. The Cham may be their traditional foe, but the Annamites look upon the Chinese as their mortal enemies. Put yourself in the position of the Annamite emperor. Would you want to find yourself faced with mortal enemies both north *and* south? You can expect no easy passage through his kingdom. If Sögatü doesn't suspect that, he's a fool."

It was as I had feared. I'd thought Sögatü's assurances had been too glib. Changing the direction of my queries, I asked, "What do you know about Champa? Sögatü didn't seem to have a very clear picture of what faces us."

"I'm not surprised. Not too much is known about it. No Chinese army, as far as I know, has ever fought there. Apart from seafaring traders, few Chinese have visited the realm. The early name given it by the Chinese, *Linyi,* seems most appropriate. I'm told that, aside from a narrow strip of coastal plains, the country consists of mountains cloaked with dense rain forest, fever-ridden and abounding in savage beasts and poisonous snakes. Not, to my way of thinking, a pleasant place to do battle."

"Do you know anything of Cham battle tactics?"

"No . . . though I've been told that they rely heavily on war elephants in their battle formations. That is common to the southern kingdoms. Mangatei's army gained experience fighting such formations in its campaign in Burma."

"I'm glad *someone* has," I observed tartly, then added, "There's one other aspect of this campaign that troubles me."

"What's that?"

"Sögatü expects us to be resupplied by sea. I can see two, possibly three, major flaws in that concept. The first is that just about every available ship in China will be utilized for the forthcoming invasion of the Island Kingdom in the East. The second is that five months hence . . . when the Month of the Dragon gives way to the Month of the Snake . . . the prevailing winds will make voyages from Canton to Cham ports difficult, if not impossible. The final reason is one not touched upon by Sögatü—the Cham navy. Do you know anything about their naval forces?"

"Not firsthand," Toghu replied seriously, "but, as seafarers, I understand that they're exceptional. They should have a formidable naval force."

He had confirmed what I had suspected and prompted a question that concerned me. "I was glad to see that you've acquired additional mortars for your artillery *touman*. What stocks of black powder and projectiles do you have on hand?''

"Providing you don't get involved in lengthy sieges, I'd say they were adequate.''

"Prolonged sieges are a distinct possibility. Actually my concern is an ample supply of powder for the mortars. When you reach Cambulac, I'd appreciate it if you would order an additional supply and have it sent to Canton for onward shipment. With luck, *some* supplies should get through a Cham naval blockade.''

"I'll do my best, but I doubt the kegged powder could reach Canton much before the Month of the Dragon. Is there anything else you'd like me to pursue on your behalf?''

I hesitated. "One thing. A personal favor."

"Which is?"

"I would be beholden to you if you would visit my quarters in the Imperial City and convey a message to Gentle Breeze. Tell her that I miss her and hope we will soon be reunited and . . .''

"And?"

"And—ah—that I much regret my churlish behavior.''

As he inclined his head in acknowledgment, a ghost of a smile brightened Toghu's normally sober visage.

Chapter Twenty

The grass-grown track was little used. From van to rear guard our column of march stretched over a distance of close to six leagues—more than a day's march in total length.

We followed down the west bank of the dun-colored Red River on its southeasterly course. When we came to a point where, on the opposite bank, a river of light-blue hue emptied into the Red River, we knew from our terrain maps that we had entered Annam. The only other evidence of a transition was that the track widened and appeared to be more traveled. Marshal Sögatü, notwithstanding his avowed lack of concern, must have expected trouble. He detailed units to scout ahead and on the flanks of our line of advance, shortened the column of march, and doubled the detachment guarding our supply train. The precautions were well advised. Almost from the day we entered Annam, our passage through the realm was disputed through almost continuous harassment.

The harassment was no trifling matter. It took many forms—ambushes, rockfalls seeming to appear natural disasters, concealed traps, and hit-and-run attacks by night. They took an alarming toll. By the time we emerged from the mountains onto the deltaic plains northwest of Hanoi, we had been reduced in strength by some four thousand officers and men killed or wounded, had lost close to a quarter of our spare mounts and unladen pack animals, and had been forced to abandon some of our vitally needed supplies. To make things even more miserable, since entering Annam we'd been subjected to almost continuous leaden skies and intermittent drizzle.

Had Kubilai's orders not expressly forbidden it, I am almost certain that Sögatü would have directed our attack against the Annamite capital. Instead, complying with his orders, we circled well to the west of Hanoi to indicate peaceful intentions. It seemed to have the desired effect. The harassment dropped down to a few minor skirmishes on our flanks. No Annamite forces sallied forth to challenge us openly. As we left Hanoi behind us and resumed our southeasterly march, we breathed easier and spirits lifted noticeably. Too soon.

Apart from fording minor streams and tributaries, we had encountered no crossings of rivers of any size. To the southeast of Hanoi this changed. We came to the diked banks of a swollen stream too deep to ford. Since it was late afternoon, and since no river craft were anywhere in evidence, we made camp along the riverbank. At first light we would send out foraging parties either to find a fordable stretch or to commandeer craft that could ferry us to the far bank.

Sometime during the hours of the ox—between three and four in the morning—I was awakened by someone frantically shaking my shoulder. It was Chang. In the orange light from a flickering single oil lamp, his features looked ghastly. "Sire, sire!" he exclaimed in a voice edged with panic. "Wake up! Hurry! The waters are rising!"

I scrambled to my feet, stumbled from my tent, slipped on the rain-slicked surface of the roadway running atop the dike, and fell to my knees. Chang and a white-faced junior officer helped me to regain my footing.

It was true. Not the river. It seemed actually to have dropped about a foot in level. But the muddy paddy fields behind the protective barrier of dikes—*where most of our troops were bivouacked*—were aswirl with rising water.

I realized what must have happened. "God's blood!" I cursed. "They've broached the dikes somewhere upstream of us." I whirled on Chang and queried, "Marshal Sögatü?"

"Safe, sire."

"Scimitar?"

Chang pointed to where my steed stood trembling on the

grass verge. I grunted in satisfaction, and looked to right and left. It was a scene of incredible confusion. Hand-held torches bobbed and wavered along the top of the dike. From what little I could see from my vantage point, men floundered beneath my gaze in waist-deep water. The darkness rang with hoarse shouts and screams of men and animals.

Turning back to Chang, I snapped, "What orders has the marshal issued?"

"None that I know of, sire."

"Take charge. See to it that men with torches are spaced twenty or so paces apart at intervals along the dike. Have soldiers gather anything dry enough to burn . . . fuel from the cooking tents, sleeping mats, spare clothing, anything . . . and have them build bonfires every two hundred paces. Detail those without torches to help men and mounts climb atop the dike. The waters can't reach this high."

Having done what I could, I strode toward Sögatü's command pavilion to report the situation as I saw it—and the action I had taken.

At first light it was reported that sand bars had emerged at a widened stretch of the river about a league and a half downstream from our position. We proceeded to that point and found it possible to ford the stream. Not until we were safely on the far side did we tally our losses.

General Liu reported to me that all but two of his mortars and a single rocket launcher lay somewhere beneath the waters of the flooded fields—along with most of the black powder and mortar projectiles.

"Can't be helped," I responded brusquely. "What losses did you sustain in men and mounts?"

"I'm not sure yet," he replied, running the back of his hand wearily across his eyes. "I'm waiting now for the final reports of the unit commanders."

When the final count was in, our losses proved more staggering than I'd anticipated. In the darkness many of the befuddled men must have stumbled into the deeper water of irrigation ditches and drowned. In those dreadful predawn hours we had lost more men, mounts, pack animals, and stores than in all the preceding weeks put together. In manpower we had been reduced by close to fifteen percent. We had few spare mounts and our supply train had dwindled by one third.

When I reported this sad state of affairs to Sögatü, he received the news in glowering silence. He stared moodily at his horsetail standard for a few moments. I could sympathize with him. We had sustained appalling losses—and had yet to face battle.

Finally, without looking at me, he growled, "Form up. . . . Resume the march."

As though to compensate in small measure for our unhappy situation, the skies cleared. Two days later, although no one was in a festive mood, we celebrated the demise of the Year of the Dragon and the advent of the Year of the Snake.

In the lunar cycle the Year of the Snake is supposed to bring conflict. It is a year known for wars and insurrections. I couldn't help but wonder if Kubilai's court astrologers had advocated this as a propitious year for him to embark on military conquests. By now the invasion of Nippon should be well under way. I wondered if it was going more smoothly than the ill-starred campaign in which I was now involved. But for a chance spin of the Wheel of Fate I would be in overall command of that expeditionary force. But for an even unhappier set of circumstances, Gentle Breeze and I, by this time, should have been somewhere in the Outremer nearing the crusader-held port of Acre. God, in His infinite wisdom, had decreed otherwise. I was far from being a happy man.

I don't pretend to understand Annamite thinking. It could be that the emperor, Tran Nhon-Ton, when apprised of the losses we'd suffered in the flooded paddy fields, had second thoughts. He might have felt that, if subjected to more harassment, we would be provoked into attacking Hanoi. It might have been that he did not want to reduce further our capacity to inflict punishment on his traditional foe, the Cham. Whatever his reasoning, from the time when we forded the river until we arrived at the Cham frontier two weeks later, we were not hindered or molested in any way.

Our transit of Annam took longer than anticipated. We did

not reach the frontier until halfway through the Month of the Tiger—the third day of March in the Year of our Lord 1281.

We were confronted by a steep-sided mountainous spur that extended to the surging sea. A Cham-speaking Chinese cavalryman explained to me that the Cham referred to the pass through this natural barrier as the "Gates of Annam."

The Chams had to have had ample warning of our approach. Patrols well in advance, we cautiously ascended the tortuous roadway leading toward the pass. It was terrain that lent itself readily to defense. We fully expected to come under attack at any moment. To our surprise the pass was not defended. Although I now know the reason for this apparent lack of concern, at the time I found it incomprehensible.

We filed through the pass and descended onto the narrow plain between the coastal mountains and the sea. The soil was sandy and sparsely foliated. There was little in the way of cover. Unless screened from view in the forested slopes of the encroaching mountains, no Cham forces were on hand to oppose our entry into their kingdom. Manifestly, that we were not being challenged both puzzled and worried Sögatü.

We continued our southward march, but with flanking patrols keeping a wary eye on the foothill approaches. Over the next two days the largely uncultivated flatland between the beach-fringed sea and the jungle-matted foothills widened somewhat, but otherwise remained unchanged. Peasants tilling the fields made themselves scarce on our approach.

On the third day we came to our first objective, Mu Cheng, a fortified town hugging the seacoast, protected on its landward side by a wide moat. It boasted, on its southern extremity, a lagoon which served as a partially sheltered haven for shipping. If Sögatü had hoped to find Chinese merchantmen and warships awaiting our arrival, he was sadly disappointed. None were in evidence either standing out to sea or within the shallow harbor.

We left behind a force deemed large enough to storm the brick-faced earthworks that constituted Mu Cheng's defenses, then continued our march to the south.

Though the mountains continued to dominate the western skyline, the coastal plain grew ever wider. It was, nonetheless, composed largely of sandy and infertile soil given over to

tufted grasses and low shrubs. Only where rivulets meandered
toward the sea was there much in the way of habitation or
cultivation. On our left league after league of unbroken wave-
swept beaches stretched as far as the eye could see. Sand
dunes bordering the beaches were dotted with stands of slender palms and feathery tamarisks. To the west the mountains
were cloaked with dense foliage. But, in between, the coastal
plain seemed unproductive—a chiefly sterile vista with exten-
sive patches of chalk-white sand that supported no plant
growth of any kind. It was depressing.

It was, I thought, little wonder that no Cham forces were
deployed to bar our advance. What puzzled me was why
Kubilai had deemed such an unprepossessing realm worthy of
conquest. Where was its wealth? Where were its defenders?
Try as I might, I could not shake off a growing sense of
foreboding.

Morale was at a low ebb. Our provisions were dwindling
rapidly. The weather had assumed a pattern to which we were
unaccustomed, and which we found trying.

The days dawned still and clear. During the morning the
sun beat down on us mercilessly. As the morning progessed,
towering clouds formed over the mountains and extended
slowly seaward. About midday the heavens opened up to visit
torrential rains upon us as thunder crashed and roared above
our ears. The rain lasted an hour or two, then the sun broke
through and the landscape steamed itself dry. In the late
afternoon the clouds gathered again and we were battered by
a second deluge. In the evening the skies cleared above us but
the clouds persisted over the mountains. Thunder rumbled in
the distance and lightning danced and shimmered in the western sky.

It might have been the weather that contributed to a problem of a much more serious nature. Our surgeons had had to
cope with a spate of casualties and illnesses, but it was not
until we passed through the so-called Gates of Annam that
they were faced with any major affliction. What was visited
upon us was what they termed "blackwater fever." It was
similar to, yet a much more virulent form of, the quartan
fever which had come close to finishing me off in the oubliette at Hama. It was an affliction that alternated between

chills and raging fever. It scythed through our ranks with grim impartiality. Our physicians could do nothing to forestall the paroxysms of fever that carried off many of those stricken with the illness. Our southward progress from Mu Cheng was marked by shallow graves.

Four days after we left Mu Cheng behind us, General Liu died in raving delirium. Even though my quartan fever had returned to plague me, I now served in a dual capacity as both second-in-command of the expeditionary force and acting commanding general of the Army of the Blue Dragon.

In mid-March we moved through irrigated farmland and reached the heavily fortified city on the northern bank of the Perfume River—Indrapura. We were fever-ridden, on short rations, and demoralized, yet still a formidable force numbering slightly more than forty-five thousand. No Cham army had dared sally forth to challenge us. Certainly we were in sufficient strength to storm and take Indrapura. Sögatü decreed otherwise.

In his decision to continue our southward march in order to secure Faifo as a supply port and to storm Vijaya, I believe Sögatü was influenced unduly by what was reported to us when we set up camp in the shadow of Indrapura's walls. Two weeks earlier a flotilla of Chinese merchantmen, escorted by a squadron of Yuan warships, had put in an appearance in coastal waters off the mouth of the Perfume River. They had been engaged by Cham naval units and had suffered heavy losses before retreating to the southeast with Cham warships in hot pursuit. Sögatü was convinced that we would find the supply ships awaiting us in Faifo.

I argued vehemently against this course of action. I maintained that there was no guarantee that the Chinese merchantmen had found sanctuary in Faifo or, for that matter, in any other Cham port. I contended that the Cham strategy appeared to be to draw us ever deeper into their realm in order to overextend our lines of supply. When they considered us to be weakened sufficiently, they would engage us at a time and place of their choosing. Indrapura, I stated, looked to be a prosperous river port that should be stocked amply with provisions. Accordingly, our wisest course of action would be to mount an all-out assault against Indrapura before disease and starvation reduced our capabilities any further.

To my surprise Mangatei supported my arguments. To no avail. Sögatü could not be swayed. With him the taking of the Cham capital, Vijaya, seemed to have become a fixation that dwarfed all other considerations.

Chapter Twenty-one

His shaman assured Sögatü that the spring equinox would see a change of fortune. On that date—leaving behind a force of some ten thousand to besiege Indrapura—we resumed our march toward Faifo and Vijaya.

We hadn't proceeded many leagues after crossing the Perfume River before the character of the countryside began to change. Once again the mountains pushed toward the coast. Not only did the coastal plain become compressed, but a saltwater lagoon a league or more in width ran down its center. Chinese-speaking Chams we had made captive near Indrapura advised us that the lagoon extended southward for a distance of some two days' march and that, at its lower extremity, it widened into a salt lake of considerable size. Beyond the salt lake we would find ourselves confronted by a mountain range that jutted outward into the sea. The saddle by which we would cross between the peaks was called by the Chams the "Pass of Mists."

Sögatü feared that if we marched down only one side of the lagoon, a Cham army could march north undetected on the opposite side not only to outflank us, but to lift the siege at Indrapura. To forestall such a tactic, Sögatü divided our force. The Army of the Silver Ram, with Sögatü at its head, would march south on the landward side of the lagoon. The Army of the Blue Dragon, under my command, would proceed along the sandy coastal strip. We would rendezvous south of the salt lake to re-form and cross the mountain pass as a single body. While I was not particularly happy at the prospect of splitting a force that now had been reduced in strength to about thirty-five thousand, I could see the logic in the marshal's reasoning. Nonetheless, I could not rid myself of the presentiment that the time and place for a confrontation with the Cham forces was nearing rapidly.

The mountain barrier, blurred by distance and partially obscured by cloud cover, had grown more distinct during the day. By late afternoon I could make out what seemed to be the lower limit of the salt lake. Beyond that the jungle-clad lower flanks of the mountains rose steeply. There was no sign of the Army of the Silver Ram. I called a halt.

It was sometime after midnight when Chang roused me from a fitful sleep. "The scouts report a Cham army forming ahead of us," he stated evenly.

I rubbed the sleep from my eyes and ran my fingers through my beard. "Could they estimate its size?"

"Not accurately. They believe it to be more than three times our number. It is being formed about two li from us . . . stretching from the edge of the lake to the seashore."

Three times our number! Of the two armies, mine was the smaller, numbering in all about fourteen thousand. That would put the Cham force in the neighborhood of forty-five thousand. The marshal's soothsayer, I thought grimly, had not erred. The equinox indeed had brought a change in our fortunes—but not necessarily for the better. Yet, oddly enough, I felt no dismay. The thought of action exhilarated me.

"Summon the unit commanders," I ordered briskly.

I had additional lamps lit and affixed to my tent poles. On a large piece of white cloth I sketched in the geographical features and the enemy formation with a piece of charcoal. I laid the cloth out on my rush mat.

When the officers were assembled, I referred to my rough map. "As you can see," I said crisply, "they have chosen their position well. Our cavalry has no hope of outflanking them unless we can dislodge one end of their line of battle. And *that* is exactly what I propose to do."

I drew a line in front of what represented the Cham battle

line. "We will form up and advance to this position, about
one li from them. Most of our cavalry will be on our left, or
seaward, flank. We will hold our position and let the enemy
take the initiative. Since they are superior in numbers, this
they will not hesitate to do."

I gave the unit commanders a moment or two to study the
map, then addressed myself to the captain commanding the
artillery *touman*. "It is unfortunate that your mortars have
been reduced to only two, and that you have but one rocket
launcher, but we'll have to make do with what you have. I
want the mortars positioned about twenty paces on either side
of my place in the center of our line . . . and the rocket
launcher about midway along our left wing. I want them
screened from view behind the front line of infantrymen.
When the enemy have closed to about half a li, I'll dip my
battle lance. That will be the signal for the ranks to part and
the mortars and launcher to fire. The mortars are to be angled
inward toward the center of the Cham formation and the
rockets aimed outward toward its seaward flank. You are to
reload and continue firing until I raise my lance. Only then
will our great drums signal the advance. Are there any questions so far?"

There being no questions, I continued. "We will advance
at normal speed until the battle is joined. Then, our right
wing will give ground slowly, while I hold fast and our left
wing advances as rapidly as the tactical situation allows. If
you see my lance canted to the right, it will mean that I want
the right flank to fall back more rapidly. If my lance tilts to
the left, it means I want the left flank to do its utmost to
increase its speed of advance. What we will be achieving is a
gradual pivoting toward the lake. The enemy will be forced to
respond and its seaward flank will shift inland. When the gap
is sufficiently widened, our cavalry will race through to join
with General Mangatei's cavalry that should be advancing on
the enemy's rear."

"How do we know, sire, that General Mangatei's cavalry
will be advancing?" Colonel Chu, our cavalry commander,
questioned.

"We don't. We don't know the present position of the
Army of the Silver Ram. We don't know whether or not it

faces a situation similar to our own. I am assuming, from the enemy strength facing us, that the Army of the Silver Ram is not opposed as we are and, once alerted to the fact that we're in action, it will advance at best speed and arrive on the scene in time to swing the tide of battle in our favor."

Chang frowned. "How will they be alerted? Are we not too distant for signaling by means of whistling arrows?"

"I am assuming that to be the case," I replied evenly. "From an hour from now until first light, we will fire a single rocket above the salt lake every half hour. Are there any other questions?"

General Fong, the commander of the right-wing forces, spoke up. "Yes, sire. In the heat of battle how are we to see your signals?"

I grinned. "My pennants should be clearly visible. In case there is any question, Chang will dispatch riders to relay my orders verbally. And I doubt that you will have any trouble seeing me . . . even in the ebb and flow of battle. I will be garbed distinctively in full armor."

When the rim of a blood-red sun edged above the eastern horizon, we were drawn up facing each other at a distance of slightly less than a li. I looked curiously at the enemy formation. I counted at least thirty war elephants spread at intervals along the forward line of battle. Never before had I seen an elephant girded for war. They presented an awesome spectacle. In the center of the formation was a magnificently caparisoned elephant larger than the others. A low-sided platform graced its back. The rear of that platform was raised to form a kind of throne. I took it that this mammoth creature served as the mount of the Cham commanding general. The distance was too great for me to make out the seated figure above whose head there reared what looked to be a tiered series of umbrellas that diminished steadily in size as they ascended upward on a single shaft. In fact, there looked to be not one, but three, figures atop the huge beast. One was seated just behind the elephant's ears and one was standing behind the seated officer holding aloft the tiered contraption that appeared to be some sort of a standard.

A twinge of envy assailed me. The Cham forces would

have no difficulty whatsoever identifying their commanding general.

The air was still. Banners and pennants hung limply. No sound came to us across the sandy stretch between our battle lines. From our ranks all that could be heard was the jingle of harness, as horses stirred restlessly, and the shuffle of nervous feet.

The cinnabar sun seemed to hang suspended for a moment before breaking free from the clutching sea. That was the signal. In our ranks, wind instruments wailed and cymbals clanged as voices rose in boastful chants. From the enemy ranks came a similar cacophony with an added accompaniment of throbbing drums and the mournful sound of conch shell signals. Then a ripple ran through the Cham ranks as the battle line started to move ponderously forward. Hoarse shouts bridged the distance between our battle lines. Our line stood fast.

When the gap had closed to about half a li, the sky was darkened by arrows winging toward us. I waited. Now!

Our ranks parted. Rockets, trailing tails of fire, swooshed toward the enemy's seaward flank. The mortars belched fire and smoke as they roared in unison. And, since the dropping of my lance point also had been a signal to our bowmen, a hail of arrows arched toward the advancing enemy.

It had been five years since I'd used the mortars and rocket launcher in field combat at Hengyang. My memory of their effectiveness on that occasion had dimmed. Now the memory flooded back as I watched the devastation visited on the Cham ranks. The advancing line buckled and wavered as the projectiles plowed into yielding flesh and bone. The screams of wounded men and horses mingled with shouts of horror. An elephant lay on its side, its legs jerking erratically. A second elephant, trumpeting in terror, thrashed about trampling everything in its path.

The artillerymen worked with practiced speed reloading the mortars and launcher and struggling to reposition the supporting *mappa*s that had been knocked askew by recoil. I glanced back toward the Cham lines and cursed inwardly. As had happened at Hengyang, the commanding general had escaped injury. Conch shells blared, the gaps filled, and the line steadied and, while ragged, continued its advance. There was no time to get away a second salvo. God's teeth, I thought, had the artillery *touman* at its disposal the eight mortars and six rocket launchers that had been in our supply train when leaving Tali, we might have halted the Cham advance and turned it into a rout.

Reluctantly, I raised my lance to the upright position. Immediately, the great drums boomed the signal and our line surged forward to meet the Cham advance.

As I dropped my visor and touched spurs to Scimitar, a wave of anticipation pulsed through me. The long-awaited confrontation with the enemy was at hand.

The battle wasn't progressing as I'd planned it. On my left, fighting raged where Chu's cavalry pressed forward with unrelenting fury. My right flank was giving ground as I'd ordered. The Chams, however, were not exploiting this apparent advantage and fighting had slackened on that flank. In the center, where I was holding my position, it seemed as though the enemy was purposely avoiding contact.

Chang rode with me almost stirrup to stirrup. Lifting my visor, I leaned toward him and shouted to make myself heard above the din of battle. I told Chang to send a rider to contact General Fong with instructions for Fong to close and engage the enemy.

As Chang wheeled to have my order carried out, I reined in to survey what I could of the confused scene. The Chams were holding firm to a battle line that stretched from the wavelets lapping on the beach to the marshy ground bordering the lake. They seem to have halted their advance. No, so slowly that it was almost imperceptible, *they actually were falling back*.

It wasn't right! At this stage of the battle the sheer weight of their numbers should be carrying them forward. The inescapable conclusion was that they were easing back by design. To what purpose? Could they see what I could not? Were units of the Army of the Silver Ram advancing to their rear? And why, in God's name, was I left unmolested?

Momentarily, the dust and swirling sand cleared and I caught a glimpse of the rearing mountains and the tree line through the milling throng. Strange! The tree line looked to be closer than it had when the battle was joined. God's blood! That was it! That was their strategy. They were falling back to draw us into the jungle. Once in that tangle of foliage— terrain all too familiar to them but foreign to us—they could cut us to ribbons at their leisure. At all costs I must avoid being lured into that trap.

I turned toward Chang, intent on issuing an order to disengage and fall back. The command did not leave my lips.

A shrill trumpeting reached my ears. Scimitar reared in sudden fright. My lance was dislodged from its stirrup socket and flew from my hand. I was thrown from my saddle and fell heavily. As I struggled to my feet and reached for my sword, I saw a war elephant, its trunk raised high and its metal-tipped tusks gleaming, bearing down on me at incredible speed. A thrown spear jolted me as it glanced off my breastplate; then, before I could regain my balance and raise my sword, the monster was upon me.

The elephant's trunk whipped around my waist. I was lifted clear of the ground. The sky and earth tilted crazily before I was hurled to the ground and consciousness left me abruptly.

Chapter Twenty-two

I have a vague recollection of a series of disjointed impressions. I must have regained consciousness briefly at some point, because I recall looking up through thick foliage at a patch of sky. I was, I think, being carried. I heard voices speaking in some unidentifiable tongue. The sound seemed to come from a great distance. I was in pain. Mercifully, darkness reclaimed me.

When consciousness finally returned, I found myself in alien surroundings. A palm-thatched roof was above me. I was lying on some sort of a raised, cushion-strewn platform. I was in a room of sorts with three sides formed from woven bamboo and the fourth side open to the elements. I heard birds singing, the sound of splashing water, and a strange sound as of a muffled drum.

I turned my head stiffly. Through the unscreened opening I saw a flame tree, a welter of greenery, and part of an ornately carved facing of gray stone.

I tried to sit up, gasped in pain, and sank back onto the cushions. A voice intruded into my befogged thoughts. Until that moment I had thought myself to be alone in the room.

"Ah," the voice said in Arabic, "Allah, the All Merciful, has seen fit to restore you to the land of the living."

I turned my gaze toward the foot of the platform. A beak-nosed bearded man wearing a *jallabah*, a smile on his lips, gazed down on me. In his cupped hands he held a wooden bowl from which steam rose lazily.

I stared up at him in stunned bewilderment. *An Arab!* God's teeth, what had befallen me? "Where am I?" I croaked in rusty Arabic.

The Arab's smile widened. "You speak my tongue. How fortunate. You are in a safe place . . . a royal retreat and religious sanctuary."

"How came I here?"

The Arab chuckled. "Part of the way slung across the back of your stalwart war-horse . . . the rest of the way borne on a litter. Considering your condition it is a wonder that you lived through the journey."

"My condition?"

"Your left arm is broken in several places—the elbow crushed beyond repair. Your left leg is broken, but will mend. Most of your ribs are cracked or broken and Allah alone knows what internal injuries you sustained when the elephant trampled you. Had it not been for the valiant companion who stood over you and drove Airavata back at spearpoint, you would have died on the field of combat and, by so doing, saved me much concern and labor." The Arab hitched up his *jallabah*, squatted at my side, and held the bowl to my lips. "Here," he said, "drink this. It will give you strength."

Memory returned with a rush. "How went the battle?" I questioned anxiously.

The Arab laughed. "I did not witness it. Like most battles, its success or failure is in the telling by those who survived it. The Chams claim it to have been a great victory despite their heavy casualties. Your capture more than compensates for their losses. Your presence on the battlefield inspired awe and fear in the Cham ranks."

"How so? I was but little in the fray."

"With good reason. They feared to approach you."

"Why?"

"None had ever seen a Frankish knight. Encased as you were in shining armor, they thought you to be a god in human form. They took you to be Shiva—'the Destroyer.' Even fallen, they thought you capable of rising to strike them dead."

"There was at least one," I observed sourly, "who overcame his fear long enough to strike me down."

"Their commanding general, Prince Sinha. He risked destruction to impress upon his troops his own invincibility."

I smiled wanly. "He must have been delighted to find I was a mere mortal."

"He didn't discover that until you were brought here and I pried you out of your metallic carapace. Yet you are no mere mortal in his eyes. Though he no longer believes you to be a god incarnate, he is firmly convinced that you are a reincarnation of a legendary warlord . . . a figure of history they call the Tartar."

"Surely you don't subscribe to such superstitious nonsense. From your remarks I take it that you have seen knights in armor before."

"As a youth I saw Christian knights at Arsuf and Jaffa, but I must confess that never did I see one garbed in armor of burnished bronze."

"How came *you* here?" I asked curiously.

"As a young man I came here aboard a merchant vessel. I had some skill with herbs and medicine. It was my good fortune to cure the king of a trifling ailment. Since then I've been the court physician. It is also my good fortune that you have survived, since I was charged with restoring you to health. Now, say no more. You need rest . . . the best medicine I can prescribe."

For a good many weeks I was left in doubt concerning my status. I was attended by the Arab physician, whose name I learned was Abdel bin Hasan, and by two of his young wives. I was bathed, fed, and treated with courtesy and consideration. My hair and beard were trimmed and I was given a sheathlike garment called a *sampot* to clothe me from waist to ankle. Against the evening chill I was provided with a quilted jacket and, against the day when the splint would be removed from my left leg, a pair of sandals for my feet. It was clothing that was both simple and practical in those climes and, as I soon discovered, clothing worn by royalty and commoners alike. The only distinction of rank was in the elaborate embroidery of gold and silver thread incorporated in the *sampot*s worn by nobles and members of the royal household.

As my ribs healed and my breathing no longer pained me, I took more of an interest in my surroundings. Eventually, when the splint was removed and I could walk again, I ventured forth from the sanctuary of Abdel's dwelling on short forays into the mountain community and its environs.

What struck me most was the contrast between the Chams and their way of life and the people and mores I had come to know and accept in the Middle Kingdom. Where the Chinese were slaves to tradition and rigidly paternalistic in their outlook, the Chams appeared to be unconventional and easy-going. Where the Chinese were industrious, the Chams seemed indolent. I suppose the climate was a factor. There was no winter season such as I had known in China. In Champa there seemed to be but two seasons—hot and wet, and hot and dry. The Chams had no need to toil endlessly in order to coax sustenance from the soil. Except where the sandy soils of the coastal plains had been leached of nutrients, the Chams were blessed with an abundance of growth. In fact their labors appeared to be directed more toward discouraging than encouraging rampant growth. Where China largely had been stripped of forests, most of Champa was cloaked with untamed rain forest where trees grew to astonishing heights and gorges were choked with a well-nigh impenetrable tangle of shrubbery.

That trees and timber products were plentiful was reflected in Cham construction. Their dwellings—palm- or grass-thatched—were built exclusively of wood. They were raised on stiltlike underpinning to allow a free circulation of cooling air and were spacious in proportions. For the most part, internal divisions within the dwellings and external protection against the intrusion of rain or mist were afforded by bamboo screening that could be raised or lowered as required. Only the residences of the nobility had windows boasting louvered shutters.

Manifestly, the Chams cared little for the privacy so prized by Chinese of substance. No high walls protected Cham property or residential compounds from prying eyes. Even the royal compound of grounds and palaces was enclosed only by a low hedge of flowering shrubs.

If the prevailing wooden construction and absence of containing walls suggested impermanence, exactly the opposite impression was imparted by the religious edifices. The temples were massive multitowered structures of enduring brick-and-stone construction. The lintels and cornices were intricately carved in bas-relief floral patterns and depictions of a pantheon of the gods, goddesses, and demigods of their Hindu faith.

Like the Chinese the Chams were dark-eyed and black of hair, but there all similarity ended. Cham skin tones ranged in hue from nut-brown to bronze. Their eyes were round, not almond-shaped, and their noses had distinctive bridges. I found the nubile Cham maidens singularly attractive—all the more so due to their mode of dress and deportment.

The *sampot* was uniformly worn by both men and women. Knotted at the waist, it sheathed the lower extremities but left the chest and breasts bare and unencumbered. Only when age or childbearing caused a woman's breasts to sag would she knot her *sampot* at armpit level. Young women displayed their trim figures and firmly rounded breasts with sensuous pride. Chinese women would have been shocked by such immodesty, and I must confess, initially I found it somewhat disconcerting. Where Chinese women of breeding were kept in seclusion from puberty onward, Cham women of all ages mingled freely with the men. This conduct would have been unthinkable to the Chinese, who would have been horrified to see men and women, youth of both sexes, and children bathing together in unabashed nudity. Gentle Breeze, I was sure, would have found the permissive customs delightful.

I questioned Abdel concerning some of the customs and practices I found rather disturbing. He laughed. Was not, he asked, a woman's body made to attract male attention? Cham women were trained from childhood to attract and satisfy men, and according to him, at puberty they underwent a ceremony wherein they were deflowered by a Brahmin priest. Chastity, he assured me, was an affront to their Hindu gods. And, he added, since I was evincing interest, I must be well on the road to recovery. He prescribed female companionship as part of my continuing therapy. Thereafter, no night went

by but that I found an attractive bed companion had been
provided me by my physician host.

The community was located in a horseshoe-shaped valley.
On three sides it was hemmed in by rounded, forest-cloaked
peaks. The open side dropped away abruptly in a series of
steep tree-mantled slopes leading down to a fertile valley that
fanned outward to the coastal dunes and the sea. The altitude
of the upper valley was not great; I estimated its height above
sea level as being not much more than two thousand feet.
Nonetheless, Abdel assured me, the combination of altitude,
towering shade trees, morning mist, sea breeze, and the
afternoon shadows cast by the surrounding peaks kept the
temperature well below the searing levels that held the coastal
regions in a relentless grip during the coming dry-season
months. The valley was blessed with an added attraction, a
waterfall that tumbled down from the western crags into a
natural basin on the floor of the valley. I could well see why
this was a favored summer retreat of the king, Indravarman,
and members of the royal family and the Cham court.

When my convalescence had progressed to the point where
I could essay modest exploration of my surroundings, I was
accompanied initially by Abdel. Soon, however, I went
unattended. While there was a military encampment near the
open end of the valley and soldiers were much in evidence in
and around the temple compounds and the mountain community,
they paid me little heed. I concluded that I was not thought of
as a prisoner. Indeed, there was no reason why I should be. I
was without weapons. I walked with a pronounced limp. My
left arm was still encased in splints and bandages and gave
every evidence of being virtually useless. I dared not venture
into the rain forest unaccompanied, and—even if I had harbored thoughts of escaping—I was so alien to the Chams in
face and form that I could not have strayed far undetected.

There could be no doubt that I was an object of curiosity.
Obviously in awe of me, the Chams kept their distance yet
did not go out of their way to avoid me. At my approach they
would clasp their hands close to their chests, bow their heads,
then, with eyes downcast, they would step aside deferentially
to let me pass. I was treated with unfailing courtesy. It was

astonishing. There could be none among them who did not know of me, yet I was accorded treatment not as a vanquished enemy but as befitted visiting royalty. They made me feel not as an interloper but as an honored guest.

The impression I formed of the Chams was that they were an outgoing people of childlike simplicity and trust—essentially a passive breed. Having faced them on the field of combat, I should have known better. Much better.

Chapter Twenty-three

In early June, Abdel informed me that the king and his royal party were due to arrive within the week. Casually, Abdel added that, soon after his arrival, King Indravarman would want to speak with me.

The royal palace was on a grander scale but differed little otherwise from Abdel's unpretentious residence. Two guards escorted me to a sunlit porch where a frail old man was seated in a high-backed chair. He was the veranda's only occupant. As we approached, he leaned forward and squinted at us myopically. When we were some ten paces from him, the guards halted and bowed deeply. When I sank to my knees to kowtow, the oldster stopped me with an impatient gesture and said in Arabic, "We need not stand on ceremony, young man." Indicating a low stool beside his chair, he added, "Come, sit by me. We have much to discuss and my hearing is not what it used to be."

When I was seated, the guards departed. I observed the aging king closely. His thinning hair was snow-white, his beardless face a mass of lines and wrinkles. The flesh at his neck, across his chest at the armpits, and on his upper arms sagged loosely. A tracery of veins stood out along his forearms and on the backs of his hands. His swollen-knuckled hands resembled falcon claws gripping the armrests of his chair. There was an unhealthy pallor to his desiccated flesh.

He wore no adornment. He was dressed simply in a vermilion *sampot* richly decorated with gold embroidery at the lower hem. His feet were bare.

"Since you speak not our tongue," the king observed in a surprisingly resonant voice, "it is well that you speak Arabic. Like my hearing, my command of Chinese dialects leaves much to be desired. Besides, like their Mongol masters, the Chinese speak in riddles."

His observations called for no comment on my part. I waited patiently for him to continue.

With his head cocked to one side the king regarded me speculatively. "So, you are the warrior they call the Golden Barbarian. My son, Prince Sinha, contends that in you the Tartar has been restored to us."

"Does he truly believe that, sire? Do you?"

The king smiled, baring well-nigh toothless gums. "It matters not what *I* believe. Sinha stands firm in his conviction and has convinced others. Now, most of my people believe that you are the Tartar returned to deliver us from our oppressors. Sinha is impetuous and often jumps to wrong conclusions, but the evidence supporting his contention is not easy to refute."

I was confused. I had the feeling I was missing some important clue to what was taking place. "Sire, it is you who talk in riddles. I came into your realm as part of an army of conquest. How is it expected that I can deliver you from your oppressors when, surely, I myself fall in that category in your eyes? Who was this Tartar you speak of? In what way can I, an English knight in the service of Kubilai Khan, possibly resemble this man you speak of?"

"You do," the king said solemnly, "in more ways than you can imagine. The Tartar was a Chinese general in the service of a foreign despot. Like you, he came leading an army bent on conquest. Although not of your coloring, he was much like you in stature. His was a noble steed much like yours . . . and not since his day has such a horse been seen in my kingdom. He introduced us to the fearsome weapons that spit fire, smoke, and death. Not since the one battle in which he employed those devices some fourscore years ago have they been used in warfare, until now. We had thought them forgotten until they were reintroduced by you. Those, Barbarian, are the facts upon which my son based his assumption of reincarnation. How, he reasoned, could anyone not guided by the Tartar's thinking have devised such awesome weaponry? Do you not find such reasoning logical?''

''The weapons, though fallen into disuse, are neither new nor novel,'' I relied gruffly. ''They were first used in the Middle Kingdom more than a century ago.''

''That well may be,'' the king said agreeably, ''but was it not you who recognized their destructive potential after all those years of disuse? I think it more than coincidence. Still, if you do not, then consider this—a fact that did not come to my son's attention until captives from your army were interrogated. Until then he knew not that you were called Chin Man-tze—the Golden Barbarian. The given name of the Tartar was Hsü Yung. The Tartar was a name he acquired in his youth and adopted from then onward. Do you not find it passing strange that in Chinese 'barbarian' and 'tartar' are synonymous? In both your cases it was a term applied derisively that came to command respect. Is that coincidence? My son thinks not.''

Hsü Yung? Why did that name sound vaguely familiar? Then it came to me. God's teeth, the Chinese warlord who was Hsü Ch'ien's illustrious grandfather! It was a fantastic coincidence. Had reincarnation not been a concept contrary to the teachings of my faith, I might have wavered. Was it possible that my destiny was in some way intertwined with that of a dead Chinese warlord? I rejected the thought as too absurd for serious consideration. Nonetheless, I would not mention to the Cham king that I had served under, and replaced in field command, the Tartar's grandson. To do so would only add substance to Prince Sinha's specious argument.

''If, sire, as you say,'' I observed, steering the conversation into safer channels, ''the Tartar came to Champa as an enemy, why do you speak of him as a hero?''

''Because he was a heroic figure in every sense of the word. He overthrew a Cham tyrant who had usurped the Cham throne. For the following two decades, though he governed in the name of the Khmer king through a viceroy of the Tartar's selection, he was the warlord who ruled this kingdom, in fact, if not in name. He took to wife a Cham princess, my aunt, in fact. They were devoted to each other. He was more than a military genius; he was a farsighted statesman who preserved Cham cultural and religious integrity and brought peace and prosperity to our troubled realm. He restructured and strengthened our military and naval forces. When, sixty-one years ago, he withdrew the Khmer army of occupation, he placed my uncle, Prince Phanra, on the Cham throne to restore the authority of our Eleventh Dynasty. The following year the Tartar willingly sacrificed his life to prevent the kingdom from being torn apart by a war we could not hope to win. It is little wonder that he was beloved in his time and that his memory is revered throughout the land.''

It was a moving account, told with feeling, yet I failed to see how the Tartar's history related to me. ''Yes, sire,'' I said, ''I can well see why you consider him a hero . . . but why does your son see me as being cast in the same mold? I am but a vanquished and crippled captive.''

''My son sees you as a symbol . . . a sign that assures us of victory. I perceive a more practical benefit to be derived from your presence among us.''

''What is that, sire?''

''The captives we questioned informed us that you stand high in the khan's favor. I have sent an emissary by sea to Canton. He is to journey to Cambulac to tell the khan that you will be restored to him, sound in wind and limb, if he withdraws his army and gives us assurance of lasting peace.''

It was an exchange I was sure that Kubilai would reject out of hand, but that was something I had no intention of disclosing to the Cham king. ''The conquest of your kingdom should be well advanced if not completed by the time your emissary reaches Cambulac. Why should Kubilai bargain with you under those conditions?''

The king's age-ravaged countenance took on added creases and wrinkles as he grinned broadly. ''That will not happen, nor do you believe it will. In open combat we are no match for your experienced, well-disciplined troops. If Sinha did not believe that earlier, he does so now. We will fight no large-scale battles. We will strike where you are weakest, and withdraw rapidly into the mountains where you dare not follow. It is not our armies you will fight, but hunger, disease, and heat prostration. It is Champa, not the Chams, that will defeat you. You must be resupplied and receive reinforcements. The winds and our navy will stop help from reaching you by sea. And, even though the Annamite emperor, Tran Nhon-ton, is no friend to us, he is even less well disposed toward the Middle Kingdom. He will contest any passage of troops and supplies through his domain. No, my young friend, the Mongols cannot win this war against us. When Kubilai realizes this—as soon he must—he will seize on any excuse that will permit him to extricate himself with honor. You will provide that excuse.''

I regarded the aging Cham king gravely. He did not know the khan as I did. Kubilai considered himself the Lord of the World. He presented terms—he did not accept them. My chances of being exchanged on *any* terms were virtually nil. Nonetheless, as long as Indravarman believed that the khan would bargain, my safety was assured. What would happen when the king learned he was in error? At the moment it was a question I did not care to contemplate.

''Am I to remain a prisoner here until the khan gives you an answer?'' I asked.

''Not a prisoner, a hostage. You can stay here if you wish, or you can accompany me when I return to Vijaya as the summer draws to a close.''

That surprised me. ''Is Vijaya not threatened, sire?''

''Not at the moment. I somehow doubt that it will be. The army that arrived too late to be of assistance to you sustained heavy losses in the rain forest when it attempted to cross the Pass of Mists. It withdrew to the north and now has Indrapura under seige. Indrapura is well defended. Mu Cheng could fall at any time, but I am confident that Indrapura can withstand a siege of long duration.''

''What of the army I commanded, my lord?''

''Under your leadership it fought with disciplined fury. With you gone it is demoralized. It is like a toothless tiger. If provoked, it will lash out in rage but not do too much damage. At the moment it is encamped on the salt flats north of the Pass of Mists.'' The king paused and eyed me speculatively. ''In case,'' he continued mildly, ''you are entertaining thoughts of trying to rejoin your army, I would strongly advise against any such attempt. You would find every hand raised against you—even though you are a symbol to my people and of value to me. Should you be discovered unaccompanied anywhere north of here my orders are that you be killed on sight.''

Chapter Twenty-four

In Kubilai's intricate game of chess, the king had not been toppled by a knight attack. I was not deluding myself with respect to the outcome. The knight would be sacrificed. Like the Tartar before me, but through no choice of mine, it looked as though I was destined to end my days in Champa.

Bleak as the outlook was, I did not dwell on it. I'd learned from experience that, as long as the body retained breath, hope should never be abandoned.

I occupied my waking hours with activities of both a physical and mental nature. Diligently, I exercised my sword arm. I restored my left leg to fitness by means of long walks and frequent bathing. As a mental exercise I applied myself to learning the Cham spoken language and its cursive Sanskrit script.

An unexpected development was that King Indravarman was intrigued by and evidenced a liking for me. Once or twice a week I was summoned to his presence. On many of these occasions Abdel bin Hasan was included in the king's invitation.

The king was a truly remarkable man. Though age was taking its toll on his body, his mind was sharp and clear. Our discussions covered a wide range of subjects.

The king evinced a keen interest in my travels and experiences. I told him about England, the Holy Land, the perils of the caravan route to Cathay, and of my life in the

Middle Kingdom in the khan's service. In turn he recounted much of Champa's more than one thousand years of recorded history, of its cultural ties with India and the Island Kingdoms of the West, of its trading ties with China and Arabia, and of its almost constant wars with its neighboring states, Kambuja and Annam.

When Abdel was with us, the discussion often turned to religion and the disciplines of the Confucian and Buddhist philosophies. Abdel was delighted that I could quote at length from the Koran. As for the king's faith, the cult of Shiva of Brahmanistic Hinduism, I learned a good deal. What I did *not* learn was whether or not the king actually believed me to be a reincarnation of his beloved Tartar.

I developed a genuine affection for the shrewd old monarch.

Early in September the royal party prepared to leave the mountain retreat and Brahman sanctuary, Ban Son. I accepted the king's invitation to ride with him in state on the sedately swaying back of the royal elephant. It was a singular honor which demonstrated to all we passed along the way that I enjoyed the king's confidence. That the king had had a reason other than the pleasure of my company for subjecting me to public scrutiny did not occur to me until many months had passed.

It was a leisurely journey. We did not reach Vijaya until mid-October. I was allocated luxurious and well-staffed quarters in the royal compound and thereafter left pretty much to my own devices.

Under other circumstances I would have found my stay in Vijaya enjoyable. Unfortunately, I was living beneath a dark cloud of uncertainty. Within a few weeks the prevailing winds would blow onshore from the northeast. It would not be long after the change of wind that the king's emissary would return from Canton bearing with him the khan's answer to the terms the Cham king had extended. All I could do was mark time and await a decision which, in no wise, could I influence.

Vijaya, like Mu Cheng, was heavily fortified on its landward side. It was a bustling hub of maritime commerce, a cosmopolitan metropolis giving evidence of great wealth. Moslem mosques, Hindu temples, and Buddhist wats reared minarets, towers, stupas, and slender spires heavenward. The towers of the Hindu temples and some of the Buddhist stupas were sheathed with gleaming gold.

The harbor was a large lagoon protected from the surging sea by towering sand dunes through which a gap to the south provided a sheltered entrance. The lagoon and docks were crowded with shipping of every size and shape—Indian, Arab, Chinese, and Cham merchantmen, small harbor craft, and lateen-rigged Cham warships. The loading docks were piled high with elephant tusks, stacks of fragrant sandalwood, and aromatic bales of cinnamon bark. Off-loading and loading of cargo went on apace. Vijaya, and its frenetically busy harbor, gave no outward sign that, well to the north, a war was in progress.

Vijaya held a number of surprises for me. To my delight I discovered that Scimitar had survived the battle intact and had been brought to the capital. He was quartered in the royal stables. To my sorrow I learned that captives from the Army of the Blue Dragon had been brought to Vijaya. Once they had been questioned, they had been put to death. The almost daily public executions I witnessed in the large square close to the royal palace gave the lie to my earlier conclusion that the Chams essentially were a passive people.

As interesting as were the sights of the city, time hung heavy on my hands. To fill in the empty hours I embarked on a project. If I was to die in this city, who would know what had befallen me? There were those in England who should know that I had not renounced my claim to my lands and title—that only cruel fate had prevented my return to press my claim. I fashioned a quill pen, borrowed an inkstick and inkpot from one of the court scribes, procured a supply of fine Chinese paper, and addressed myself to the task of chronicling my life from that day in May when I set forth from Oxford for Ravenscrest up to the present dire predicament in which I found myself.

The document was intended for Brother Bartholomew and for whomever he chose to show it to—providing, of course, that it ever reached Coombs Abbey. In support of the petition he should have entered on my behalf, the good monk might wish King Edward to see the chronicle.

As my story unfolded I could not but wonder if Brother Bartholomew, or *anyone* in England, would believe it. Even to me who had lived it, it seemed the stuff of which dreams and myths are fabricated.

So absorbed did I become in my scribbling that I hardly noticed the days and weeks flying by.

When the news reached me in mid-December, it came from an unexpected source.

A servant interrupted me at my writing to tell me that someone wished to see me. I nodded absently and continued writing. It was not until a discreet cough alerted me to someone's presence that I looked up. When I did so, I dropped my quill in astonishment. My visitor was none other than Niccolò Polo.

"Master Polo!" I gasped. "What brings *you* here?"

"I came at the khan's request to discuss matters pertaining to commerce with the good merchants of Champa."

I looked at Niccolò in bewilderment. He was dressed in high felt boots, an ankle-length cloak, and wore a close-fitting cap. Except that his hair and beard were grayer, he looked much as he had when last I'd seen him some years earlier. It wasn't his appearance that I found startling; it was that he was here at all on a mission such as he had just described. "But," I retorted questioningly, "isn't China still at war with Champa?"

"War," he replied sententiously, "need not disrupt legitimate trade."

"Mmm. Why have you sought me out? How did you find me?"

"You were not hard to locate. You appear well-known throughout the city." He glanced around appraisingly and added caustically, "and appear to be doing well."

I ignored the implied slur. Coming from Niccolò Polo, whose sole motivation seemed to be profit, it could have been taken as a compliment. "But that doesn't explain why you sought me out," I said evenly. "I have no hand in trade."

"Normally, de Beauchamps, I don't mix in matters that do

not concern me,'' Niccolò said haughtily, "but because my
son seems well disposed toward you . . . and because you are
a European and a Christian . . . I've made an exception in
this instance. I have come to give you a grave warning. How
you treat it is entirely your affair."

"Warning? About what?"

"When I left the capital some months back, the khan was
in a towering rage. The invasion he had launched against
Nippon was a disaster. His fleets were scattered and suffered
appalling losses when they were struck without warning by a
terrifying storm. On the heels of that news he learned of the
heavy losses sustained by your armies in Annam and Champa.
That this campaign is virtually stalemated, he blames on you.
You have been accused of treason. Rank and titles have been
stripped from you. Any property you had has been confiscated.
Your concubine was sentenced to death. Should you—"

"*What!*" I exclaimed. "What is that you said about Gentle
Breeze?"

"Gentle Breeze? Oh, your concubine. Why he should con-
demn to death a lowly concubine defeats me . . . unless he
thought her in some way party to your treason. Still, he *did*
decree her death. And, as I was about to say, should you set
foot in China it means your certain death, as well."

I stared at him dumbly for a moment, then mumbled, "I
. . . appreciate your going to this trouble, Master Polo. Now
. . . please leave me."

For some time I sat at the table, my head bowed and my
hands clenched tightly before me. I was numb with grief.

Then the tears came and dropped unheeded on the page
beneath my hands. I sobbed aloud in anguish. Why? Mother
of God, why had she been taken from me?

In helpless rage I beat my right hand again and again upon
the tabletop—and cursed God.

The letter was handed to me by a servant the following
morning. Niccolò Polo must have given it to the servant
before leaving. I imagine that the servant, seeing me in such a
distraught state, had feared to intrude.

I recognized the cramped handwriting immediately. It was

that of Brother Bartholomew. I broke the seal and read the letter within. It was dated 15 June 1278.

The letter was brief. The monk stated that he had complied with my request, but though the king was sympathetic, he had stated flatly that nothing could be done unless I appeared in person to present my claim. By way of explanation Brother Bartholomew added that Edward was embarked on wars with both Scotland and Wales and needed the support of his barons. Since Simon de Broulay, Earl of Croftshire, was a powerful figure with much influence among the barons, it was only reasonable that King Edward would not want to offend him.

Brother Bartholomew made no mention of Ethelwyn, who I assumed must now be the Countess of Croftshire, but he did devote a few lines to young Thomas. The lad, the monk stated, was a strapping eight-year-old who was, in every way—in coloring, physique, and mischievousness—the very image of what I'd been at that age.

I folded the letter and put it back in the envelope. God's teeth! I had dispatched my letter to Coombs Abbey in the summer of 1275. It had taken six and a half years for the reply, written more than three years ago, to reach me. How far away, how very far away, England seemed—and how distant now the indiscretions of my youth. I smiled wanly. Brother Bartholomew had avoided saying it directly, but he had hinted broadly that he knew Thomas de Beauchamps to be my natural son.

I walked over to a brazier in the corner of the room. I dropped the letter on the glowing coals and watched it curl at the edges, char, then burst into flame. It was a useless reminder of a past long gone and best forgotten.

Chapter Twenty-five

My summons to appear before the king did not come until the first week of January. To my surprise he received me privately.

He came directly to the point. "Your erstwhile patron has disavowed you."

"I know, sire."

His eyebrows lifted slightly. "Oh. How come you by this knowledge when my emissary returned only this morning?"

"A Venetian merchant, sire, who enjoys the khan's confidence and patronage."

The king's lip curled. "Oh, him. The one who was so anxious that the strained relations between the khan and me should in no way diminish the flow of cinnamon, ivory, and rhinoceros horn to China. Yes, he *was* here some weeks ago. I understand he has gone now to visit Kambuja and the Mon kingdoms. What was it he told you?"

"That I am blamed for the lack of military success in Champa and have been labeled a traitor. Kubilai has taken from me my rank and titles and confiscated all that I owned. The Venetian warned me against returning to China."

"Good advice . . . if you had any choice in the matter. So Kubilai holds you to be a traitor, does he? I may have done you a disservice when you traveled south in my company. News of that must have reached the khan. He has spies everywhere. However, the Venetian doesn't seem to have been fully informed—or did he tell you of the khan's demands?''

"He made no mention of demands, my lord."

"The khan commands me to take you into custody and to return you to China with a cangue secured around your neck."

It was worse than I'd anticipated. I was to be subjected to humiliation before being put to death. "Why are you telling me this, sire? Why did you not simply have me seized by my guards?"

"Because, Barbarian, I have changed my mind about you and have no intention of complying with the khan's demands."

I could scarcely believe my ears. "But, sire," I protested weakly, "won't defying Kubilai put Champa in further jeopardy?"

"Whether I defy him or not, we are in jeopardy," the king retorted dryly. "You are incidental to his plans. Though he talked of peace with my emissary, Kubilai is even now massing a great army in Southwest China . . . a greater army than has heretofore been known to history. Its purpose is to avenge the insults inflicted by the Annamites, complete the subjugation of my realm, then move on to conquer Kambuja, the Mon kingdoms, and the Island Kingdoms of the West. That I believe to be his purpose."

I saw it now clearly. I had perceived it dimly earlier, but suddenly it was clear to me. Indravarman was right, but only partially so. Kubilai's plans were of even greater scope than the king imagined. The khan already held Burma in thrall. The conquests Indravarman mentioned were but a prelude to a march on India. What Kubilai sought was a secure maritime link with Persia. For it not to be subject to challenge, he would have to establish Mongol suzerainty over every realm that exercised control of sea frontiers along the route. It called for conquest of staggering proportions.

"How," I questioned, "do you intend to defend Champa against this plan of conquest, sire?"

"I'll temporize by sending tribute to Cambulac. I'm sending an envoy to the Annamite emperor suggesting that we form an alliance to counter the common threat. Beyond that there is little I can do but raise and train a much more effective army than we can field at present. The difficulty facing me, Barbarian, is that while my people have the will to fight, they lack experience and military skill. They are not to blame. As was my father before me, I am a man of peace. Apart from minor border skirmishes, we have been at peace with our quarrelsome neighbors for an entire generation.''

I think I knew the answer to my next question before I asked it. ''If I am not to be sent back to China in chains, sire, what have you in mind for me?''

''A proposition. For me the sands of time are running out. Prince Sinha, who will succeed me, is an able administrator. Unfortunately, he is not a skilled military commander. Nor is there one of note in the entire realm. If you would consent to raise, train, and command a Cham army, I am prepared to offer you the rank of marshal and make you a prince of the realm. This is not a sudden decision, Barbarian. I have had it in mind since soon after our first meeting in Ban Son. What say you?''

''I am flattered, my lord, but what makes you think that your soldiers would respond to my leadership?''

A smile lifted the corners of the king's lips. ''Your Chinese and Mongol troops were loyal to you, were they not? And here, you must remember, the people firmly believe you to hold within your flesh the spirit of the Tartar. They would follow you without question.''

''Perhaps, sire. It is a tempting offer, but a grave responsibility. Have I your leave to give the matter thought before giving you an answer?''

''By all means. Let us say that we will meet again one month from today. I think I have *that* long to live and reign.''

I was faced with an agonizing choice. What the king did not know was that Gentle Breeze's execution had been a terrible blow to me. It was as though my very life had been taken from me. I did not fear death. I think I would have welcomed its release. What I did fear was that I no longer had the will to fight—that I would not be equal to the responsibility he proposed for me.

There was another consideration. Could I, in good conscience, take up arms against my former comrades in arms of the Army of the Blue Dragon? They had served me loyally. Did I not owe them loyalty in return?

I owed nothing to Kubilai. By his action against me and, in particular, against Gentle Breeze, he had forfeited any respect I might have had for him. There was nothing but burning hatred in my heart for the arrogant Mongol. To revenge myself and exact a price for the death of the woman I had loved, I should oppose the khan. But was my hatred for one man sufficient motivation? The Cham were not my people. I had no roots in this realm beyond a liking for their aging king. Tempting as was his offer, was I nothing but a mercenary who sold his sword to the highest bidder?

I decided I'd had my fill of war. It was war that had cost me the life not only of the woman I loved, but of many good and true companions. I no longer had the heart for combat. If Gentle Breeze had been at my side, I might have thought differently. But she was gone—and with her had gone my strength and confidence.

But what alternative did I have? War, in fact, was all I knew. It was at that point that a longing to return to England swept over me.

I pursued that line of thought. What was there for me in England? A son who knew me not and whom I could not claim as mine without doing him harm. God's teeth, in a few weeks he would turn twelve. Soon, he would be knighted and his lands would be joined to the de Broulay estates. If I returned to claim my lands and title, what would become of Thomas? Did I have the right to rob him of what he thought to be rightfully his? Was he not flesh of my flesh? Did I not owe him something?

Day after day I was besieged by doubts and plagued with indecision. I paced my rooms, walked for hours on end in the palace gardens, and, at night, slept fitfully.

Finally, I arrived at a decision. England was where I belonged, even if I made no attempt to claim the lands and title rightfully mine. If I was fated to live by the sword, my fealty belonged to my liege lord, King Edward.

All I had to do was persuade King Indravarman to that point of view.

Chapter Twenty-six

The king squinted up at me, then inclined his head slowly. "I feared you would reject the offer. You are right . . . it is not your concern. I can appreciate your desire to return to your homeland ere age catches up with you. The years pass all too quickly. Yours is the course of wisdom, but I shall miss you."

"And I you, sire."

"When is it that you plan to leave us?"

"The winds favor a westbound passage. I'll leave as soon as I can arrange accommodation on an Arab merchantman."

There remained the problem of payment for my passage. Abdel agreed to purchase Scimitar. The price he offered was considerably higher than I'd anticipated, but I raised no objection. I needed the gold too badly to let pride stand in my way.

My choice settled on a well-found vessel measuring some ninety-five feet from bowsprit to rudder post. Her destination was Basra, by way of Serendib and Kulam Mali. When I paid her a visit, she was taking on a cargo of sandalwood, camphor, and cinnamon. The loading was expected to be completed within the week.

The turbaned ship's master met me when I came aboard. He salaamed deferentially, then escorted me to a spacious cabin in the after section of the vessel.

"It more than meets my requirements," I protested gruffly, thinking more in terms of cost than comfort. "I've little by way of baggage. Have you something smaller—more suited to my needs?"

The captain smiled unctuously. "This was the cabin chosen for you, effendi. You'll find it all too cramped during the seven-month voyage. It's the best we have, I fear."

I tried not to show my bewilderment. "Chosen for me? And who, pray, did the choosing?"

His smile vanished. His face reflected uncertainty. "I know not his name, effendi. He was one of the king's ministers. He selected this cabin as befitting your rank and station . . . and paid for it in advance."

Minister? Which one? It mattered not. Whoever he was, he'd acted simply as the king's agent. I smiled tightly. "Then I'm sure this cabin will do admirably."

When we emerged onto the deck, the ship's master took leave of me. I stood for a moment by the offshore rail gazing unseeingly at the busy harbor.

What had prompted King Indravarman's generosity? If I'd earned his gratitude by performing some service, I could have understood his solicitude. But I'd rejected the proposal he'd advanced. Apart from that, I'd entered his realm bent on conquest. That fact alone should have earned me nothing but ill-will, if not execution. Could it be that the king actually believed me to be the Tartar incarnate? Or was it that my continuing presence in his domain could become an embarrassing political liability?

I gave off posing myself such riddles. Who can fathom the megrims of a monarch?

When I returned to the palace compound, I sought out Abdel.

"The king has seen fit to pay my passage to Basra," I said.

"I know. He discussed it with me some days ago."

"I'm properly grateful, but I've no need of the space allotted me on shipboard. I've no possessions to speak of."

"You've somewhat more than you realize, my friend. Unless you wish to leave them behind, there's your bronze armor, your weapons and shield, and the saddle you had fashioned for your war-horse. I imagine you'll have need of those items in the course of your travels.''

I was taken aback. "But I thought them lost on the battlefield—except, that is, for the armor. Surely that was damaged beyond repair.''

"Not at all. On Prince Sinha's instructions all your possessions that could be found were gathered up. As for the armor, it so intrigued Cham artisans that they restored it as best they could. I think you'll find it functional.''

"But the saddle," I demurred, "—that goes with your purchase.''

Abdel's teeth flashed a wide grin. "I've no use for such an elaborate contrivance . . . a socket for the butt of your battle lance, loops to hold a battle-ax, stirrups much too long for my legs.''

"That's another matter, your proffered price for the stallion. In all good conscience I cannot now accept such a sum.''

Abdel laughed. "Of course you can. That's not too high a price to pay for such a noble steed. Besides, the name you bestowed upon him appeals to me.'' The physician turned to cut off further protest, took a few steps, then added over his shoulder, "Oh, I almost forgot. A visitor awaits you in your quarters.''

"Who?''

"I know him not. A somewhat bedraggled Christian holy man.''

I was speechless. Could Abdel possibly mean Brother Demetrios? The Nestorian was the only Christian cleric known to me.

"God's blood!" I blurted when I'd recovered the use of my tongue. "What are you doing here?''

The friar rose to his feet and chuckled. "That's hardly the way to greet an old friend. I'm not a ghost, Edmund.''

I grimaced weakly, then strode forward and embraced the friar. "Forgive me, little father. It's quite a shock. I thought never to set eyes on you again. How did you get here? What brings you here? Wha—''

Brother Demetrios cut me short with upraised palms. "Hold, Edmund," he said with an admonishing laugh. "All in good time. We arrived only this morning aboard a Cham merchantman out of Canton. We came specifically to seek you out. It has been a long and arduous journey.''

''We? Who else is in your party?''

The friar beamed. ''A small group of fugitives from Cambulac whose wish it was to find you . . . though I can't imagine why. I joined them somewhat tardily in Turfan, and guided them hither. On arriving here I was elected to come ashore and make inquiries concerning your whereabouts. Happily, you weren't hard to find.''

I was nonplused. ''What fugitives?'' I asked testily.

''Wong Sin, Ah Hsing, Gentle Breeze, and—''

A wave of dizziness engulfed me. My knees turned to jelly. I groped for the balustrade and would have toppled from the porch had not the friar reached out to steady me.

''What ails you?'' he asked anxiously.

''I . . . I was told she was dead,'' I mumbled dazedly.

''Who? Gentle Breeze? Who told you that?''

''Niccolò Polo. He visited Vijaya some months back. He told me she'd been sentenced to death . . . her only fault being that she was my concubine.''

''Ah!'' The friar's face cleared. ''What Niccolò told you was true. She *was* sentenced to death. Her crime, in Kubilai's eyes, wasn't that she was your concubine. It was bearing you a son when he'd expressly forbidden her to have your child.''

The friar's disclosures were coming too fast for me to take them in. ''What son? I knew naught of her pregnancy. Why . . . why didn't she tell me? How could it have come about? She was always so careful.''

''It was no accident, Edmund. She wanted desperately to bear your child, e'en though she knew full well the risk she ran. When you returned from Korea, she threw caution to the winds. It wasn't until you came back from Shangtu that she was sure she was quickening. She *would* have told you, but you gave her no chance. You lashed out at her with unjustified accusations—then stormed out in anger.''

''I know,'' I muttered contritely. ''The accusations were not without justification, but they should have been left unsaid. I've regretted the outburst from that day to this. But tell me, how did she escape Kubilai's sentence of death?''

"General Toghu risked his career, and his life, to get word to her. She escaped with the newborn infant bare minutes ahead of the arrival of the guards sent to take her into custody."

"Where did she go? Where did she hide?"

"Friends of Wong Sin hid her and the baby until he could get them out of the city."

I don't think that it was until that moment that what Brother Demetrios had told me really penetrated. Gentle Breeze was alive! She was here in Vijaya—with our child! My son! Happiness flooded my being.

Getting to my feet, I said, "Come! Take me to her. I—"

Brother Demetrios placed his hand against my chest and gently pushed me back against the balustrade. "Not so fast, lad, not so fast. She isn't going anywhere. There are a few things that should be clarified before you meet with her."

"What things?"

"Regardless of what you think, she did not break faith with you. Not once. The precious stones are a good example. Kubilai didn't learn about the gemstones from her. He did so through a slip of the tongue on my part."

"How so?"

"When I returned to Cambulac, I accused Maffeo Polo of chousing me out of my share of the caravan profits. He told me blandly that I'd been hired to guide the caravan and that, having been duly reimbursed for my services, I shouldn't have expected to share in its profits regardless of any bargain struck following Orsini's death. I would have accepted that had not Maffeo added that he'd learned through a reliable source in Changsha that I'd purchased a large quantity of gems. Since, obviously, I'd swindled your army, what need had I for profits from the caravan trade goods?

"In anger I blurted out in my defense that I'd bought those gemstones at your behest. It must have been through the Polos, thanks to my indiscretion, that Kubilai learned of your purchase."

The gemstones weren't the contentious issue. In an attempt to steer the friar away from the subject, I said tersely, "I suspected that something like that had taken place. I believed her when she denied having given that information to Kubilai.

But you still haven't answered my earlier question. How did she manage to flee Cambulac?"

Brother Demetrios eyed me speculatively for a moment before answering. "She stayed with Wong Sin's friends for some weeks until the hue and cry lessened. Then Wong Sin and his number-one wife smuggled her from the city disguised as a boy. With her hair cut short and her breasts tightly bound, she passed for a boy . . . at a distance. The baby was supposed to be Ah Hsing's. It must have been awkward, since Ah Hsing had no milk and Gentle Breeze had to nurse the child at frequent intervals. They went north, not south, passing through the Great Wall at Kalgan. From there they bribed passage with a northbound caravan going to Urga, then westbound to Jargalan. They left the caravan at Tayshir. Eventually, they reached Turfan. It isn't a route I'd care to follow."

"Didn't Kubilai suspect Wong Sin of complicity?"

"I suppose he did when Wong Sin disappeared, but until then Wong Sin and Ah Hsing stayed on at your residence. Since Wong Sin had faithfully performed certain services for the khan, he wasn't suspect initially. When the search was broadened to include Wong Sin, I imagine they looked for him along the principal caravan route to the south and west."

"So in Turfan, they sought you out and persuaded you to join them."

Brother Demetrios grinned. "In a manner of speaking, yes. Actually, I wasn't there when they reached the oasis. I was on my way back from Khotan, where I'd gone to buy jade."

"Why Turfan? Was she seeking refuge with her family? Surely the Mongols would have anticipated that."

"Perhaps she hoped to see her mother, and introduce her to her grandson. Her mother had died during Gentle Breeze's absence. However, Gentle Breeze was alive to the danger. Don't forget, she was still disguised as a boy. She made no attempt to contact other members of her family."

"But she *did* contact you. Weren't you being watched?"

"Maybe earlier. Not then. I'd just returned from Khotan, by way of Kashgar. In any event Gentle Breeze didn't contact me directly. Ah Hsing located me on her behalf."

"What did she want of you?"

"Gentle Breeze was determined to seek you in Tali. She wanted my advice on how to reach that isolated region."

"But by then I was no longer in Tali."

"I knew that. I'd heard that the expeditionary force was on its way to, or already in, Champa. I persuaded Gentle Breeze to go instead to Canton whence we could go by sea to Vijaya . . . or to some other Cham port."

I rubbed my beard with my right hand. "You traveled the entire length of the Middle Kingdom without incident. That doesn't seem possible. Weren't you stopped anywhere along the way?"

"We were stopped. Quite often, in fact. But we had two things in our favor. As you probably know, a large army is being assembled at Nanning. It will be commanded by Kubilai's son Togan, and is rumored to be the largest army ever fielded, some half a million men in strength. By virtue of that fact there is troop movement all through the Middle Kingdom, particularly in South China. That state of confusion worked to our advantage."

"You mentioned two things working in your favor."

The friar reached down the neck of his sweat-stained cassock, tugged at a leather thong, and brought forth a metal plaque. I recognized it immediately as the khan's safe conduct given in Venice to Count Orsini by the Polos. "This," Brother Demetrios said with a dry chuckle, "proved useful. Without it, even with Gentle Breeze still masquerading as a boy, we might have faced difficulties."

"So you reached Canton unmolested. Didn't anyone recognize you there?"

"*I* was recognized, e'en though we didn't enter the city proper. We stayed with—ah—friends in the shantytown outside the city walls. It was there, in wineshops frequented by seafarers, that Wong Sin and I learned a good deal, though not all of it might have been truth. We heard that the invasion launched by Kubilai's armies against the Island Kingdom in the East had met with disaster. The invasion fleet was battered by a storm of unprecedented fury. In Champa, Sögatü's expeditionary force had fared little better. It was rumored that the failure of Sögatü's campaign was laid to a military blunder made not by the marshal, but by his second-in-command,

General Chin Man-tze. Gossip had it that the mighty army
being raised at Nanning would move first against the Annamites,
complete the subjugation of Champa, then be launched against
the Kingdom of Kambuja.''

"Your seafaring friends appear to be remarkably well
informed. It doesn't surprise me that I've been made the
scapegoat for the stalemate in Champa. I knew that would be
the price of failure even before I left Shangtu.''

"That's not all. It was rumored that you'd defected to the
Cham and that Kubilai had demanded that you be returned to
China in chains.''

I smiled thinly. "I didn't exactly defect. I was wounded in
battle and made captive. King Indravarman, however, not
only chose to ignore Kubilai's demand, but offered me a
military post. Had I accepted it, you would have arrived to
find me in command of all Cham military forces.''

The friar's eyes widened. "Why didn't you accept?''

"A number of reasons,'' I answered evasively. "I chose
instead to return to England. In fact I've just come from
inspecting the quarters assigned me on an Arab merchantman
bound for Persia. Had you arrived a week from now, you'd
not have found me.''

"Then we'd have booked passage on another ship and
followed in the hopes that we would catch up with you along
the way.''

"*We?* What of the caravan you intended to put together?''

"The trade goods are safely stored in a *makhzan* in Turfan.
The caravan can wait for my return to the oasis.''

"It's just as well, then, that you found me before the dhow
sailed.'' I moved from the balustrade, but, once again, Brother
Demetrios stopped me.

"There remains another misconception to be resolved,
Edmund. In your mind you still believe she betrayed your
trust concerning General Hsü Ch'ien. She—''

"What I told her was confidential,'' I interjected curtly.
"She was the only living soul to whom I made that disclosure.
I believed her when she said she'd not told Kubilai of that
conversation, but she discussed it with someone. That indiscretion cost Hsü Ch'ien and his family their lives.''

"You gave her no chance to explain. She discussed what

you'd told her with me, but only *after* Kubilai had learned of Hsü Ch'ien's contemplated treason from another source.''

I stared at the friar in confusion. "What source? Who else could have known what Hsü Ch'ien told me in confidence?''

"His principal wife. He'd taken a Korean concubine and his wife was furious. Thinking to do him harm, she told the wife of a Korean official of Hsü Ch'ien's treasonous thinking. It is through that source that Kubilai learned of Hsü Ch'ien's contemplated defection at Hengyang.''

It was a startling revelation. I stared gape-mouthed at Brother Demetrios. Mother of God! Could she ever forgive the wrong I'd done her?

Chapter Twenty-seven

As the boatman sculled Brother Demetrios and me across the wrinkled surface of the harbor, I was prey to confused emotions. I was both elated and apprehensive. Beneath the loose cape I was wearing over my waist-knotted *sampot*, I nervously massaged my stiff elbow.

Forsooth, since Ban Son I'd not given much thought to my disability. I'd grown accustomed to the affliction. My shoulder muscles functioned adequately, and though numbed, my left hand had lost but little of its grip. Without giving it thought, I exercised my left hand and wrist by flexing and unflexing my fingers. The elbow, of course, was useless. I accepted that, and the muscle wastage of my upper arm, as an inevitable consequence of my crippling wound. I had to live with it; I didn't have to dwell on it. Yet, as we neared the anchored Cham merchant ship, I was suddenly acutely conscious of my infirmity.

How would I appear in her eyes? Would she find me much changed? What of her? Would I find that motherhood had altered her in face and form? I angrily put such thoughts from me. Outwardly, we'd both have changed. We'd not seen each other for close to two years and much had happened in both our lives. I should not be thinking of such a superficiality as outward appearance. I should be giving thanks to God that she'd been restored to me. Nothing else really mattered.

Yet, unaccountably, the closer we got to the anchored vessel, the more uneasy I became.

Appreciating that I was under emotional stress, the friar did his best to divert me. He kept up a steady stream of innocuous chatter and seemed not at all offended by my preoccupation and lack of response.

Cargo-laden, the Cham merchantman sat low in the water. A rope ladder dangled over her side amidships. I mentally calculated the distance from waterline to gunwale capping to be no more than eight feet. Suddenly, this distance became inordinately important to me. With luck I could reach the gunwale from the deck of the sampan and swing myself aboard without disclosing the fact that I was partially disabled. I'd been wearing my cape since early morning. Up to now I don't think that Brother Demetrios had noticed that I favored my left arm. The last thing I wanted was to ask for his assistance in order to board the vessel. This became all the more important, since I could make out Gentle Breeze standing in the waist watching our approach. I recognized this anxiety as being childish. She would learn of my infirmity soon enough. It was just that I wanted to demonstrate that my injury was of little consequence.

When the sampan nosed alongside, I motioned for the friar to precede me. He scrambled up the ladder and disappeared from view. The sampan, relieved of his weight, rose a few inches in the water. It was enough. I reached up, got a firm grip on the gunwale capping, put my right foot on the bottom rung of the ladder, then swung myself up and over the gunwale. Regaining my balance, I turned to face Gentle Breeze.

She stood a few paces from me. Her deep-violet eyes were brimming with tears, some of which spilled onto her cheeks. Her lips trembled. For the life of me, even with her hair shorn close, I couldn't see how anyone could have taken her for a boy. She was so beautiful that it made my breath catch in my throat.

I stood there like a country bumpkin, unable to move. It was as though my sandals were nailed to the deck. I blinked my eyes to fight back tears of happiness.

Gentle Breeze was the first to move. She ran to me,

clasped me around the waist, and pressed her face against my chest. Her shoulders shook with silent sobs as she clung to me. I circled her slim waist with my right arm and held her close. We stood like that for some time, both of us trembling and unable to speak.

I reached up and gently tilted her head back. "Thank you, Lord," I murmured reverently as our lips met in a lingering kiss.

I know not how long we stood there clinging to each other, oblivious of all around us. It seeped gradually into our consciousness that we were not alone. Reluctantly, we drew apart.

Brother Demetrios stood a few paces from us, beaming. On the deck Cham sailors had paused in their labors and were grinning fatuously. Some paces away stood Ah Hsing. In her arms she held a squirming, sandy-haired child.

I looked at the infant wonderingly. Ah Hsing lowered the child to the deck, whereupon he walked falteringly but determinedly toward Gentle Breeze. She knelt down and held out her arms, scooping him up when he teetered within her reach. Rising she held the infant up for my inspection.

"Your son, my lord," she said proudly.

"Mmmm—ah . . . he can walk!"

"He *is* almost two years old, my lord."

I opened my mouth to dispute this assertion, then closed it, grinning shamefacedly. I'd forgotten that Asiatics consider a child one year old at birth.

The child subjected me to critical scrutiny, then tangled his pudgy fingers in my beard and gurgled delightedly.

"Isn't he beautiful?" Gentle Breeze said softly.

"Boys aren't beautiful," I answered gruffly. "That only applies to the gentler sex. His mother is beautiful. He's—ah—handsome."

The baby tired of tugging at my beard, looked at me disapprovingly with wide gray-blue eyes, then turned and buried his face in his mother's shoulder.

I reached out with my right hand and wonderingly touched the soft hair that curled at the base of his little skull. "What do you call him?"

Gentle Breeze's teeth flashed in a smile. "He was christened Emun Demetrios."

"*Christened?*"

"Yes. Brother Demetrios told me you would want that. He officiated at the ceremony."

I glanced toward Brother Demetrios and grinned broadly. The friar said nothing, but nodded approvingly.

Turning back to Gentle Breeze, I said, "Emun Demetrios de Beauchamps! It's a fine name, little one. A proud name. I'm sure he'll do it great honor." Then I changed the subject by asking briskly, "Where's Wong Sin?"

"Belowdecks."

"After the lengthy voyage you must be anxious to set foot on solid ground. Have Wong Sin see to the packing of your chests. We'd best get ashore before the noontime rain o'ertakes us."

"Chests?" She laughed softly. "I left our residence in Cambulac in rather a hurry, my lord. Everything we have with us fits into four saddlebags. It will take but a moment to assemble our effects."

Gentle Breeze issued rapid instructions to Ah Hsing, who scurried off to do her bidding. Brother Demetrios went belowdecks to gather up his belongings. Gentle Breeze, little Emun, and I were left alone. She turned to me, a worried frown on her face.

"What happened to your arm, Emun?" she asked anxiously.

My cape still hid my left arm from view. I doubted that she'd seen it, but she'd sensed its lack of response. I grinned crookedly. "It's nothing to worry about, little one. In battle I had an unfortunate encounter with a Cham war elephant."

"*War elephant?* What's that?"

I laughed. "You'll have to see one to believe it. And then you'll wonder how I escaped with my life." I pushed back the cape, exposing my malformed arm.

Her eyes grew wide. "Oh!" she gasped. "Does it pain you?"

"It did when the bones were knitting. Not now. It was the king's personal physician who attended me. He did an excellent job." I demonstrated by twisting my hand from side to

side and flexing my fingers. "Had it not been for Abdel's
skill, I'd probably have lost the arm above the elbow."

"Are . . . are you sensitive about it, Emun? Do you wear
the cape to hide it?"

Generally, I didn't even think about my stiff arm. I'd
donned the cape earlier that morning when I'd gone to visit
the seagoing dhow. But the morning had grown warm, yet I
was still wearing the cape. I *had* tried to hide my infirmity,
both from Brother Demetrios and from Gentle Breeze. I'd
done it reflexively, in a futile attempt to delay the revelation.

Reaching up, I untied the cape at the neck and draped it
over my shoulder. I smiled self-consciously. "I'm not normally sensitive, little one. I suppose I didn't want to shock
you."

She moved close to me and let her fingers slide tenderly
along my injured arm. Her voice quivering with emotion, she
said softly, "All that matters is that you're alive, and that I've
found you."

Forsooth, those were the very words *I* should have used.

As the boatman sculled us shoreward, Gentle Breeze and I
sat side by side facing the sampan's blunt-nosed bow. Above
us the clouds were building, but the sun shone with dazzling
brightness on the palm-fringed beach ahead of us.

Gentle Breeze stirred within the encirclement of my right
arm. She looked up at me, her eyes wide in disbelief. "Those
women . . . on the beach? They're dressed like you—in that
. . . that?"

I grinned. *"Sampot."*

"Does everyone wear that? Is that *all* they wear?"

I laughed. "Almost always, except in this season of rains
when some of them don capes or jackets against the evening
and morning chill. You'll find it garb admirably suited to this
clime."

"Do you expect *me* to go bare-breasted?"

"You will. You'll get used to it, little one."

Sliding my hand beneath her loose shirt, I cupped her
breast and gently squeezed its nipple. She pressed her hand
over mine and giggled.

Chapter Twenty-eight

From where I stood by the veranda railing I could hear Gentle Breeze crooning as she tucked Emun in for the night. I smiled and breathed deeply of the soft evening air.

In the space of a few short hours everything had changed dramatically. I was having no small measure of difficulty in adjusting to the altered conditions.

It was as though I'd been groping in Stygian gloom, fettered by fear. I'd stumbled blindly into obstacles that had assumed terrifying proportions. Now, suddenly, it was as though a lighted torch had been thrust into my hand. I could see. The fearsome obstacles had become naught but trifling impediments. The phantasmagoric ogres of imagination had disappeared like thinning smoke, or retreated to the far shadows. I once again could stride boldly forward with renewed confidence.

But in what direction?

I mentally reviewed the arguments I'd marshaled to convince myself that returning to England was my wisest course. They were conspicuously lacking in validity now that Gentle Breeze and I were reunited.

I'd told myself that I was a stranger in an alien land. God's teeth, that had held true for the past decade in the Outremer, Syria, Turkestan, Cathay, and now in Champa. It hadn't bothered me unduly then, why should it now? I'd told myself that I belonged in my native land among my own people. That certainly was true, but what would I face on my return to

England? I'd played down what well could be odds stacked so heavily against me that I stood no chance of winning. Examined realistically, what were those odds?

I would have arrived in England virtually penniless. To have pressed my claim for the return of my lands and title, I would have needed money. Perhaps a good deal of money. It was almost a certainty that Simon de Broulay, at the instance of Ethelwyn of Hebb, would have acted in support of his stepson to oppose my claim. King Edward had dire need of de Broulay, one of England's most powerful barons. Lacking revenues and unable to call on men-at-arms, what need had Edward of me?

If, out of a misplaced sense of obligation to my bastard son, I'd renounced my claim, what then? I'd told myself that I could live by my sword. But could I? I'd commanded an army far larger than any fielded by England, but would that count for anything in Edward's eyes? I'd campaigned in Asia, but did that qualify me to campaign against the Irish, Scots, and Welsh? Moreover, I boasted a crippled arm and was approaching middle years. I had to face the fact that, in all likelihood, neither Edward nor any other nobleman would want my services as a knight-at-arms.

If I produced my almost-completed chronicle in support of my claim to battle experience, I feared it would meet with naught but derisive laughter. It would be considered at best a hoax, at worst the ravings of a madman. The only hope I had of the account being taken seriously was if I returned to England a wealthy man.

Now I had others to consider. I could not subject Gentle Breeze and our son to possible, nay probable, penury and humiliation. My prospects would have to be reviewed in the light of the changed conditions.

The alternative would be to accept King Indravarman's offer and remain in Champa. I would hold the highest military rank the kingdom could bestow, and into the bargain I'd be made a prince of the realm. Gentle Breeze would share the honor of my exalted station. Emun would be raised as befitted royalty. It was tempting, yet it had inherent drawbacks.

What would happen when death claimed the aging King and Prince Sinha ascended the throne? As of now the prince was in awe of me. Would that hold true once the reins of power were firmly in his hands? Would he see me as an ally—or as a threat to his position of authority? I suspected the latter, which had been one of my chief reasons for rejecting Indravarman's offer. Did I have the stomach for the power struggle I felt must follow inevitably on Indravarman's passing?

What if I were to make my acceptance of the offer conditional? At the moment the kingdom was faced with peril. Could I place a time limit on my services, as I'd hoped to do with Kubilai? If I accepted on the basis of release from obligation if and when the kingdom was no longer threatened, would the king agree to such terms?

There remained one vital question: Was the king's offer still open to me?

So engrossed had I become in these sobering reflections that night had crept up on me unnoticed. An onshore breeze had sprung up and now was strengthening. Wind soughed through the plantain trees in restless gusts. Stirring palm fronds rasped and rattled. I shivered and glanced toward the sky. Westward-moving clouds partially obscured the crescent of a waxing moon. Rain would soon follow.

Turning from the balustrade, I strode toward the doorway giving access to the residence. I paused within the doorway yet still outside the pools of light cast by the bean-oil lamps.

Brother Demetrios was reclining comfortably in a nest of cushions. Gentle Breeze was seated cross-legged in front of him. She was laughing delightedly at some sally the friar had made. My heart lifted. God's bonnet, how beautiful she looked in the soft lamplight.

I'd arrived at my decision, but would say nothing of it until I had talked with King Indravarman on the morrow. I stepped into the circles of light and sank down beside Gentle Breeze.

"Ah, Edmund," the friar said, a broad smile lighting his cherubic countenance. "We were just talking about you. I just now remarked that adversity sits well on you. For a vanquished enemy you appear to be doing well. Extremely well. These quarters are nothing short of luxurious and your serving wenches are delightful creatures."

"Perhaps you should convert them to your Nestorian faith," I responded with a chuckle.

"A worthy project, but when I leave, who will minister to their spiritual needs?" He hiccuped, stretched, yawned, and added apologetically, "Forgive me. I fear I ate overly much of your spicy fare. My couch beckons. It's been a long full day."

"That it has, little father, that it has."

He rose unsteadily to his feet, smiled at us benignly, then stumbled off in search of his sleeping quarters.

I watched his retreating back with affectionate amusement. "I doubt the food was any more piquant than that served you aboard the Cham ship which brought you here," I observed. "I should have warned the Nestorian tosspot about the potency of the rice liquor brewed here in the Cham capital."

Gentle Breeze looked at me inquiringly. "Was I wrong to have him christen Emun?"

"Huh?" The question confused me. "By no means! Why do you ask?"

"He's a Nestorian. You are a Catholic."

"They're both Christian faiths."

"Is there no difference then between your faith and his?"

I rubbed my beard reflectively. "There *is* a difference, but I must confess that it's unclear to me. Brother Demetrios once tried to explain the divergent viewpoints. I'm afraid I wasn't too attentive. Nestorius was a Christian patriarch of Constantinople who contended that Jesus played a dual role and that the Virgin Mary was His maternal parent only in a purely temporal sense. For this heresy Nestorius was banished. His followers were persecuted and sought refuge in Persia, India, and Cathay. That, of course, happened a long time ago, almost nine centuries in the past, and it led to an accommodation whereby the differences were reconciled. Did you know that Kubilai's grandfather, Genghis Khan, professed to be a Nestorian Christian?"

Gentle Breeze's face wore a look of perplexity. "No, I didn't know that. But if the Nestorians believe that your Jesus was both man and god, where does that differ from the Catholic faith?"

"We believe in the Father, Son, and Holy Ghost, one and indivisible, the Holy Trinity."

Gentle Breeze looked, if anything, more baffled. "I don't understand."

"Neither do I," I admitted frankly, then added loftily, "There are many things that must be accepted without question as matters of faith."

She looked at me uncomprehendingly. I could hardly blame her. How had we stumbled into this abstruse morass? It had started with her questioning the friar's competence with respect to Emun's christening. I grinned sheepishly.

"These are questions best left to learned theologians," I said contritely. "As for Brother Demetrios, e'en though he narrowly escaped defrockment, I can think of no other to whom I'd as lief entrust the spiritual well-being of our son."

The cloud of uncertainty left her face, replaced by a relieved smile.

Taking her hand in mine, I rose to my feet. "Come, little one, it's high time we, too, sought our couch."

She stood up hesitantly. "Emun . . ."

"What?"

"I couldn't find the bathing chamber."

"Oh," I said, realizing what was bothering her. "I'm not surprised. There isn't any."

She colored. "What am I supposed to do? How can I bathe? There wasn't much chance to cleanse myself on the ship."

"Here, the people bathe in outdoor pools. Men, women, and children of all ages bathe together."

"I couldn't do that! I'd die of shame!"

"No, you won't. It takes time to get used to it, but the Chams thinks nothing of nudity."

"Maybe they don't," she said heatedly, "but I do. What am I supposed to do *now*?"

I relented. "Have you a cloak of some kind?"

"Yes."

"Fetch it. There's an urn beneath the eaves to catch rainwater. We'll use that for your ablution."

She left me and returned in a few minutes draped in a

woolen traveling cloak. I led the way toward the veranda, then stopped and turned to face her.

Touching her cloak, I said, "Isn't that one of—"

"Yes. I had to remove some of the gems from this one and give them to Wong Sin. He needed them to buy ponies, pay our way with the northbound caravan, and hire a Tartar guide to conduct us from Tayshir through the mountains to the outskirts of Turfan. Had it not been for your foresight in having me sew gemstones into our traveling cloaks, I don't know what we'd have done."

Oddly enough I'd given no thought to the cloaks. In my mind I'd considered them irretrievably lost. It was a relief to know that the valuables they contained had been instrumental in saving my son and his mother. I breathed a silent prayer of thanks.

We stepped forth onto the rain-drenched planking of the veranda, at the far end of which the protecting overhang stopped short and an earthenware urn almost as tall as Gentle Breeze was positioned to catch rain that cascaded downward from the eave trough. I guided her there, and held her cloak while she stood alongside the urn and used a dipper to sluice water over her naked body.

"Whoof!" she gasped. "It's freezing."

I grinned. "That's why the Chams bathe in the sun-warmed waters of their pools."

Shivering, she quickly soaped herself from head to toe, then rinsed herself with water dipped splashingly from the brimming urn. Dripping, teeth chattering, she stood in a widening pool of water. I wrapped her in the woolen cloak, then hustled her directly to my bedchamber.

Discarding the sodden cloak, I took a large towel from the low table by my couch and rubbed her vigorously while she, with a smaller towel, dried her tousled hair. Gradually, her shivering subsided as her flesh took on a pinkish glow.

I stepped back a pace or two and looked at her admiringly. She let the small towel drop to the mat, ran her fingers through her unruly, still-damp hair, and smiled at me mischievously.

"Why are you gawking at me, my lord? Do you find me much changed?"

I regarded her critically. Her face, neck, forearms, hands, and feet were sun-browned. Her brown-nippled breasts were fuller yet still upthrusting much as I remembered them. She was as slim-waisted as before but her hips and lower belly seemed to be more softly rounded. A thin tracery of stretch marks was visible on her abdomen and upper thighs if one looked closely. In all she looked much as she had when first she'd appeared in my field tent. God's bonnet, that had been almost seven years ago. It hardly seemed possible.

My lips twitched in a faint smile. "No, little one, I find you little changed . . . though, as I recall, when last I saw you your jade gate was not masked with curling hair."

She glanced down at the soft triangle of hair and laughed softly. "I would have removed it had an opportunity presented itself. I've had little privacy over the past months. I hope your half-blind monk won't find it *too* discouraging."

"I can assure you," I said as I undid the knot at my waist and let the sheathlike *sampot* fall to the floor, "that he'll be able to grope his way to the jade gate through that tangle of foliage. I have every confidence in him."

"I trust your confidence is not misplaced," she said sweetly.

Chapter Twenty-nine

King Indravarman was delighted when I advised him that I'd had a change of heart. Evidently, he guessed what had caused my abrupt about-face. He congratulated me on my reunion with my infant son and concubine and bade me extend a welcome to them on his behalf. He also evinced keen interest in the Christian holy man who had accompanied them.

By now I should have been used to the rapidity with which such information reached the seat of authority, yet I must confess I still found it disconcerting. As had been the case with Kubilai, very little escaped the Cham king's attention. Like the Mongol emperor, King Indravarman maintained a pervasive network of informants. But what I found particularly unnerving was that the friar and Gentle Breeze had been in Champa less than twenty-four hours and all the conversations that had taken place between us had been conducted in Greek or Mandarin Chinese. It was conceivable that there were those among my servants who were conversant with the latter tongue, but it was inconceivable that any were Greek-speaking. I thought that the most likely source of Indravarman's information concerning the relationship existing between Gentle Breeze, Emun, and me, had come from Chinese-speaking officers on board the Cham merchantman.

Indravarman wasted little time on pleasantries. He came quickly to the point. My promotion to marshal of the Cham ground forces would be announced that very day. This made me responsible to the king for procurement, recruitment, training, deployment, and tactical employment of all the ground forces. Nominal command of the armies, however, would still be vested in the heir apparent, Prince Sinha.

This was a restriction I'd not anticipated. I could foresee grave difficulties arising from such a dichotomy of command authority. My face must have mirrored those misgivings because Indravarman hastened to assure me that the prince's command was largely ceremonial in nature. It was a traditional royal prerogative. The assignment and promotion of officers, however, would be at my discretion, and notwithstanding the prince's presence, tactical command in the field would be mine, and mine alone.

Despite these assurances, I envisioned a number of areas where problems could arise. As long as I was responsible directly to Indravarman, and enjoyed his unqualified support, these obstacles could be overcome. But what would happen when Indravarman was removed from the scene?

It brought to the forefront of my mind the single major objection I'd had to his proposal, now magnified by the condition of the heir apparent's nominal command. The king, peering at me anxiously, must have understood from my hesitation the root cause of my dilemma.

"Barbarian," he said quietly, "I am told that the force Kubilai is raising to send against Annam, and Champa, is greater than any army previously known to man. It may well be that we cannot survive an assault of such magnitude. In your leadership, *Siao Hu,* lies our only hope for survival. My son holds firm in that belief. He will not oppose you."

Siao Hu? In our earlier conversational exchanges the king had spoken Arabic. Later, as I'd become more fluent, our discussions had been in the Cham tongue. This was the first time I'd known him to employ Chinese. In the Mandarin dialect *Siao Hu* translated into "young barbarian." It also could be interpreted as "young Tartar."

The king's gaze remained fixed, yet he seemed not to be looking at me so much as through and beyond me. His voice strengthened. "Our gods have favored us. Vishnu, the Preserver, has restored to you your son and his mother. In so doing he has graced us with your continuing presence. Shiva, the Destroyer, will grant you the strength and wisdom to defeat our Mongol foe.''

I shifted my position uneasily. I liked not this allusion to divine purpose. I cleared my throat and interrupted the king with a statement of intent. It was time for me to clarify my position.

"If my knowledge of the strength and weakness of Mongol tactics can serve you to advantage, so be it," I said rather more sharply than I'd intended, "but it must be clearly understood at the outset that, regardless of the outcome of the coming struggle, a time will come when I must take leave of you, and Champa.''

Indravarman shook himself and focused his myopic gaze on my face. His lips twitched in a semblance of a smile. "Of course, my son. When that day comes, we will not detain you.'' He lapsed into silence for a moment, then continued briskly. "But now, there is much to be done. I will advise the high priest to prepare for the rites that will bestow on you royal status.''

"I'm deeply honored, sire, but would not my military rank suffice?''

"Oh, no! Military command at that level is reserved for those of royal station. The two go hand in hand. The royal umbrellas can only be conferred on a king, or a prince of the realm. Didn't you know that?''

"No, sire, I knew it not.''

"The ceremony will take place a few days hence. The high priest must settle on the most propitious date and time. Have you any further questions?''

"Just one. My accommodation aboard the Arab merchant-man, *Al Zabag*, was paid for by a minister of your court. Should he not now be advised, sire, to retrieve that sum?''

The king's face creased in a smile that revealed the carious stumps of his remaining teeth. "It is a trifling matter. If he does not wish to remain among us, perhaps the Christian holy man might like to journey westward in your stead.''

When I left the palace, I strolled meditatively in the park-like grounds of the royal compound. One thing was now abundantly clear. Although he'd not openly admitted it, the king's belief in reincarnation was every bit as much a part of his being as it was of Prince Sinha's. Like the prince, King Indravarman was convinced that the spirit of Champa's revered Tartar lived on in me.

I lingered in the shade of a giant flame tree pondering the ramifications of the king's inadvertent disclosure. It shed light on a number of things that had puzzled me. It explained the deferential treatment I'd been accorded since my capture. Undoubtedly, it was the reason for Indravarman's rejection of Kubilai's demand that I be returned to Cathay to face charges of treason. What was harder to explain was just why, once I'd rejected Indravarman's generous offer of military employment, he'd accepted my rejection without demur and, in fact, had done everything possible to smooth the way for my departure? One explanation for that seeming paradox came to mind. To have held me in Champa against my will would have defeated the king's purpose. He'd prayed to his gods that I would have a change of heart. Now, he believed those prayers had been answered.

The Chams believed that the Tartar had delivered their realm from almost certain disaster. It defied logic, but they seemed to believe that I, through some miracle of transmogrification, could repeat the performance in this their hour of darkest peril.

I didn't return directly to my residence. I sought out Abdel bin Hasan to negotiate the return of Scimitar. Not finding the physician at his residence, I waited for his return. The noontime rain had set in before he put in an appearance.

"I have just now come from the palace," Abdel said, smiling broadly. "The king is in excellent spirits. He's prancing about like an arthritic satyr. Your acceptance of his proposal did him more good than any nostrum I could have prescribed."

"He has a childlike faith in my military genius," I said, smiling wryly.

"Well, you can't blame him. There's none other in the realm with your knowledge of Mongol strategy and tactics.

With you to lead them, the Cham armies should be successful in defending the kingdom.''

"I wish I shared your abiding optimism. You don't, perchance, believe in reincarnation?''

Abdel laughed. "No, but the Chams do. To a man. Believing you to be the Tartar incarnate, they'll follow you to the very gates of hell . . . and beyond.''

"They may well have to.''

Abdel's laughter subsided to a chuckle. "I presume the purpose of this visit is an attempt to talk me into parting with my recent purchase.''

"Exactly.''

"You'll be expected to ride a war elephant into battle.''

"I expect that . . . but I'll have a good deal of traveling to do between battles.''

"So you will. Ah, me, Allah giveth and Allah taketh away. The stallion is a noble steed, but perhaps too grand for a humble healer. He's still in the royal stables. Take him with my heartfelt best wishes.''

"Thank you. I'll see to it that your gold is returned this afternoon.''

I waited for the rain to slacken before returning to my residence. When I did so, I was informed that Brother Demetrios, accompanied by Wong Sin, had gone to search out Chinese and Arab traders in the commercial quarter of the city. They came back to the residence scant steps ahead of the evening downpour.

I took the friar to one side and informed him that I'd committed myself to the employment Indravarman had proffered.

Brother Demetrios inclined his head approvingly. "The course of wisdom. Have you told Gentle Breeze of this?''

"Yes. As a matter of fact, I'd said naught to her about having arranged a westbound passage. Did you?''

The friar shook his head. "Nary a word. In fact, Edmund, I rather suspected you might take the king up on his offer now that you and Gentle Breeze have been happily reunited.''

"It leaves a cabin going begging aboard *Al Zabag*. The accommodation is bought and paid for. The king suggested that if you didn't want to stay in Champa, you might like to avail yourself of the passage."

Brother Demetrios shuddered. "God forbid! I'm no sailor. For most of the three-week voyage from Canton to here, I was deathly ill—e'en when the sea was relatively placid. A seven-month voyage would be the end of me. No, I'll stick to the ponderous swaying of a Bactrian ship of the desert. Besides, I don't fancy wending my way back to Turfan by way of Persia."

"You're welcome to stay here as long as you wish."

"An offer not lacking in appeal. I find the country and its people strangely fascinating. But Turfan calls. My trade goods await loading on camels. I should tarry here no longer than is necessary."

"To attempt a northward journey through Champa and Annam is out of the question. You've no choice but to return by sea to Canton and journey overland from there. The winds won't favor such a voyage for another nine to ten weeks."

The friar beamed. "Then I've two full months in which to savor the delights of this enchanting realm."

Chapter Thirty

The weeks flew by.

A Brahman high priest officiated at the ceremony which inducted me into the Cham royal house. As a prerequisite I had to take a Cham name. Derived phonetically from my surname, I became Prince Bo Chom.

Plans I'd made to visit units in the field were held in abeyance awaiting the dry season. There was, however, more than enough to occupy my time close to the capital. An army encampment just outside Vijaya was expanded to accommodate a veritable flood of new recruits.

I commissioned agents to scour the countryside in order to procure horses—to be more accurate, the sturdy little mountain ponies which were all that was available in the way of mounts. I intended that the initial training would concentrate on mounted bowmanship. I didn't expect to duplicate the performance of Mongol or Mongol-trained cavalrymen. What I hoped to achieve was sufficient mobility to counter the outflanking tactics of Mongol cavalry. There were decided advantages of the Cham battle formation, based as it was on the formidable war elephant, but its greatest single disadvantage was a lack of flexibility.

Appreciating that I soon would be absent from Vijaya for extended periods, I spent as much time as I could steal from my military duties with Gentle Breeze and Emun.

Gentle Breeze soon overcame her initial bashfulness. She

adopted the *sampot* as a mode of dress, e'en though for some weeks she modestly kept her breasts hidden by a loose shirt. As the weather warmed, she abandoned the shirt and soon was uniformly tanned a golden brown from the waist up. It took her somewhat longer before she could bring herself to shed her *sampot* and venture into the bathing pool before the onset of dusk.

In a surprisingly short space of time she had learned enough words in the Cham tongue to carry on broken conversations with the Cham servants. Such was Gentle Breeze's infectious good humor that she quickly became a favorite with all who came in contact with her. It had been long absent, but laughter now echoed beneath my roof.

Emun seemed to grow before my very eyes. His steps became more confident with each passing day. Imbued with insatiable curiosity, he was into everything. He kept up a steady stream of unintelligible chatter—which Gentle Breeze and Ah Hsing professed to understand perfectly. To me this seemed highly improbable. Gentle Breeze spoke to him in Turkic, Ah Hsing in Mandarin Chinese, the servants addressed him in the Cham tongue, while I, determined he should learn the language of my homeland, conversed with him in Norman French.

His mother adored him. Ah Hsing was devoted to him. Captivated by the mischievous sandy-haired imp, the servants doted on him. To me he was a source of joy and wonderment.

One evening Brother Demetrios came upon me talking solemnly to my son in French. The friar listened for a moment, then commented, with a broad grin, "He's going to be quite a linguist."

I rose from my squatting position and responded with a dry chuckle, "He shows signs of marked precocity. Would you believe it, little father, already he can say 'da da' in four languages."

Ah Hsing, who was never more than a few paces from her beloved charge, swooped in and scooped up Emun. She shot me an accusing glance, as though to let me know she was rescuing him from the contamination of my paternal presence.

Turning to Brother Demetrios, I queried, "We see little of you these days. How do you occupy your time?"

"There are diversions aplenty in this fair city. Then, too, I've been dabbling in commercial ventures."

"What sort of ventures?"

"I've purchased three bales of medicinal-grade cinnamon bark and a sizable quantity of rhinoceros horn. Both are commodities which fetch astronomical prices in Canton. I'll turn a tidy profit. The thought of that should allay the misery of seasickness."

"Why does rhinoceros horn command a high price?"

"You don't know?" the friar asked incredulously, then added, "No, at your age, I suppose it's of scant interest. 'Tis said to impart miraculous rigidity and stamina to the one-eyed monk."

"Does it?"

Brother Demetrios rubbed his bald pate and grinned ruefully. "Not noticeably."

Toward the end of May the weather underwent its seasonal transformation. The errant winds were light. No rain had fallen at midday. Fleecy clouds hung lazily suspended in an azure sky.

The time of parting was almost upon us. Within a few days, when the trails and cart tracks had dried sufficiently, I would head north to inspect the army encamped near the Pass of Mists. It would not now be long ere the friar's ship set sail for Canton. I chided myself for not having acted sooner. I was anxious to talk with Brother Demetrios. I had an important request to make of him.

On the veranda at my side, forearms resting on the balustrade, Gentle Breeze stood with her gaze fixed on the grounds spread out beneath us. The garden was a riot of color. The majestic flame trees were ablaze with orange-red blooms. A spraying clump of bougainvillea was clouded with dark-red blossoms. Frangipani trees added contrast with their delicate creamy flowers. Through the stately palms the western peaks etched a soft backdrop of smoky purple against a blue-green sky. A bronze disc of evening sun stood just above the mountaintops bathing Gentle Breeze and the crowns of the flame trees in golden light. Beneath the spreading branches of the trees deepening shadows lengthened.

"It's beautiful," she breathed raptly.

I glanced sideways at her, drinking in the curve of her cheek and the swell of her firm breast. Her hair, still damp from bathing, had grown almost to shoulder length. In the warm glow of evening sunlight she looked like a gilded goddess.

Her reaction to the scene was unexpected until I realized that it was the first sunset she'd witnessed since her arrival in Champa. Up to now the mountains had been obscured by gathering clouds heralding the onset of the evening rain.

I slid my right arm across her bare shoulders and said amiably, "Yes, little one, it *is* lovely."

She snuggled close to me and sighed contentedly before straightening. "Enough, Emun. 'Tis high time your son was bedded for the night."

I grinned. "I suppose it is. In the season now upon us, twilight lingers. By the way, didn't Brother Demetrios say he was joining us for the evening meal?"

"Yes. He should be here any time now."

I walked with her to the salon and watched her as she continued purposefully through the archway leading to the bedchambers.

In the salon the servants were setting out the lamps and placing chopsticks and dishes of condiments on the low table. In the corner was the brazier, which would not be needed to dispel the dampness for the next six months. My gaze came to rest on the writing table, atop which was a sandalwood box inlaid with ivory. Beside the box were my inkstick, porcelain ink dish, and some of the quill pens I'd fashioned. Smiling faintly, I walked to the table and opened the sandalwood box. Within was the unfinished chronicle of my adventures and misadventures. The manuscript had gone untouched since the day, more than two months ago, when I'd hurried to my residence to find Brother Demetrios impatiently awaiting my return.

My smile widened as I riffled through the written pages stacked within the camphorwood-lined box. How important the completion of the written account had seemed, particularly when I had thought Gentle Breeze had been taken from me. How unimportant it seemed now that she'd been restored to me. As I gently lowered the lid, I supposed that one day I would complete the document, but the element of urgency had been removed from the project.

It was almost as though the closing of the box were a signal. I heard footsteps on the veranda planking and turned to find Brother Demetrios entering the salon. He paused when just within the doorway to wipe sweat from his brow.

"It has turned much warmer," the friar commented.

I laughed. "We're embarking on the hot dry season. If you think this is bad, you should be here two or three months from now. Luckily, you'll be long gone ere the inferno o'ertakes us. When *does* your vessel sail?"

"Three days hence. I've just now come from seeing to the safe stowage of my cargo."

"Before you go, I've a favor to ask of you."

"Oh. What might that be?"

"In your capacity as a man of the cloth, I'd like you to unite me with Gentle Breeze in the holy bonds of matrimony."

For a long moment the friar regarded me in silence. Finally, he said gravely, "Do you realize what you ask of me, Edmund? I hope you are not contemplating this step simply to legitimize Emun Demetrios in the eyes of the church."

"No," I replied seriously, "though it's a consideration that has not escaped my attention. I fully appreciate what it is I ask of you. Gentle Breeze, forsaking all others, will become my wife in the eyes of God and man."

The look of uncertainty that had clouded the friar's countenance was replaced by a pleased expression. "Then nothing, my son, could give me greater pleasure than the granting of your request."